Chronicles of the Infected
Zombie Attack
Zombie Defence
Zombie World

Non-Fiction
How to Write an Awesome Novel
Horror, Demons and Philosophy

You Owe Me

Rick Wood

Blood Splatter Press

Also By Rick Wood

The characters in this book are fictional, but the events are inspired by extensive research into the lives and events of real-life incels who have committed murder.

"If I can't find one decent female to live with, I will find many indecent female to die with. If they are intent on denying me life, I will have no choice but to deny them life."
   - Death Note of Scott Paul Bierle, 2018

"The ultimate evil behind sexuality is the human female."
   - Manifesto of Elliot Rodgers, 2014

"The incel rebellion has already begun."
   - Facebook post by Alex Minassian, 2018

Prologue
Excerpt from the Manifesto of Dayton Dankworth

I'M A GREAT CATCH.

A great fucking catch.

A better fucking catch than YOU deserve.

You have *no idea* what you've missed out on!

You'd have been lucky to have someone as charming, and happy, and classy as me. I have great taste; all my clothes are expensive and from high-end stores – and I have money, too! You should see my BMW... But you won't because you're arrogant selfish bitches, wearing your short skirts and giggling, waving your long blond hair and thinking that means you can *fuck everyone over*.

And then you justify *fucking people over* because *you* frequently *get fucked over*. But guess what? That's what happens when you choose to date DICKS! They *fuck you over*, you ungrateful wench! *You* choose to date morons, then *you* moan about how they are morons – THAT is how fucking stupid you are!

You date the kind of blokes who spend all day in the gym drinking protein shakes then ignoring your calls and treating you like shit when you could be with someone *so* much better – but

1

you don't even know it because you're too far up your own fucking arse to see beyond the vapid empty men your vapid empty mind is drawn to.

You could have had *me*.

ME!

But instead you chose THAT.

The kind of man who calls me a four-eyed freak then shoots his shiny white teeth in your direction before luring you into his bedroom with promises he won't fulfil.

I would fulfil my promises.

I *always* fulfil *all* my promises.

And I'm kind, dammit! So fucking kind. I'd have treated you nicely, and flattered you, and taken you to fancy restaurants, and been grateful for you. Instead, you chose someone who doesn't even like you, and will just dick all over you as soon as you become an inconvenience.

This is all *your* fault.

YOUR fault.

If you'd have just looked my way – JUST ONCE – you'd have seen what you were missing. I go out into town wearing a smart blazer, pulling up in my BMW, and sit at the bar with expensive whisky looking smouldering as fuck with my cool-boy expression – and STILL you don't come up to me, or talk to me, or approach me. Instead, you let them approach you, with their stuffed pants and their limpdick strut and their arrogant jokes. They aren't even funny, yet you laugh, tossing your hair back and thrusting out your cleavage. Have you no pride? No fucking pride? None at all?

You would never have to get your tits out for me. Not in public. I'd have treated you better than that. I'd have shown you that you can dress modestly and still be sexy as fuck. And I'd have driven you everywhere, been nice to your mother, and paid for your dinner. Instead you choose a guy who turns out to be a dick, then bemoan the fact you only attract dicks.

But I am right here.

I am not a dick. I am a gentleman. I'm charismatic, I'll get on with your friends, take you to fancy places, show you what it means to be pretty. AND I'm intelligent. You'd no longer have to force conversation with vapid minds who cannot grasp the finer points of life. I'd talk to you about Aristotle and Shakespeare. I'd quote sonnets and love poems. We'd discuss literature and films. We'd have such great conversations. Instead, I see you pretending to laugh, putting your hands on his biceps, tittering like you're in love even though you're not. You sluts always sound so fucking fake when you laugh.

I'm funny as fuck. Really funny. Like, actually funny. Not pretend funny like whatever meathead you open your legs for.

And there's no need to open your legs until you're ready with me. I'll wait. Weeks, if I need to. Months, even. Because it's not what I'm here for. I mean, I'm a man, and I want it – but I'm here for *you*. I just have manners.

That's another thing the men you choose are missing. Manners.

FUCKING MANNERS.

I see them in the bathroom when I'm washing my hands. They spend more time with their reflection than the urinal. Tensing their muscles. Talking shit about sport with other guys who talk shit about sport. No one actually likes sports, they just talk shit about it to be all manly and macho and shit. I don't need to do that. Because I don't pretend.

It's all MAKE BELIEVE you see.

But you don't see, do you?

You'll never see.

I'll remain alone, with nothing but my virginity for company,

3

and you'll remain with the wrong men, forming the opinion that *all* men are the *wrong* men.

Fuck off with your stupid judgement. It's your fault for having bad taste. I've been here all along, waiting for you, but where have you been?

Fucking all the fuckboys, that's where.

And I'm angry. Of course I'm angry. I AM VERY FUCKING ANGRY.

And now it's time.

You brought this on yourself.

You will know this by the time I'm finished.

You. Brought. This. On. Your. Self.

If you'd have just spent time getting to know me, who I am, what I can offer, instead of the fucking CHADS you FUCK instead, you'd have seen who I am. I sat at the bar, waiting for one of you to approach me, but you weren't bothered. And now look. Now you're going to have to pay.

Forced prostitution would have solved this, but no, you fucking feminist nazi fucks get all fucking sensitive about it – but it's easy for you, isn't it? You can fuck without force! What about me, huh? WHAT ABOUT ME? You can fuck whoever you want because you're a woman. All you need to do is pop out the house and there'll be a million fucking men just waiting. You don't even have to be that good looking or that much of a catch, they'll just fuck you.

And I wouldn't have been like those men. I would have treated you with respect. And now...

You owe me.

You did this to me.

I gave you a chance.

So don't blame me for what comes next. Blame yourself. And blame your boyfriends. And blame your friends.

You Owe Me

This could have been so different, and it PAINS me that this is what you've brought me to.

By the time I'm done burning the world down, you're going to have wished you had given me a chance.

Just remember that what comes next is not my fault. What I do now is not my fault. Everyone who suffers as a result is not my fault.

It's *yours*.

The Day of the Twenty-First

Chapter One

It had just gone half past midnight and the lights were off.

Usually, one of Dayton's housemates would leave the hallway light on. This meant that, when they arrived home separately later that night, probably drunk, a little light would guide their way. But on this night, the lights were kept off.

It wasn't because of their neglect, or forgetfulness, however. The last housemate to leave had indeed left the light on when he stepped out of the door, wearing his smart shirt and jeans, with money in his pocket and phone in his hand. He'd locked the house and strolled down the street, whistling a tuneless song, giving no thought to what was going to happen when he arrived home.

The light was off because Dayton had turned it off, shortly after his third and final housemate had left.

It occurred to him as he waited in the dark that not even one of his housemates had wished Dayton a happy twenty-first birthday, but it didn't matter. Today wasn't about his birth. It was about his retribution. And it was going to be glorious.

He took his time, knowing he had a while until anyone returned. He made himself some tea – canned ravioli on toast – and sat at his computer for a while, staring at the forum that gave him so much comfort. He typed the last words of his manifesto, saved it, and exported it as a PDF to ensure no one could amend his message – he wanted it to be read exactly as he intended, down to every word and every unintentional grammatical error. He hadn't proofread it because he liked how it sounded like a rant; he was angry – nay, he was furious – and he wished for people to understand this when they read his words.

He shut his laptop lid. Killed the lights. Took his hunter's knife from under the bed – a curved eight-inch steel blade with a sharp point – and held it for a while. It was heavy, but so it should be. It made him feel powerful. Taller. Bigger. Greater.

He went to the bathroom and stood in front of the mirror. He could see little of his face, only the eye that was lit by the moonlight through the window, but he didn't mind the darkness – he loved how the shadows made him appear sophisticated. His skin looked so much better at night, yet women in nightclubs never seemed to notice.

He'd make them pay.

They would all pay.

He lifted the knife and posed with it in a few different positions. Pointed upwards. Held above his head like he was a Jedi about to fight a Sith Lord. At his side like he was an action hero walking away with fires raging behind him. Then he extended his tongue and placed the curve of the blade against it, like he was so tough that he wasn't scared about pricking his mouth. The way he looked made him chuckle; the sound of which would make any rational stranger feel disconcerted.

He left the bathroom. Opened the fuse box and turned off the main switch, then stalked down the stairs and stood in the darkness of the hallway. It was nine forty when he took his position, and whilst his housemates usually stayed out late, they could return at any time. And he would be ready.

But an hour passed, and there was no movement. He kept imagining how the first person would die. Where he'd stab them, how many times, whether they'd fight back, whether it would be messy, how much blood there'd be. He cared little about his housemates, and he wouldn't bother killing them if they lived somewhere else – but he needed them gone so he could use this house. It was to be his den, his layer, his dungeon. And he could have none of them in the way.

Growing tired of the hallway, he decided to wait in the nearest bedroom. Clark's bedroom was on the bottom floor, nearest the front door. He nudged the door open and entered, leaving it ajar, hiding behind it.

Clark's bedroom made Dayton angrier. There was an open box of condoms on the desk, messy clothes dumped on the floor, and his bed was unmade. An empty pizza box with dirty crusts perched on top of a computer tower. The wall had a bikini model calendar pinned to it, showing last month's dates. Pictures of his family were stuck to the door beside pieces of blu tac where other pictures had fallen off and not been replaced. How could women go for such men? They were imbeciles. This man was unclean and uncultured. Nothing like Dayton.

This bedroom provided the clearest evidence that Dayton was justified. That today's events were inevitable. That he had no choice.

Another hour passed, and another, and Dayton waited in the darkness, his eyes on the window. He was eager, but knew the need to be patient. He would not be reckless. He was not like other men; he was not a beast, he was a gentleman, and he did not begin his ventures irresponsibly.

Finally, shortly after half midnight had passed, there was a movement under the street lamp outside. Clark's red drunken face passed the window. He was striding fairly well for someone who'd been out drinking, but he had that wayward look in his eyes that often appeared after he'd had a few.

He failed to get his key in the lock at first, and it took a bit of scraping on the door to find it. It eventually churned, and he opened it, mumbling, "Why the fuck is it so dark..."

Dayton heard Clark try the light switch. It didn't come on. Clark swore again under his breath and shut the door behind him.

He treaded through the hallway with heavy steps, walking into the living room with his shoes on. So uncultured. After a minute or so, his footsteps into the kitchen were followed by the sound of a lager can being opened.

Dayton stepped out of the bedroom and stuck to the shadows. He moved slowly, each step particular and precise, and crept across the hallway, performing his role as the predator. He stopped at the edge of the living room, watching Clark in the kitchen hitting buttons on the microwave, and Dayton scoffed silently at his roommate's stupidity.

Dayton hovered, watching, his knife behind his back.

When Clark walked past him, Dayton would do it. He just had to wait.

Except, he couldn't, as Clark turned around, jumped, then exhaled, and stayed where he was. "Shit, Dayton. I didn't see you there."

Dayton remained in the shadow. Clark squinted to make him out.

"What are you doing?" Clark asked. His bemusement was clear, but Dayton didn't move.

Clark looked around, then looked back, perplexed.

"Dayton, what are you doing?"

Clark stepped out of the kitchen and into the living room, but paused a few steps away. He seemed cautious, but Dayton didn't think Clark was intelligent enough to be cautious. The man was not smart like him; he didn't have the awareness to be wary.

"Why are you just stood there?"

Dayton didn't answer. Just watched.

Clark shrugged his shoulders. "Fine. Do you know what's going on with the electricity?"

Clark searched the darkness for an expression in his housemate's face. Dayton gave none. Clark tried laughing to ease the tension, but stopped, and ended up sighing, perhaps deducing that Dayton was just being his usual weird self.

"You are a fucking freak," Clark declared as he rolled his eyes and shook his head. He turned away and slurped on his beer.

Dayton leapt forward, lifted the hunter's blade high above his head, and brought it down into the back of Clark's neck with all the force his weak body could muster. Clark screamed, colliding with the floor, and Dayton struck him again in the neck and the back before Clark realised what was happening.

Clark, still being the physically superior one, rolled onto his back, and tried using his arms to fight off Dayton – but Dayton continued his frenzy, slashing at Clark's arms, piercing Clark's chest. The blood dribbled out his skin, oozing and leaking in a way that felt so satisfying to watch.

Clark punched Dayton's hip and knocked him a little off balance. This facilitated the fatal blow, as Dayton fell forward a little and, instead of striking Clark in the chest as he intended, he struck Clark in the throat, and the knife sunk deep into the flesh.

Clark yelped, but only briefly. It was a little embarrassing. His eyes widened, and he grabbed his throat as he suffocated.

Dayton stood back and watched his housemate. He'd never seen someone's eyes as they realised they were about to die, and it was something to behold. There was a resolved panic in them, a humiliation that mimicked the way Dayton had felt through his many years. His entire life had been an extended moment of humiliation; he saw that feeling reflected in Clark's eyes as he stared helplessly up at the killer who refused to help him.

Clark died, and Dayton dragged his body into Clark's room by the feet. It was quite a struggle with his weak, gangly muscles, but he managed. He shoved Clark's body under the bed and waited for the next housemate.

Like previously stated, there was little emotion in this kill – it was a means to an end. A necessity. Dayton wasn't bothered about his housemates; they were just collateral damage he had to endure. Something that had to be done.

So he hid behind the door and waited for the next one to arrive home. He was patient, despite his eagerness to move onto those he really felt deserved it. He'd waited a long time for this day, and if he stuck to his plan, then it would occur exactly as he intended.

Just two more housemates to go, then the carnage will truly begin.

He sighed at the thought. It was going to be beautiful.

Before the Twenty-First

Chapter Two

Dayton Dankworth weighed four pounds exactly when he was born, seven weeks early and before the nursery was ready. Already he was pathetically small, and a huge inconvenience.

His family was a relatively successful upper-middle-class unit, who liked to show off to those who hadn't done quite so well just how successful and upper-middle-class they were. His father, Brian, was a film director – though not normal films; he directed art-house films, which basically means it was pretentious shit that confused most people, but allowed critics and academics to read into all the nuances that were put there for the sake of being arty. Brian was much admired and earned a generous wage, even if none of his movies made any sense.

His mother, Delilah, was an actress – or at least she'd tried to be. She met Brian when she was playing the butt double for his leading lady. Even though their first night together was convenient sex Delilah hoped would help to secure her a better acting role and advance her career, they ended up falling in love, and were excited to get married –

either that, or their lifeless, monotonous relationship was easy to maintain, so they settled for marrying each other because it was the simplest choice. Really, is there much difference?

When Dayton was born, she stepped back from her acting career to take care of their child while witnessing the many successes Brian was achieving in his career. Even though she'd never verbally consented to this, she played the part well, and encouraged him from afar, keeping the child out of his office so he could work at the weekends, and standing outside the studio on filming days so their baby's wails didn't interrupt the shoot. His films were mostly successful abroad, where subtitles would give the film an air of artiness and prestige, but weren't too popular in Britain where he made them. People would either be too polite to pass opinion, or declare it to be a load of shite and laugh at it with their friends. It was rare that negative opinion affected Brian, but on the days that it did, Delilah was there to reassure him he was wonderful and make the world right again. When asked, she would tell his admirers how marvellous it was that he could live out his dreams, and he would always smile and agree, and bask in the light of her praise. Her dreams were never mentioned – either that, or he'd assumed her dream was to be a mother and raise a wonderful family; something she initially deemed to be a tremendous success. Nevertheless, he made enough money that she didn't need to work, so she fell into the routine lethargy of a docile, subservient wife who never complained; the kind that men like Brian craved.

As Dayton grew into a toddler, the boy would spend a lot of his time organising his toys rather than playing with them. He would put his building blocks into piles of the same colour, or categorise his dinosaur toys into types of dinosaurs, or organise his books into size order. He could read at a young age, but his speech was delayed, and it took him quite a few years to start putting sentences together. Brian was more concerned about Dayton's height than his speech, so when the child turned two, they took him to the doctor out of fear that he might have dwarfism - or 'midgetitus' as his father referred to it. The doctor laughed out loud before telling them he was "just a small kid," and that they should "just get on with it."

Delilah found out she was pregnant a few days later, and they stopped fretting about Dayton's size, instead celebrating the imminent arrival of a new baby. They had a girl, named her Cassidy, and told Dayton he was going to be a wonderful big brother. When Cassidy turned two, they were almost the same size, and Delilah would push them around in a two-seater pram, and people would ask if they were twins. Dayton was too young to realise he felt humiliated, but he did, and for that reason, he refused to respond to the annoying strangers, and often tried to hit them should they get close enough for his small arms to reach.

Dayton's first memory came when he was five. He and his younger sister would have baths together, and he'd marvel at what she was missing, confused what had happened to her. Delilah would wash them, then play games with toy ships and rubber ducks. She would use a bubble bath with pictures of sailors and pirates on, then they would use them as toys, inventing backstories and voices for each of them.

Dayton would one day look back on this bath as the day he peaked. It was the first and only time he'd ever seen a female naked in the flesh, and he hated that this was the best it was ever going to get.

But for now, he bathed in the childhood innocence that

he would someday miss, back before he knew people were awful and deserved nothing but scowls and judgement. Someday, he would look at others with contempt, and judge the human race as being unworthy of its place on earth, and as nothing but archaic, primordial animals who are far from the most intelligent species on this planet. Those days, however, were years in the future; for now, he enjoyed splashing the water over his sister and the happiness he gained from making her giggle. Her chubby cheeks would light up, her bright face framed by her curly hair, and he would feel content that he'd made another person happy. That feeling did not last long.

When he started school, he spent most PE lessons crying. Even though they were playing sport with very little contact, he still hated how rough the other kids were. He would stand still while people kicked or threw balls around him and, whilst the teachers tried to encourage him at first, they ended up just ignoring him. It was easier to let him be a radiator child, as unnoticed as the heater against the wall, than to make a fuss out of his lack of participation. Besides, it didn't help that he was so much smaller than the other kids, and they could barge him out of the way so easily.

His height never bothered him until he was on one of many holidays his family took abroad. They went to places like Barbados, and Hawaii, and the Maldives, and Costa Rica, and Tahiti, and he was especially excited when they went to Florida; there was a big theme park and he wanted to go on all the big rides. He queued for hours with his dad, watching other boys his age as they were let on the ride with their dads, laughing and enjoying themselves.

But when they arrived at the front of the queue, Brian was told his son couldn't ride.

"Can't ride?" Brian demanded. "What do you mean, can't ride?"

"He's too small."

"Too small! There are plenty of kids his age getting on the ride."

"It's not about age, sir."

The pimpled teenager pointed to a picture on the wall next to him. It was a cartoon of a freckled ginger kid with braces, pointing at 120cm on a two-metre ruler, with a speech bubble by his open mouth displaying the text *you must be this tall to enjoy this ride*. Dayton was quite a bit shorter than where this irritating picture was indicating.

"Well, surely a few inches don't matter?" his dad pleaded. "We've been queueing for hours."

"I understand that sir, but these signs were at the beginning of the queue where you could have—"

"Are you saying we came all the way to Florida for this damn ride and you're not going to even let us on it?"

Dayton remembered little else of what was said, but he remembered how red his father's face became. He'd never seen Brian that red or angry before – at least, not until now. Someone much older had to rush over and intervene; a middle-aged man who looked pathetic wearing the cap and polo shirt all the workers had to wear, and who did not take kindly to Brian ridiculing him for the minimum wage he earned. When the man threatened to have Brian escorted off the premises, Brian finally gave in, grabbed Dayton's arm, and marched him away. Brian's fist could fit all the way around Dayton's spindly bicep, and it hurt, but Dayton said nothing.

Dayton appeased his dad by saying it didn't matter, and his dad said little for the rest of the day. But it did matter. Dayton felt devastated. He'd waited all summer to go on that ride, and they weren't letting him on when plenty of boys his age were being allowed on. It just wasn't fair.

This was the first time Dayton felt the sting of injustice.

It filled him with rage, and he wished to punish everyone else for making him feel this way. He scowled at the other children as they shared their experiences, glaring at them as they showed each other the photos they'd bought of themselves mid-ride. They were laughing at the silly faces each other had pulled, and Dayton thought of the silly face he'd been practising all summer in preparation.

He longed to hurt his peers in the worst possible way for the pain they made him feel. It would be a feeling he'd come to know very well throughout his life.

Chapter Three

Julia Roberts had never done a nude scene.

Her legs at the beginning of Pretty Woman were a body double's, as was any glimpse of intimate flesh in any of her other movies. She'd survived an entire career as an actress in Hollywood without having to expose her body to secure a job, and for this reason, she was Delilah's hero, and the actress she wished to emulate. Unfortunately, emulating her wasn't so easy; even when Delilah began searching for her first acting jobs, and she auditioned for independent films that only paid her expenses, most of the producers required her to show some skin.

Delilah refused. She was going to maintain her integrity, just like Julia Roberts. She was going to be a feminist, and she would not let anyone push her into showing what she didn't want to. But the more she told this to producers, the more they turned her down; it seemed Julia Roberts was an anomaly.

She wouldn't believe it at first. But, when she was alone, maybe sitting in the bath or watching television, her mind would wander over the subject, and she'd try to think of another actress who'd managed to keep their clothes on in front of the camera throughout their entire career – and she could not. She would even look up the filmography of her favourite actresses, trying to reassure herself, searching with fading hope, only to find that one film where they'd shown a breast, or their buttocks, or a large slab of bare, intimate skin. It was usually early in their career, before they had earned the power to say no.

Delilah hated this. It felt like nudity was a prerequisite to success, and if she wished to have an acting career, Delilah was going to have to show something.

She consoled herself to this fact, as her determination to become an actress overrode her pride. But she was still going to retain some dignity, so she only agreed to show a little. Even so, as soon as she became willing, a whole new world of possibility opened up, and the jobs started coming in. She could even quit her job as a barmaid, and was delighted that she'd no longer have to serve drinks in seedy bars to lecherous punters who molested her with their eyes.

A few months went by, and she was finally enjoying the life she'd dreamt of since she was a little girl. It was great. No, better than that – it was magnificent. She was acting for a living and, even if she had to show a bit of her body now and then, she could finally write in her tax form: *Occupation – Full Time Actress.*

But it wasn't enough.

Eventually, the work dried up, and she had bills to pay. So she showed a little more. Then even more. Then even, even more. Then a lot. Until, one day, she found herself frequently working as a nude double for better known actresses – the kind who were so coveted that producers were willing to pay someone else to be their legs, or bum, or breasts.

This ended up becoming Delilah's job, and she found herself needing to do it more and more to pay the rent.

She hated it. There'd always be a few extra men on set on the days she went in front of the camera. Like the IT guys she'd never seen before, or the caterer who was conveniently delivering a sandwich before lingering by the door. They never seemed to have a job to do, they were just there, watching, waiting. She despised them for it, but never felt she could say anything. And, to make it worse, they always made the set cold to make her nipples hard, and her flesh would be armoured with goose pimples, and she would feel pathetic, and exposed, and empty.

There was only one director who ever addressed this. A director who demanded that people who didn't need to be on set go back to doing their jobs, and that the temperature was turned up, and that Delilah had an assistant to give her a robe between takes.

That director was Brian.

She liked him for it. And, honestly, the first time she slept with him, it was to advance her career, knowing that he could bring the possibilities of a real acting job – but she found herself drawn to his passion. The way he became more animated when he talked about his next film idea. The way he believed she could be anything she wanted to be.

He proposed after ten months, in their kitchen, with a ring that didn't fit. It felt odd, as neither Brian, nor Delilah, had ever wanted to get married, but she said yes. Looking back, she couldn't be sure if it was out of obligation or love, but she convinced herself she had no doubts, even though it was something she'd never wanted. As a little girl, Delilah did not dream of white weddings and dresses and walking down the aisle. She dreamt of red carpets and Hollywood stars and her face on a big screen.

She had a sole ambition, and she was determined to follow it – she was going to change the world with her performances. But she fell pregnant after a year, and her caesarean scar meant no one would employ her as a nude double anymore. But Brian said she didn't need to work as a nude double, anyway – why keep demeaning herself? She was a mother now. That was her job. Best put all her energy into that.

And that's what she did. She stood at the side-lines and watched other women become his leading ladies, marvelled at the brilliant job they did in every take, and tried not to envy how much praise he doted on them. She remembered receiving that praise, and she remembered how it felt. She wondered if that leading lady would sleep with her husband to get ahead too. She wondered whether she trusted him enough not to worry.

Years went by – seven, in fact – and the resentment grew. She wasn't aware of it, and neither was he. It hid away with the other voices at the back of her head; the ones that told her she wasn't good enough, and that she would screw up her children, and that she should lead a much better life than this. Until, one day, unbeknownst to her, the feelings she didn't know she had surfaced, and like a volcano that had been squashed and pressurised for centuries, she erupted, and the lava fled through their home, destroying everything they had built.

Dayton witnessed the argument. He was in the room for the beginning of it, then his father asked him to go to his room as his parents needed to discuss something. He left, but he didn't go to his room; he stood outside the door, ear against wood, listening to everything that was said. He never realised how much his mother had given up for him, and how much of it was his fault. And he never realised how hard his father worked, and how little his father felt she appreciated that.

Dayton asked his mother the next day if they were going to break up. She wore a pitiful smile as she crouched down in front of him, took his hands, and promised that they would not break up. That it was just an argument, and sometimes couples argue. They were too strong for that, and they loved him too much to put him through such an ordeal.

They had a very different conversation ninety-five days later, when Delilah and Brian took Dayton for a walk on Cleeve Hill, then sat him on a bench overlooking the surrounding villages, and announced that they needed to talk. They'd taken him out for ice cream first, and he sat on the uncomfortable wooden slabs with the taste of vanilla and hundreds and thousands still on his tongue. He'd never be able to eat ice cream again, because it would forever be associated with this moment; nor would he ever be able to drive past this hill, or set foot on its grassy mounds, or see sheep grazing the fields like the ones nearby him, as they would remind him of the feeling of being sucker-punched as his world fell apart.

"You know that Mummy and Daddy love you, don't you?" Delilah said, cradling Cassidy who was too young to be a part of this conversation.

He gave an absent nod. She only ever referred to herself in third person when he had done something wrong, and he wondered what she was going to tell him off about.

"And what we are about to tell you has nothing to do with you," Brian said. "It is entirely about us, and it's important that you know that."

This wasn't a telling off. Dayton was confused. What were they on about?

"I'm afraid that Mummy and Daddy..." She glanced

upward, meeting her husband's eyes, and a moment of weakness passed between them. "...are getting a divorce."

The words echoed in his mind. A divorce? He'd heard of it. Some kids at school had parents that were divorced. But not him. He didn't have divorced parents. His parents were different from their parents. This couldn't be right. They must be wrong. It wasn't true.

His mother and father kept talking about logistics, and reassuring him it wasn't his fault, and that sometimes mummies and daddies just have to make a decision. Their words were unclear, like Dayton was underwater, and he couldn't quite make them out. The way the words were delivered stuck in his mind more than the words themselves, as they were both sat in a way that was so unlike them, and even when he became an adult, he could recall the specifics. His mother was sitting on the edge of the bench, as far to one side as she could, with half of her posterior perched on the edge, and both hands clasped together, and she could have easily slid off at any moment. His father, who usually sat back with his legs wide apart, sat on the edge of the bench as well, with his knees tight together, and his hands clasped like he was praying, despite the way he always ranted about religion. Everything about the way they sat was unnatural and forced, and though he couldn't have articulated it at such a young age, the unfamiliarity of it made him feel as nauseous as the news itself.

The following week, he, Cassidy and Delilah moved out, and Brian remained in the house where the ghosts of their family still haunted the corridors. Their new flat was considerably smaller, and it was close to lots of other flats, and the street felt more crowded. He saw his father on weekends, but it felt strange to return to the house where he'd felt so warm, only to find it so cold. It was emptier now, with more space, and it felt wrong.

His mother reverted to her maiden name and referred to herself as Delilah Cartwright. This confused Dayton. Why would his mother want to have a different surname from him?

This was the first great betrayal Dayton ever experienced, and he couldn't understand it. His parents had deliberately hurt him, and he couldn't fathom why. This deception was an insult to his trust in them, and he took it very, very personally.

Delilah and Brian were the first people to show him how abhorrent the human race truly was.

Chapter Four

DAYTON DREADED WEEKEND TRIPS TO HIS FATHER'S house. It felt weird calling it his *father's* house rather than *his* house, but that's what it had become – it no longer felt like home, because it no longer had the unity it had destroyed. It was like a veteran soldier returning to empty battlefields where their comrades' bodies lay. They had endured warfare, and now they were left to roam amongst the remnants of disaster.

Cassidy, however, loved going at the weekend. She was too young to realise that her world had imploded, and she saw it as going on a holiday every few days to see her dad. She would leap into his arms, and they would play on the climbing frame Brian had bought for the garden, or on the trampoline, or on the swing – some of the many new toys that seemed to appear in the months since Delilah had moved out. Dayton wasn't impressed by the climbing frame, or trampoline, or swing, and he would sit on the garden bench wearing a scowl that never seemed to penetrate his dad's insistent good mood.

"Would you like to come join us, son?" Brian would ask.

Dayton would fold his arms and shake his head, leaving Brian and Cassidy to continue playing and laughing. This was another thing Dayton hated that had become commonplace since his parents began living in different houses – terms of endearment such as *son,* or *junior,* or *boyo.* He despised how they seemed to be littered in conversation, and his dad rarely asked a question without one.

Then there was another big change that Dayton hated as well – before, he'd had the flexibility to play however he wished on the weekends, but now, Brian always had activities for them to do. Dayton couldn't understand why, and he'd partake in Brian's scheduled fun with a stiff demeanour and dead expression, longing for Sunday night when his mother came to collect him. These attempts included an inflatable play land, a football match, crazy golf, go karting, rock climbing, a zoo visit, museums, craft workshops, hiking, theme parks... Cassidy loved every activity, but Dayton found himself exhausted at the end of the weekend, and resented the way it all felt so forced.

Then, one day, the activities stopped. They arrived at the house on Friday evening, waiting to see what they would be up to that weekend, and Brian said there were no plans. He had to work. They could occupy themselves, then Brian would be back for dinner. So Dayton played computer games on his dad's old PC, and Cassidy spent time in the garden on the climbing frame. A few weekends later, Brian wasn't even there, and they had a child minder waiting for them, as he was filming in another country. He kept promising he'd bring them to set, but never did.

Meanwhile, Delilah was using her free weekends to work extra shifts at her second job. She'd ended her relationship with her husband with excitement that she could reignite her acting career; his dreams would no longer be in the way of hers. But she needed to buy food. And clothes. And furniture. And pay for school trips. And electricity bills. And gas bills. And water bills. And ensure the rent was paid on their three-bedroom flat. The one that embarrassed Dayton. The one he would tell kids at school was temporary. Because his dad had loads of money, and his parents were going to get back together, and they were going to use all their money to buy an even bigger house, and that house would be bigger than any of them could imagine.

Then came the weekend where Dayton and Cassidy arrived at their father's house, and there was a woman there. One they'd never met before. Pretty, but like she came from a faraway land. Her skin was a different colour, and when she said hello, she had an accent. One Dayton didn't recognise.

Brian sat Dayton in the same chair he'd sat in as he listened to his mother pack their belongings, and his father explained the situation.

The woman's name was Nala. They were engaged. They were getting married. She was moving in. To their house. The one where Brian and Delilah had started their life together. And their family. The one where Dayton had grown up with both of his parents there, together. This new woman was now going to be in the bedroom Brian had once shared with Dayton's mother. Dayton almost asked whether Nala would wear his mother's clothes too, but he didn't. He said nothing. Cassidy, however, was excited, and he hated her for it.

To fill the silence, Brian told the story of how they'd met. Nala had auditioned for a part in Brian's movie. He'd suggested that he could really help Nala's career. He was going to get her lots of auditions. Feature her in his films. And, as they worked together, they fell in love.

When Brian finally stopped speaking, he left a silence, waiting for Dayton to speak, an expectant expression like this was wonderful news and he was waiting for Dayton to join in the enthusiasm. When no response was forthcoming, he said, "Well? What do you think, bud?"

Dayton simply looked at his father and said, "Can I go now?"

Brian reluctantly nodded, and Dayton ran upstairs to his old room. The one he used to live in.

Now, when they arrived every weekend, and his father was off filming or working – which was most weekends – it was no longer a child minder who was waiting for them. It was Nala. And he didn't understand what the point of them going there at the weekend was if they were just going to spend time with this strange woman. And he hated how much Cassidy enjoyed playing with her new stepmother. And he hated how strict she was, and how she limited his time on the computer, and how she made him keep his elbows off the table during dinner, and how he had to take his shoes off when he entered the house. And, most of all, he hated how his mother's home was now a tiny flat, with tiny bedrooms, and radiators that cranked as they heated, and showers that took minutes for the water to get hot, and an oven that his mother had to light with an extra-long match.

Nala was the enemy. Cassidy was the enemy. Delilah was the enemy. And Brian wasn't anything – he just wasn't there.

Dayton didn't involve himself with the games Nala and Cassidy played. He didn't interact with his mum when she rushed them to school as she was late for work. He didn't speak to the boys at school who were all too loud for him. And the girls at school... well, they weren't part of the same reality. They played with the other boys, running around the playground, giggling and acting and showing off, like what they were doing was such fun they had to shove it in Dayton's face. They played kiss chase, and the girls would run after the boys who screamed as they ran away, and every boy in the class except Dayton was a target, and it took over the playground for an entire lunchtime. Dayton stood at the side of that playground, leant against the wall, watching the commotion. It was like he was watching something on the television with the volume down. He knew it was there, but he didn't really understand it, so he just left it on in the background. He wasn't a part of the games the girls played, and he convinced himself he didn't want to be.

Cassidy and Nala could have their games. The girls at school could have their games. And Delilah could have her tired evenings falling asleep in front of reality television shows because her two jobs and extra shifts had left her too tired to interact with her son.

Dayton wasn't bothered. It didn't affect him. It just happened. Sure, it wasn't ideal, and he would change it if he could, but it didn't matter. He already knew he was destined for great things.

The Day of the Twenty-First

Chapter Five

THE NEXT HOUSEMATE APPROACHED THE HOUSE AT 2.42 a.m.

He stumbled slightly from side to side, using a lamppost to hold himself up, presenting a distant smile at his drunken predicament. Dayton watched as Samuel struggled to open the gate that led to the house, ultimately deciding to climb over it, trying too hard to keep himself balanced and avoid falling into the small mound of weeds and thorns that took up their front lawn – if one could call a small patch of over-grown grass a front lawn.

Samuel took out his keys, even though the door was unlocked, and placed them in the keyhole. He twisted them, which locked the door, and he appeared confused about why it didn't open. He twisted the keys back, unlocked the door again, then opened it with a smug satisfaction in his grin.

He mumbled something as he entered. Dayton couldn't decipher the words, but it didn't matter. He was pleased that Samuel was so inebriated. It would make this easier. He stood in the darkness of Clark's room, his feet inches from

Clark's wide dead eyes, watching Samuel pass the doorway. Samuel was singing to himself; an eighties rock song Dayton vaguely recognised as something his dad used to listen to in the car. He emerged into the shadows of the hallway and followed Samuel into the living room, his hunter's knife held above his head with both hands, the blade pointing downwards.

Samuel paused by the sofa, leant over it, placed both hands on the arm, and struggled not to heave as he kept himself balanced. Dayton was stealthy and quiet, but he needn't be – Samuel was barely aware of what his own body was doing, never mind what someone was doing behind him.

Dayton edged forward and lifted the knife higher. He'd originally been numb to what he was doing, seeing his housemate's death as a necessity rather than a desire – but as he approached Samuel's back, he recalled all the times this prick had demeaned him. Samuel frequently had female visitors, and he made a point of having loud sex in his bedroom so the entire house could hear it; his housemates would chuckle about how Samuel was having a good time – but Dayton did not see it this way. To Dayton, it was an insult; a jibe at his lack of female attention; an act of gloating for what Samuel could achieve, and Dayton could not. So when Dayton approached his nemesis, methodical in his thoughts, he felt encouraged by a glower of rage that festered like a sickness in his belly, and a shiver of fury that travelled across his skin, through the tip of his fingers, and into his knife.

Dayton, much to his own surprise, roared as he brought the blade down onto Samuel's back. He penetrated Samuel's flesh easily, but had to push harder to force the blade through the muscle – or, at least, what Dayton assumed was muscle; biology had never been his best subject. Samuel's body convulsed, and he lifted his right arm into a claw, and he arched his body as he looked upwards. His yelp of pain was delayed; he seemed to have little awareness of what was happening. Dayton retracted the blade, lifted it high above his head again, then shoved it downwards as hard as he could, this time forcing it into the flesh within an inch of the spine. He tried to tilt it slightly to penetrate the bone, wondering whether inserting it into the spine would render Samuel unable to move, much as he'd heard it might, but struggled as Samuel tried to stagger away, but fell as he did, collapsing onto the floor like a dying worm, his hazy instincts compelling him to flee, but the shock rendering him hopeless.

Once again, Dayton retracted the knife, lifted it high above his head, and brought it down on Samuel's back.

Samuel, however, was taking too long to die. Despite how much hatred Dayton held for the guy, he had far more ambitious targets he'd fantasised about tormenting, and he wished to despatch of Samuel quickly. So, for the last time, he lifted the blade high, and aimed for the back of the neck. He'd never been good with his aim – his father once took him to a bow and arrow activity when he was a little kid, and Dayton couldn't even hit the target board, never mind land the arrow in its centre. Perhaps he just needed greater motivation, because he found his aim now, and he lodged the blade far into the throat, much to his own surprise. He left it there and stood, waiting for it to be over.

The carpet in front of Samuel's mouth quickly became stained with red. He coughed up mouthfuls of blood as he struggled to breathe, and blood oozed out of the holes in his back until his shirt was a soggy maroon colour.

"What the fuck?"

Dayton abruptly turned around, surprised to see his third and final housemate in the doorway behind him, staring at Dayton with his mouth hanging open. This housemate, Marcus, appeared unable to move, stuck in the moment and rendered static from the shock.

Dayton turned back to Samuel's body, which had stopped wriggling, and yanked his knife out of the flesh. It was stuck like the sword in the stone, but Dayton proved himself worthy as he twisted it and extracted it from the corpse. By the time he'd turned back around, Marcus was not there, and was running toward the front door.

Marcus had just turned the door handle when Dayton caught up with him. He ran into Marcus, slamming him against the wood, forcing the door shut and Marcus to his knees.

Dayton locked the door.

Marcus, however, despite being a little drunk, had the awareness to turn and run back through the house. Dayton pursued his target, but struck his knee against the shoe rack and stumbled. As he fell, he lunged his blade forward and sliced the back of Marcus's heal.

Marcus screamed and fell onto the stairs. He tried to ignore the pain, pushing himself to his feet; Marcus was a big fella, and could probably have taken Dayton if it came to fisticuffs, but survival instincts took over the part of his brain that produced rationality, and his panicked thoughts urged him to flee.

But flee, he could not.

Dayton pounced on Marcus and swiped the knife across his throat before he could lift his arms to block it, leaving a line of blood on his skin.

Marcus slid down the stairs and suffocated on the bottom step. He grabbed his neck and tried to press on the wound, but there was nothing that could stop the bleeding, and he could only stare upwards, eyes wide, at Dayton, as he suffered.

Dayton stood over the dying fool with his feet on either side of his hips. This was the first time in his life that he felt like the alpha.

But he didn't have time to stand here and watch Marcus die, despite how much he relished the opportunity. He had more to do by the end of the night, and he needed these bodies out of the way if he was going to use this house as his torture palace.

He returned to Samuel, grabbed his feet, and dragged him across the living room, through the hallway, and into Clark's room. Samuel's dead body was heavy and tough to move, but Dayton gritted his teeth and shoved it under the bed with Clark's body.

When he returned to Marcus, the squirming had stopped, and the body was empty. Dayton did the same with this housemate, except the space under the bed was full. This was a conundrum, and one that required considerable thought. He didn't want anyone to suspect anything when he brought them back here – at least, not until he'd begun their torture – but Marcus's dead body was hardly inconspicuous.

In the end, Dayton shoved Marcus under the desk and shut the door to Clark's room, making a mental note to avoid letting anyone into this room when he returned.

Soon, he would have a shower and wash off the blood. He'd shampoo his hair, lather his body, and towel dry himself. He'd put on a smart blazer, a nice pair of fitted jeans, and a neat polo shirt. He'd comb his hair to the side and admire his reflection. He'd look smart, and would struggle to understand why any woman would not choose to go home with him. He was a great catch, dammit, and the world was stupid not to see that.

But first, he had to get the house ready; he didn't want any of his captives running at the first sign of blood.

Then he would need to proceed to the most important part of all.

The uploading of his manifesto.

Before the Twenty-First

Chapter Six

SHORTLY AFTER DAYTON'S NINTH BIRTHDAY, DELILAH dropped him and Cassidy off at his father's house, but she didn't leave straight away. She watched Dayton trudge up the path as Cassidy ran on ahead to hug the woman who shared her old house with her old husband. She watched Dayton as he forced himself through the door, his head down and his hands in his pockets, dismissing the excited embrace between Nala and Cassidy.

Once her children had entered the house, she hung back a few minutes, then stepped out of the car. She walked the familiar path to where her old life had died; there seemed to be fewer weeds around the walls, the grass either side of the path was freshly cut, and the jeep in the driveway was sparkling clean. She hesitated, exhaled, wondered why she was doing this, then remembered her son was important and she had no choice, and rang the doorbell.

Moments later, Nala opened the door and stared expectantly at Delilah.

After Delilah said nothing, Nala prompted her, "Can I help you?"

Delilah realised she was scowling and made a concerted effort to stop. "Is Brian in?" she asked.

"No, he's not. Can I help you?"

"Do you know when he'll be back?"

"No, he's away filming at the moment. Can I–"

"Will he be back today?"

"I don't know. Who are you?"

"What is the point of me dropping the kids off to spend time with him if he's not even going to be there?"

Nala looked confused, then realisation settled over her, and she nodded in understanding. "You're Delilah?"

"Yes."

"He told me you might be like this."

"Like what?"

"Irrational and angry."

She unintentionally blurted out a snort of laughter. "Is that what he said, is it?"

"Was there something you wanted?"

"Yes, I need to speak to Brian about our son. When will he be back?"

"It might not be until tomorrow."

"Tomorrow?" She still couldn't believe he wasn't there to spend time with his children, and was instead leaving them with this new woman.

"Is this about Dayton?" Nala asked. "Cassidy? Can we discuss anything?"

Delilah didn't fight her scowl this time. "No. His parents need to discuss it."

She turned and strode away before Nala could engage her in a battle of wits. Honestly, she was furious – she didn't drop the children off to spend time with her replacement. But whatever. It didn't matter. She had bigger conversations to have with Brian.

She didn't return to her car. Instead, she carried on walking through the estate, nodding at neighbours she used to know as she scrolled through her phone to find his number. There was a sinister familiarity in the route she took – she used to walk this way after a fight with Brian to calm herself down before returning to offer an apology she didn't mean. She realised how much she missed this estate – the houses were big, the neighbours smiled more, and there was so much more space in the street. But she could never return to it now. It was tainted, and the memories conjured by a bush, or a lamppost, or a street sign, where their children rode their bike for the first time or laughed endlessly after a joke, hurt.

She selected Brian's name and put the phone to her ear. It rang, and it rang, and it rang, until eventually, his answer phone responded, and his smarmy voice announcing that he could not answer provoked a pang of anger.

She texted him: *Answer your phone. It's urgent.* Then gave it a few more minutes. She rang, and after a few rings, he answered.

"Delilah? Is everything okay?"

"Yes," she said. "I need to talk to you about our son."

"What's happened? Is he okay?"

"Yes. He's with Nala. I think he'd rather be with you, but that is where he is."

"You said it was urgent?"

"It is. I'm going to have Dayton tested."

There was a pause. "Delilah, I'm on set, if this isn't urgent–"

"It is urgent. It's about our son."

Brian sighed. "Fine, is he ill?"

"No. I'm going to take him to see a psychiatrist. I've been

speaking to his teachers, and we think Dayton may be high-functioning autistic."

"He might be *what*?"

"High-functioning autistic."

"Don't be so ridiculous. He's a sensitive kid, and a little moody, but he's not... whatever it was you said."

"How would you know, Brian? When was the last time you spent time with him?"

"Are you calling to guilt trip me?"

"No. I'm just pointing out that you're not around enough to see the signs."

"What are these *signs*, Delilah? Please, do tell me."

Despite the evident sarcasm, Delilah recounted the symptoms she'd mulled over for many evenings. The way Dayton must put his clothes in certain places of his room, and in certain piles, and that if they are not in the correct place, he buries himself in the corner of the room, covers his ears, and screams. How every time they were in town, and there was a large crowd, Dayton would stiffen, refuse to move, and even cry. The way his teachers often found him unresponsive when they asked him to do something, such as to stop repeatedly tapping his pens in a way that annoyed the other students. The way that, every time the noise of a room would get too loud, he'd cover his ears and repeat the words *I'm not here, I'm not here, I'm not here.* The way he would enter the classroom and hide somewhere, such as a cupboard or behind a plastic skeleton, and refuse to come out until the end of the lesson. The way he refused to eat food cooked by other people, which was difficult when they were at a friend or relative's house and he found himself unable to touch the meal before him; Delilah had even got in the habit of bringing sandwiches for Dayton just in case. The way that, if his items on his desk were not symmetrical to one another, or were touching, he would start hitting his head against the wall.

After the explanation, there was a silence Delilah couldn't fathom. It felt hostile, and the longer it went on, the more she wondered why she'd been foolish enough to think he would help.

"I think you're overreacting," Brian eventually said. "He's a weird kid, yeah, but kids often are. He'll grow out of it."

"He's not a weird kid, Brian. He needs help."

"I've not seen any of this, Delilah. He's fine when he's at my house. Maybe it's something you're doing?"

"How would you know if he's fine at your house? When are you there?"

A sigh, then Brian said, "I'm on set. I need to go."

"Fine. Enjoy your filming. I hope the actresses can see through your bullshit."

He hung up without saying another word. She realised her walk around the estate had turned into a march and she was panting. She stopped and stood still, glaring at her phone, her mind full of thoughts whilst also, oddly, being empty of them.

She did arrange a meeting with a psychiatrist for Dayton, but Dayton refused to enter the room. When the psychiatrist came out to talk to Dayton, he refused to speak. She begged Brian for help, once against texting him to answer his phone as it was urgent – only, this time, he didn't. Over time, the idea became lost, and Delilah just found herself appeasing her son as best as she could and taking the complaints from school with a numb smile, too busy having to work to pay the bills to give the time to Dayton he deserved.

Dayton did not know the conversation between his

parents had ever taken place.

Chapter Seven

Delilah tried to help Dayton become more sociable.

Oh, how she tried.

She set up many, many playdates for Dayton, but it never seemed to work. He rarely gelled with other children, and when he did, his conversation was strange, and parents seemed uncomfortable with the interactions Dayton had with their child.

There was Jason, for example, whose mother had become friendly with Delilah at the school gates. In school, Jason and Dayton coexisted without awareness of the other's presence, and Jason had a large group of friends he'd spend his break times with, playing tag, or football, or showing off in front of the girls – something boys did even at an age where they didn't know what they were showing off for. Dayton would spend his time hidden in a corner of the playground, or behind the bike sheds, or in a small alcove out of the way, and wouldn't emerge until the break time was over. But, at Jason's house, they were forced to be together, and the mothers watched expectantly, waiting for conversation to ignite or games to ensue, as if you could force or schedule friendship.

Jason tried. More than most kids would. He asked Dayton if he wanted to play with his big digger toy, or his remote-controlled jeep, or his trampoline in their large garden. Dayton, however, could only listen to Jason's list of potential play objects with envy. He didn't have a big digger toy, or a remote-controlled jeep, or a trampoline. The flat his mum rented was on the third floor, and there wasn't even a communal garden, let alone one of their own. So he remained silent, glaring at each offer with a resentment that festered, until eventually Jason gave up, and went outside to play on the trampoline by himself.

Delilah watched Dayton as she feigned interest in polite conversation about the PTA and the governor's meeting and how positive Jason's parents' evening was – she didn't mention Dayton's parents' evening, where she'd heard the words *unusual* and *social recluse* a lot. Her son watched Jason on the trampoline, seemingly unaware of the glare that was smeared across his face, and she observed it with a wariness she knew she held but could not find an explanation for. There was something in the way her son stared at the other child that made her worry. And, when Dayton stood up and began marching toward the trampoline where Jason did yet another somersault, Delilah was off her chair and pursuing her son with no rational reason why.

But she could not get to her son in time.

Dayton leapt upon the trampoline, approached Jason whilst he was in the middle of an air spin, and pushed him. Jason landed on the metal bars that ran the circumference of the trampoline then cried out as he collapsed on the ground.

His mother's scream was intense and nonsensical. She leapt to her feet and sprinted across the garden like she was about to take off. Jason was on the ground, grabbing his neck, howling in pain, in tears.

His mother, nursing his neck and dialling 999, looked up at Delilah with an intense scowl and spat the words, "What did your son do?"

Delilah grabbed Dayton's arm and dragged him out of the house as the woman's distressed demands at the emergency service to hurry echoed throughout the large corridors.

Delilah saw Jason's mother at the school gates a few weeks later. She attempted to apologise, but was ignored, and backed away as she saw Jason leaving the school with a cast on his neck.

The next time she set up a playdate, she ensured it was with a child who did not have a bigger house, or grander toys, or a better life. She found another child and a single mother, living in a smaller flat, in a worse part of town. This woman was a colleague, and had a daughter, who Delilah assumed would be kinder to her son than a boy might. They sat together in the kitchen whilst Dayton and Daisy sat in the dining room. Delilah watched from afar, trying to figure out her son's body language, concerned about the way he didn't make eye contact with the girl, wondering why he didn't smile back when Daisy smiled at him, and confused at why he kept flicking his knee in a repetitive motion.

Little did she know that, despite the smile Daisy plastered across her face, her questions did not match the pleasant nature she presented.

"Why do you smell so much?" she asked Dayton.

Dayton smelt because he hated baths and threw a tantrum if Delilah tried to get him in the shower. He didn't like feeling wet, or when his fingertips wrinkled, or what it was like when the water attacked his face so harshly.

"Why does no one like you?"

Dayton didn't know how this girl knew no one liked him. She didn't go to his school, and he saw it as strange that she had this information. He grew concerned that she might be a spy, or might have been watching him, or that she was in cahoots with the kids at school who always told him that no one liked him.

"Why do you look so poor?"

Dayton looked down at his clothes. The girl was well dressed, with a bow in her hair and a neat, light blue dress. Dayton wore the same t-shirt he'd worn for the past three weeks as he refused to let his mother wash it – he was attached to this t-shirt, it was his favourite, and he would scream when his mother tried to take it off him.

"I am so much better than you," the girl said.

This sentence triggered something in Dayton – a rage that, at such a young age, he struggled to understand or articulate, but it spread through his body, tingling his fingers and toes, forcing his lip to quiver, and for his eyes to leak as he shouted, "Shut up!" and pushed Daisy with both hands into a cabinet full of plates, which came smashing down on the girl.

Delilah tried to apologise but gave up quickly. She spent most of her time apologising for her son, and she was growing tired of it. She couldn't help what her son was like, so why did she keep having to beg other people to forgive her for it?

When she returned home, she had a text message from her ex-husband. Expecting some kind of vitriol, or another dig at her wish to have Dayton tested for autism, she opened it, and marvelled at the words. Rather than any form of nastiness, it was a simple, emotionless text message, letting her know out of courtesy that they were selling the family home they'd previously bought together, and notifying her of the new address she had to take her children to every weekend.

She looked up this address on the internet. The house was even bigger, and with more bedrooms. It had large gates that led to a ridiculously big driveway, and the garage was grand and housed at least three cars. Its garden could fit her flat several times over.

When she dropped Dayton and Cassidy off that weekend, and watched Nala open the gate to greet them – of course Brian wasn't there – she gazed at the house her children faded into with an ache in her chest she couldn't justify.

A few weeks later, she made a final attempt at organising a playdate for Dayton. This time, it was an organised get together at the village hall, run by a group of parents who had high-functioning children who were on the autistic spectrum. Hoping these people might understand Dayton's quirks, she took him there and sat silently in the circle as the chairs filled up. Once the leader arrived, they suggested they let the children play whilst the adults talked.

It was brilliant.

It was the first time she'd ever been able to unload. Everyone in this group had children who presented similar symptoms to hers, and she could identify and relate to almost everyone's stories. They shared anecdotes of failed playdates just like hers, and moments of having to explain their child to other people without knowing how to explain it. Dayton and the other children didn't interact much – in fact, very few words were passed between any of them – but they organised play bricks together, searched through the toy box to inspect all items, and played with an abacus of all things.

After the session, one of the other parents she'd become familiar with kept talking to her, and Delilah suggested a cup of tea at her flat. The woman agreed, and they left together with their sons walking side by side but saying nothing. Eventually, once they settled on the sofa, the children started speaking, though Delilah couldn't hear much of what they were saying.

Toward the end of the evening, as Delilah left the bathroom and was about to begin her return to the living room, she paused by the two children to overhear what they were saying. Dayton rarely conversed with another child, and Delilah was intrigued by what these two had in common. It turned out they were speaking about dinosaurs and games and their favourite crisps. It was wonderful.

Then their conversation turned to silence, a moment of solemnity descended between them, and the air between them felt a little grimmer. After a few moments, Dayton interrupted the silence to say, "This isn't my real house, you know."

"Huh?" replied the boy.

"My real house is much bigger than this. With a *huge* driveway, and a *massive* garage, and like, *a million* rooms."

"Where is it?"

"It's where my dad is. I'm not poor. I'm rich. Just not... here."

Delilah didn't react, telling herself it was kid-talk. But it didn't work. She felt it hard, in her chest, and she almost fell to the floor, but held herself up, refusing to wear the pain on her face.

She forced herself to feel numb over it, but it festered. And it festered. And it festered.

Did he really feel so much shame about their life together?

She worked all week. Then she worked at the weekend while Dayton and Cassidy were at their father's. Then she worked in the evenings of the weekend. She scraped and saved to afford this flat, and its rent, and its water, and its heating. She gave up her breakfast most days to spend the money on after-school clubs Dayton appeared wholly impartial to. But to her son, it was nothing. This was not his real life. Because he was ashamed of it. He was scared someone would think it was his home.

And as she looked over the walls she worked so hard to pay for, and the dinosaur wallpaper she put up in his bedroom to make it more welcoming, and the blue she painted the living room to make it seem calmer, and the carpet she laid because the landlord refused to replace the carpet that was decades old and it kept pricking her bare feet – she felt ashamed too. Just as Dayton did. Because it was nothing like the life she wished she could give him.

She never went back to that group again, and she never saw that woman again. She'd already given them her number, but after she ignored a few text messages and a few calls, they stopped trying. And she and Dayton continued as they always had. In silent absence, in a flat that was too small, and a life that wasn't big enough; dropping him off at the big house before going to work on a Friday night, where she'd cleaned offices or served beer to arseholes who told her to smile more.

She never pursued a diagnosis after that. The betrayal was too hard, and although she wouldn't admit it, she felt he didn't deserve it. She loved her son without hesitation, make no mistake of it – but, if she was honest with herself, which she rarely was, she wasn't sure how much she liked him.

Chapter Eight

Rules never made much sense to Dayton.

At least, not some of them.

He understood the sensible ones. Don't play with matches, look both ways before you cross the road, always put the lid back on a pen or it will go dry... the ones that were logical. But there were so many rules put upon him, and from such a young age, that he grew tired of being stifled every time he questioned one of them.

An example was the assemblies at his primary school when he had to sing hymns. The headteacher would put the lyrics on the screen, the music teacher would play the piano, and everyone would blare out the words at the top of their voice. Except Dayton. Because the lyrics made no sense. On one occasion, they claimed 'He' had the whole world in his hands, but He clearly did not, because otherwise the world could not rotate, and His body would block out the sun. Another hymn demanded that one should dance wherever they may be, because He is the Lord of the Dance, but Dayton didn't want to dance, and what's more, none of the students were dancing, so clearly there was no sensible reason to be singing about the need to dance. Then there was the one about some person called Hosanna having to sing, and they demanded that she sang over and over again, and that she did it to the Servant King – but a king cannot be a servant, because they are a king. Yet, however many times he pointed out to his teacher that the words were illogical, they accused him of being difficult or talking back, and they punished him.

Another example was school uniform. He'd grown up watching television, and most shows came from America where they didn't wear school uniform, so it was immensely confusing when the day came that he had to wear one. His school forced students to wear ugly uniforms with grey blazers, beige shirts, and maroon ties. It made for a dull combination, and it reminded him of the kinds of clothes he saw old people wearing. He hated it, but when he took his tie and his blazer off, the teachers would tell him to put them back on, then shout at him when he refused. He was doing the work they'd asked him to do, so why did it matter?

But, despite these misgivings, some of the school rules reassured him. Drinking milk at break time made sense – otherwise messier students might spill theirs over his work. Putting your hand up when you would like to say something made sense – otherwise everyone would speak and it would be too loud, and he'd have to cover his ears and shake his body to make it stop. Having your pencil case with you made sense – other people who didn't kept asking to borrow one of his pens, and he hated lending people pens, as they either wouldn't return it, or would return it with a chewed lid which would render that pen unusable.

It was at his father's house when his misgivings toward rules became a big issue. Not with any of his father's rules, of course, as he was usually away filming. It was Nala's rules. She had a lot of them, and they weren't always easy to adhere to, and she would quickly lose her temper when Dayton didn't obey. Especially at dinner times.

Dayton never began his dinner straight away. He had to organise it first. He did this by ensuring every item of food was separated from the other. If he had a plate of sausages, beans, chips, and bacon, he would ensure they were all sorted into their own parts of the plate. Nala had this dreadful habit of draping the beans over the other items, which meant Dayton had to spend a while scraping the bean sauce off the other food. Then he had to sub-organise each category of food into size order. The biggest chip would be at the left, and the smallest at the right.

One particular dinner time, in the thick of summer, when the air outside was sticky and fans kept appearing around the house, Dayton was still organising his food by the time Nala and Cassidy had almost finished theirs. They only had a few hours of light left, and Cassidy was keen to go outside and play on the new climbing frame – but Nala had a strict rule at dinner times: no one leaves the table before anyone else. She insisted it was rude, and that they should wait for others to finish. But Dayton was taking a long time, and Cassidy was growing restless. She wriggled from side to side in her seat, kept staring outside the glass dining room doors to the garden, and kept pushing out irritated sighs. Dayton thought Cassidy was being annoying. Nala, apparently, did not.

"You need to eat that," she told him.

Dayton didn't respond. He was too busy organising his pieces of chicken into size order, which required more analysis – there were two pieces that were similar in size, and he was having to look really closely.

"Don't put your face so close to your food."

Dayton knew she was talking, but he didn't register it. He held the first piece of chicken inches from his eyes, then the second, inspecting them like a detective might inspect a clue through a magnifying glass. Eventually, he lifted his head and concluded that the second piece was smaller.

"Dayton, eat your dinner."

He picked up his knife and fork, but he still didn't eat. Since he'd been scrutinising the size of the items, an oozing of bean juice had escaped the bean section of the plate, and had penetrated the space between his chips like a squirt of water escaping through a crack in a dam. This wouldn't do. He began scraping the bean juice back again.

Nala stood, grabbed his plate, and took it away.

"Hey!" Dayton cried as he chased after her.

She put her arm out to block him and held the plate out of reach.

"You know what?" she said. "If you want to play with your food, maybe you don't get any food."

She pressed her foot on the bin pedal, prompting it to open its wide mouth, and scraped his food down its gullet.

Dayton stared, his body tensed, weak in his demeanour.

"I'll do you something else," she said. "And it will be ready in half an hour."

Dayton sat at the table. He did not leave. It was too stressful; dinner time was at seven, and it was now forty minutes past seven, meaning the time was wrong. He could not leave the table until this was rectified.

It was a quarter past eight when Nala put a plate in front of him. Barely boiled broccoli and tinned new potatoes sat beside each other on the plate. He hated both.

"You're old enough to behave properly now," she insisted, and this became her go-to phrase when she enforced her rules. She wasn't the only one to have this belief either – the rules at school became stricter as he grew older as well, and he became as miserable at school as he was in Nala's company. He was in the top year of the junior school now, and whilst his peers had the strut of older kids who owned the school, Dayton remained a recluse, hiding until break time ended.

Then the day arrived when he was determined to change this. He'd spent his life up to that point in a desperate endeavour to remain unnoticed and unaffected – but now he hated the thought of being forgotten. Within an afternoon, he'd decided that he wanted to be one of those boys that mattered. The ones that everyone swarmed to at break time and asked what game they were going to play. He had never felt this urge before, but it came on suddenly and strongly, an aching yearning to be one of them. To be a winner.

When his mother picked him up that day, he saw the other boy's mothers bringing their skateboards with them, and those boys rode them all the way home, so Dayton begged his mother to buy him a skateboard. It took a few days, but she did – though it was not a skateboard like the other boys had. Those boys had shiny skateboards with cool designs on the bottom – his had scuffs down the side, and some image from an outdated television show he didn't recognise on the bottom. Still, he was determined to learn, and he spent an entire weekend on his dad's drive, teaching himself how to ride.

Late afternoon on Sunday, just as he thought he was getting the hang of it, he grew in confidence enough to skateboard down the street. It only took a few minutes for him to collide with a lamppost and his face to collide with the pavement. There was blood on the ground, and he could feel a throbbing on his cheeks, and he wanted to run to his mum.

Knowing she wasn't there, he just ran into the house, up to his bedroom, and shut the door.

When he arrived at school on Monday, the boys laughed at the big red bump on his cheek.

He tried bringing his own hobbies into school instead, and asked the boys if they wanted to trade stickers for his sticker album. They said yes, and he tingled with excitement. He brought his sticker album for his favourite sci-fi movie into school the next day, then they started asking which players he had, and came up with all these names he didn't know. After a while of being grilled and remaining silent, he realised the boys were collecting football stickers. He went home and asked his mother if he could watch a football match. She laughed and said she couldn't afford the channels – and, besides, he didn't like football.

When Dayton began senior school, he didn't fare much better, and his attempts were just as futile, such as the time he bleached his hair. The coolest of the boys had bright blond hair, and everyone said he bleached it, so Dayton decided he'd do the same. He found some of his mum's hair dye in the bathroom cabinet and, assuming all hair dye would turn his hair blond, he applied it. When Delilah arrived home that evening, she was aghast to see her eleven-year-old son with bright white hair. He looked like the child form of a wizard, or like his hair had prematurely aged. She held back her surprise, stifled her laughter, gave him a cuddle, and asked if he'd like her to do something about it. He said no. Said he liked it.

The next day, everyone was in hysterics – and the boy Dayton had attempted to emulate guffawed so hard he struggled to stay on his feet. Even the teachers held a hand over their giggles.

Dayton refused to go to any lessons, and they had to call

his mother to pick him up. Unable to lose the money, she had to take him to work and get him to sit in the corner while she cleaned the office.

But the worst was still to come.

That day, Delilah gave him a hair rub, a kiss on the forehead, and reminded her son that she loved him. She told him that, whilst he had to go to his father's house for the weekend, the instant he was home on Sunday, she would fix his hair for him, and he felt reassured that he wouldn't have to return to school with this on Monday. Delilah dropped him off at his father's – who, of course, was not there again – and gave him a sweet smile as he left the car.

The gates opened, and he trudged up the driveway as his sister galloped ahead. Nala opened the door and took Cassidy into her arms, as she often did. Someday, Dayton would look back at this and feel ashamed of his sister for loving Nala so much, but right now, he was too young to understand he felt such a way.

Then he approached Nala, who, almost in slow motion, twisted upwards from her crouch in front of Cassidy, turned her body toward Dayton, widened her mouth, and used one hand to cover it and the other hand to point. The laughter caused her to bend over and smack her knees. He hated how even her laughter was in her foreign accent, and that such a person would dare laugh at him.

After comforting a tearful Dayton on Sunday night, Delilah phoned her ex-husband.

"Where were you this weekend?" she demanded.

"On set. It's been a real doozy, we're way behind."

"And what about your son? When are you going to see him?"

"Oh, don't start, Delilah."

"Don't start? I drop him off every Friday and pick him

up every Sunday, only to find he has spent the entire time with his stepmother. Not *you,* his stepmother."

"Nala does a great job looking after them."

"But she's not you, Brian! They are not there to see her, they are there to see *you.*"

"Are they though?"

This took Delilah by surprise. She was expecting all kinds of retorts and abuse from him – such exchanges had become part of the way they communicated – but she was not expecting him to challenge the fact that Dayton wanted to see his father.

"What do you mean?" she asked.

"Cassidy, fine, yes, she wants to be here – but Dayton? Even when I am there, it's like I'm not. He spends all meal times rearranging his food, spends all afternoon staring into space, organises his toys instead of playing with them with me. He doesn't even want me to read him a story, Delilah. Does he want to be here?"

"If you were there, and were making more of an effort–"

"Then he'd carry on being the same little freak he is now."

She allowed the silence of her reaction to echo down the phone. "Freak?"

"Look, Delilah, I have to go, they are calling me back to set."

"Your son is more important than what they are calling you back to!"

"Uh huh, I got to go."

"I will not keep dropping him off every weekend just to spend it with your wife, Brian."

"Fine, why don't you stop dropping him off."

Grammatically, it may have been a question, but he

delivered it as a statement. Flat, and with little emotion aside from the impatience he evidently felt.

"I'm going, we can carry on with this later–"

"No, Brian," she said coldly. "If that's really how you feel, there's no need to carry on with this conversation at all."

"Goodbye." He hung up.

Next Friday, when she drove to Brian's house to find Nala standing in the doorway, ready to receive Delilah's children, there was only one child that came out of her car.

Nala hugged Cassidy, then looked up, expecting Dayton to be there. But he wasn't. She locked eyes with Delilah, sitting in the car outside, looking in at the life she used to have, their dead eyes meeting like enemies after a battle.

Nala seemed to understand. Or, at least, she didn't question it. There was a little confusion, but no resistance.

She welcomed Cassidy inside and shut the door.

Delilah drove away, and their weekends continued like this from then on.

Chapter Nine

Dayton's birthday took place in August, so he was always the last in his class to reach that year's milestone. It also meant that it was the summer, and his peers were either away on holiday, or not interested in going to the weird kid's birthday party when they could be at home on their games console, or kicking a ball around with some friends. So, to avoid any potential upset, Delilah simply didn't organise a party, and instead opted for a smaller affair. In the weeks building up to Dayton's twelfth birthday, she'd put money aside in a pot so she could take him and Cassidy to the local fast food burger restaurant. Dayton appeared excited at first, but spent most of his time analysing the contents of his burger, and scraping onion and gherkin onto his napkin.

Still, when September came around, Dayton approached it with the optimism he often did. He'd had six weeks' distance from school, and in that time, he'd attempted to reinvent himself. He was no longer the cooky weirdo who hung around on his own. He was going to wear his shirt untucked despite his teacher's protestations, like the coolest kids did. He was going to gel his hair. Talk about cool things. Walk with a suave stride.

But when he returned to school to begin year eight, everyone seemed to have changed in a way he hadn't. The other boys had grown taller, and some of their voices were deepening, and their shoulders were becoming broader. The girls were different too – there was more makeup, more skirts, and some of them even had lumps on their chest. Dayton was still small, little, and undeveloped. His body hadn't started these changes yet, but he felt like it should have. He'd learned about puberty, and his mum had brought him a book he'd read cover to cover, mostly focussing on the page about how to talk to girls and how relationships develop. He spent quite a bit of time on the page where there was a diagram of a female body, marvel-ling at the breasts and the pubic hair; it seemed so alien to him.

They had PE on their first day – but, being the first day, no one had their kit, so they were to sit on the floor of the gym and listen to information about which sport they were doing first and which kit they'd need to bring. Then they were sorted into boys and girls, then sorted again into three lines that dictated which set they'd be in – high ability, medium ability, or low ability. Dayton was placed in the third line behind a boy who kept chugging his inhaler like it was cocaine, and in front of a boy whose massive glasses seemed to magnify their eyes.

After a few minutes of sitting gormlessly, waiting for the lesson to end, he realised a group of boys in the line next to him were sniggering in his direction. He turned and looked at them, envying the way they were so naturally sociable – they interacted with an ease Dayton struggled to achieve. And they were so much taller than him too. This felt like an insult. He should be tall, but he was not, and it was just not right.

"Hey, Dayton!" one of them shout-whispered. "You got a bird yet?"

The rest of them sniggered, one of them even snorted. They didn't hide this from him, as if he was too stupid to notice that they were laughing.

"A bird?" Dayton said, wanting to show that he was like them. "Like a pet?"

Their sniggers grew into something hysterical, and a few of them fell onto their backs from the force of their laughter.

"No," said the boy again, struggling to speak amongst the giggles. "Have you got a girlfriend?"

Dayton looked down. Should he lie? If he said he did, would they respect him? Would he be able to prove it?

"Yes," he said, then changed his mind. "No. Maybe."

"Make up your mind, Dankworth!"

"Yes. She goes to a different school."

They laughed again, and he knew they saw through the lie, and he felt pathetic and little and stupid for even attempting to convince them.

"Do you bash your bishop over her?" another one of them said. This did it – they all fell over each other laughing, failing to keep each other aloft.

"Do you stroke your salami to her?" another said, and they kept rolling around, clutching their bellies.

"Is she taller than you?" another asked.

"No."

"No? What is she then, five?"

Dayton turned away from the laughter. He didn't want to hear it. They kept asking him questions, but he became catatonic. When it was time to leave the lesson, the group of boys did so, still laughing and repeating things Dayton had said. Dayton didn't move; he remained gormless and static, glaring at his feet.

When he arrived home, he went straight to the computer and searched *How do I make myself taller?* It said to eat well and get rest, but he already ate well and slept a lot. He tried stretching himself in his room, as if he could increase his height through sheer willpower. He'd seen pictures of basketball players, and they were tall, so he showed up to basketball club – but as soon as he entered the changing room, the same group of boys were there, and immediately laughed at him, so he left.

Craving consistency and routine, he would sit on the same bench every lunchtime and eat his lunch. From this bench, he could see the fields where the boys played football, and he could see the alcove by the art block where the girls hung out. As the weeks went on, he noticed the boys who'd teased him hanging out with these girls more and more. He even noticed some of them kissing, and the girls would giggle, and they seemed to like it.

Dayton knew he was expected to like girls too, but the thought of having to kiss one of them someday caused him such anxiety that it made him shake. He imagined leaning in and pursing his lips, and it caused such terror that he couldn't finish his lunch.

Even so, he felt like he was meant to have a girlfriend. Those boys had girlfriends, and it felt like an accessory that he should have, like a bag or a coat. But he couldn't talk to one, never mind ask one out. It wasn't that girls were mean to him like the boys were – in fact, they were quite nice, and they sometimes even said hello, though never when the boys were watching. They just felt intimidating. They were all taller than him, and he was aware on some level that they didn't see him as a love interest, or even a friend, but like someone else's dog; one they'd pat on the head as they passed it on the street.

Yet they liked those mean boys. And he grew to resent them for it.

Dayton was never anything but nice. He was shy, and said little, but he still treated those girls with manners and gentleness.

And how did those boys treat them?

Like they were worthless; something to use and discard.

He always overheard the girls talking about being cheated on, like the gossip excited them, or like the soap opera of their lives kept it interesting, and Dayton wondered whether they liked the boys being mean. Which was ridiculous. Why would anyone like someone being mean to them?

For Dayton, this was evidence that the human race was stupid. That people were just uncivilised animals, and that they needed someone like him to guide their decisions. He daydreamed about one of those girls coming to him for advice, and him telling them they needed to spend more time with a boy who's going to be nice to them. Like him. But they never did. Instead, they persisted with those boys, changing which boy they were 'going out with' almost every week. He craved their attention, though he didn't admit it to himself, and he resented the boys for winning by being horrible. It wasn't how the world should work.

When he found out those girls were going to the school disco, he saw it as an opportunity. Perhaps if he went, they'd be more comfortable asking his advice in a more relaxed, sociable setting. It took all the courage he had to attend, but he put on a shirt his mother ironed for him, and ignored her beaming smiles as she dropped him off and kept repeating how good she thought this was for him.

He stood in the corner with a can of fizzy drink he'd

bought from one of the teachers for a pound – they were in the corner of the school hall with a sign on cardboard reading *Tuck Corner,* and he found it weird to see his teachers wearing jeans and taking money. Still, he stood in this corner, and lit up when those girls arrived, then deflated when he saw the boys behind them. Even so, there were moments when the boys went outside, or to the toilet, and left the girls alone, meaning they had the opportunity to come talk to him. He was ready with advice, anticipating their approach, eager to tell them what he thought.

But they never even looked his way.

He stayed in that corner all night, and they didn't approach him even once.

At the end of the night, when he was feeling dejected and angry, ruminating about how horrible the world was and how nasty humans were, one of the older girls approached him. She wore lipstick and a dress that showed off the curves of her buttocks. She smiled in a way that looked so grown up. She asked him what his name was.

"Dayton," he replied, staring at her warily.

"Would you like to dance, Dayton?"

He panicked. He hadn't planned for this. Hadn't expected it. Didn't know what to say. Was it a prank? A joke? Were the boys going to laugh at him?

But the boys were dancing with those other girls, and they weren't even looking his way.

Without waiting for an answer, the girl said, "Come on, Dayton," took his hand, and guided him to the dance floor.

Her hand was soft, and it felt strange in his. She stopped him in the middle of the dance floor, placed his hands on her waist, and put her arms around her neck. He felt tingles throughout his body, and an uncomfortable growth in his briefs. This was incredible, unlike anything he'd ever known, and suddenly he didn't care about those girls anymore.He caught the glances of the boys from across the hall, and they stuck out their lips and nodded as they nudged each other. It was the first time he'd received their affirmation, and it felt incredible; he felt like he was high, and he could not stop grinning.

This girl, pretty and sweet, did not stop staring into his eyes and smiling. She swayed to the side, and his body felt stiff, but he tried to mimic her movement. It felt stupid at first, but he sunk into it, and when he let his inhibitions go, it felt magnificent. If he had to have a girlfriend, could she be his?

The song ended, and she stepped out of his embrace. He wanted to hold on to her, clutch onto her waist, but she didn't let him. She gave him a kiss on the cheek, and a wink, then said, "Thanks, Dayton," and left.

Dayton could have flown into the sky right then and there. He could have fought a million armies. He could have run up any hill.

He'd never felt anything like it.

But, after a few minutes of waiting for her to return, she didn't. He stood at the side of the dance floor, waiting for her to re-approach him and continue their dancing. They'd only had one song together – surely if she was to be his girlfriend, she'd want to dance for more?

After another two or three songs finished, and the boys stopped admiring him and continued laughing at him for his solitude, he decided he'd go find this girl himself. He marched out of the hall, looking around, and spotted her with her group of friends outside.

"That was really sweet of you," her friend said.

"I know, I just felt so sorry for him," the girl replied.

Dayton paused behind her, about to tap on her shoulder

and ask her why she hadn't come back in – but their conversation attracted his attention.

"What was his name?"

"Dalton I think? Daily? Darren? I don't remember."

"He's a bit weird."

"Yeah, but I always see him hanging around on his own. I felt so bad that he'd come to the disco and didn't even have anyone to talk to."

"Aw, you're so sweet. When's Bret getting here?"

"Oh, he didn't want to come – I'm going to his house after. His parents are out, so we're going to have some fun."

Dayton didn't tap her on the shoulder. He didn't even move. And, even though he was standing directly behind the group, not a single one of them noticed him. His small stature and his shy nature made him exceedingly unnoticeable, and that was never more apparent than now.

It was sympathy.

She'd felt sorry for him.

She didn't want to be his girlfriend. She didn't like him. She didn't care about his feelings.

She just felt bad that he was standing on his own.

He backed away and watched her leave with Bret, her boyfriend, probably her age, probably much taller than Dayton, and probably obnoxious and nasty and horrible, just like those other boys.

His mother had raised him to be kind. Nice. A gentleman. To treat people well. To be polite.

None of those characteristics were benefitting him.

Girls only went for scoundrels. Bastards. Boys who would mistreat them. Boys who made them miserable.

Girls made poor choices.

This was the lesson he learned that day.

And, no matter how lovely and kind and gentle he was,

he would not get a girlfriend, as girls were too stupid to choose the lovely, kind and gentle boy. They were animals, attracted to the alpha who would hurt them the most, and not to the one who would love them and treat them well.

It was almost as if they needed someone to control their love life and dictate who they dated. It would be in their own best interest. They'd be less hurt for it. And those boys would be the ones who couldn't get a girlfriend, and Dayton would laugh at them for it.

Already, at twelve-years-old, he considered himself wiser than everyone he knew.

The Day of the Twenty-First

Chapter Ten

WHEN IT CAME TO CLEANING THE HOUSE, DAYTON FELT anxious. Killing his roommates had been the simple part, but this... he'd never cleaned anything before, and he didn't know what to do. There were bottles under the sink, and each of them had a label, but beyond that, he was at a loss. Still, it was crucial that the house did not raise suspicion – if he was to bring potential targets back here then it would need to be spotless. A red stain on the carpet or the furniture might ruin his element of surprise.

With a grunt and a sigh, he plodded through the living room and into the kitchen, and crouched before the sink, his leg muscles twinging under the strain of a movement he wasn't used to. A crusted spaghetti stain, most likely from Clark's breakfast – yes, he had spaghetti for breakfast; yet another reason Dayton hated the guy – was stuck to the outside of the cupboard door. He pulled the door open and there, before him, was the waste pipe connected to the washing machine, mould against the far wall, and several bottles meant for cleaning. Most of them had a lever at the top to allow for squirting. There was a rag draped over one of them. And they were all bright colours – green, red, orange – as if someone was trying to make cleaning fun.

Cleaning was never fun.

When he was a kid, he used to hide when his mother went into cleaning mode, shutting himself in his room with his music loud. If he remained in the living room, casually watching television, she would ask him to do stuff – *Oh Dayton, can you just take this to your room? Oh Dayton, can you take your hoody off the chair? Oh Dayton, can you put your school bag in the cupboard?* – and he had learned to recognise the signs, often when she stood in the middle of the room with her hands on her hips, chewing her lip, scanning her surroundings, and had learned to escape before the cleaning started.

For now, he was going to have to learn. There was bleach. Mould remover. Disinfectant. Carpet cleaner. Glass cleaner. His infallible logic suggested that carpet cleaner would be best to use, considering the mess was mainly on the carpet. So he took the rag, squirted the potent liquid, and scrubbed away.

After ten minutes, his arms were tired, and he had made little progress. It felt as if he was just rubbing the blood further into the carpet. He'd managed to remove the surface layer, but beyond that, the stain wasn't going.

He stood. Huffed. Decided he'd just pre-warn anyone he brought to the house that he'd spilt tomato sauce everywhere, and not to worry about it. That meant he didn't have to clean anymore, which was a relief, and he returned the cleaning products to their place beneath the sink. The day was moving along, and he was keen to get started; his arms were tingling in anticipation, and his legs were bouncing in excitement.

But there was one more thing he must do. One more

piece of preparation to complete before the carnage could unfold.

His manifesto.

He climbed the stairs to his room and sat before his computer. He opened his Word document and scanned its contents. It was ten pages long, and he didn't have the time to go through it all again, but he was confident he'd included everything he needed.

And finally, the video.

He opened the camera app on his computer, positioned the webcam toward him, and admired the image of the neat-looking, well-read, educated chap that appeared on the screen. He was an attractive fella, if he said so himself, and the entire world was going to regret not seeing how superior he was.

Everything he wished to say was in his manifesto, so he didn't need to say much, but he still had a few final words he wished to convey verbally. He'd rehearsed them quite a few times over the past week. Every night when he closed his eyes, every day he went walking, every drive he took, every game he played, every bowel movement he had, he would go through these words and polish them until they were ready to be spoken.

He hit record and let it all come out.

"I am Dayton Dankworth. I am a kind, gentle man. I am a loving soul who would make a woman very happy. I am better than every one of you who cannot see this. And today, you are going to learn your lesson."

He readjusted himself in his seat. Grinned. The adrenaline was starting. He was just getting going.

"I've heard many of you discussing the red pill ideology for a while, and whilst you think you are right, you are misguided. It is the black pill you must consider. Your red pill allows women to dominate a society where they are our inferiors. The black pill, if you should choose to take it, shows you why they need the guidance of someone with a mind like mine."

He reached out and took a sip from a glass of water. He wasn't thirsty, he just thought it looked powerful to make his audience wait. Like he had so much authority, it wouldn't matter if he interrupted his battle cry to needlessly rehydrate.

"I am a charming, friendly, kind man. Yet I have learned that no amount of charm, friendliness, or kindness will have any effect on women who only want mindless men with beefed up bodies and vacuous, empty heads. You are too inferior to choose your mate, and you need someone with higher intelligence to dictate this to you – this much is evidently clear."

He took a large sniff in through his nose, and made his expression appear as grave and serious as he could.

"Your Chads and Staceys have put the Betas away for too long, and now we are coming out to play. By the time this day is through, you will understand that we will not take this anymore. From now on, we refuse to cope."

He lowered his head, allowing shadows to travel over his eyes.

"I attach my manifesto to this video. Read it well and understand my reasons. Once the Beta Uprising has started, there will be no turning back. I call on all my comrades to join me. You know what to do."

He stopped the recording.

He sat back. He felt powerful. It was surging through his body, pricking his veins, energising him; he was full of vigour, full of life, and he was keen to get started.

He didn't need to watch the video back. It was good

enough. He felt it. He'd nailed it in one take. No one would fail to understand his message after that.

He attached the PDF of his manifesto to the video, hit upload, and let the internet do its thing.

Feeling high, unformidable, full of authority, he rose to his feet like he'd flown off his seat, and strode out of his room and down the stairs, taking them two at a time. This man was too brilliant to waste his time on taking all the steps.

He collected his car keys. Collected his hunter's knife. Admired his suave appearance in the reflection of the hallway mirror. Fuck his skinniness, fuck his short stature, fuck his scrawny posture – he dressed well and looked smart dammit, and he was going to fucking rule.

"Yeah!" he shouted at his reflection.

He got high off the energy of the man looking back at him.

"Yeah!" he shouted again.

The man was bouncing from foot to foot, eager, enthused, invigorated.

"Fucking yeah!" he shouted. Nodded to himself.

He was psyched up. Galvanised by his ideals. Aroused by the sight of his large, curved, sharp blade that had already taken three insignificant lives.

With a final jump of vitality, he swung open the front door, kicked it shut, and marched to his car.

The sun was rising, and the day was only just dawning.

It was going to be a day that, to his supporters, would go down in legend.

Or to his haters, in infamy.

And to his mother, who had already seen the video and left several missed calls on his phone, in endless tension.

He smoothed down his collar, put his keys in his pocket, and left the house. The knife went under the passenger seat as he climbed into his BMW. Sitting behind the steering wheel in this car made him feel superior, and he was certain it would attract attention.

Dayton put the car into gear and pulled away. The screech of his engine woke the residents of the street as he shot down the road, driving into the morning's cool embrace, ready to give the world the carnage it deserved.

Before the Twenty-First

Chapter Eleven

It was on a frosty Tuesday afternoon in winter, after Delilah had spent ten minutes scraping ice off her car windows and even longer waiting for the air conditioning to clear the windscreen, when she received a worrying alert on her phone. She had just paid for her week's shopping, was due back at work in half an hour, and was trying to return a trolley with a dodgy wheel that kept trying to veer off in random directions when her phone pinged.

Her last transaction had taken her into her overdraft.

This made no sense. She had an Excel document on her computer where she budgeted everything – if she didn't, she couldn't be sure what she could afford. She hadn't gone over the amount she'd allocated for her weekly food shop, so how had she gone into her overdraft?

She returned to work but struggled to concentrate with it on her mind. She put on her yellow gloves and wiped down tables, scrubbed out toilet bowls, and mopped stained tiled floors, all while wondering how she could have exceeded her budget. She was already struggling to pay her bills and pay for food. Could it be identity theft? Could the supermarket have double-charged her? Could her calculations be wrong?

She finished work, picked up Cassidy from school, then picked up Dayton. She drove them home, with Cassidy nattering on about all the things she did at school – she'd painted a picture and her teacher had loved it, then she'd finished all the work in maths, and she'd scored during netball club – whilst Dayton sat in the same silence he kept every day, staring out the window with his eyes glazed over. She took them home, fed them, bathed Cassidy before putting her to bed, then checked up on Dayton, who was playing a fighting game on his games console. Then, when she finally had a moment for herself, she sat down at her computer to figure this out.

She went through her bank statements, and there was nothing irregular. No outgoing payments she didn't expect. No extra charges. She couldn't figure out what it was until, after two glasses of wine, she saw it.

The child support payments from Brian were only half of what they had agreed upon. They had been so for several months, and her bank balance was lower as a result.

She didn't waste any time. She picked up her phone and called their house. Nala answered.

"Hello?"

"Hi Nala, is Brian there?"

"Who is this?"

"It's Delilah, is Brian there?"

"No, he's at the studio. They are editing–"

"Okay."

She hung up. She didn't care what he was doing, she just needed to talk to him. She dialled his mobile number and put it to his ear. It rang out. Of course it did. Why would he answer her when he's busy with his project?

She slammed her phone on the table. The fingers of her right hand crumpled up a thin cardboard drinks mat whilst the other dug into her leg. She didn't care about the pain. If anything, it helped.

She texted Brian *ANSWER YOUR DAMN PHONE,* then slammed the phone on the table again.

Sitting back, she ran her hands over her face, through her hair, and looked over the life she'd built. Toys scattered over the floor. Dishes to be done. A drip from the tap that she tried to ignore as she couldn't afford a plumber.

She checked the time. It was gone nine. She turned her gaze to Dayton, who was still playing his game on the television.

"Dayton, it's time for bed."

He didn't respond.

"Dayton."

Nothing.

"Dayton!"

She strode over to him and stood in front of the television.

"Don't ignore me," she said. "It's bedtime."

"I just have a bit more to do."

"No – you know what time your bedtime is, you should have finished by now."

"But Mum..."

"Save the game and switch off or I'll unplug it."

He huffed. She stepped out of the way, he saved his game, and he turned off the games console. He marched to his bedroom, hands in his pocket and a scowl tattooed to his face. She supposed she should get used to these strops – his teenage years weren't far away. Still, she felt bad. She shouldn't take out her frustration on him.

Once he'd slammed his bedroom door, she returned to the table and rang Brian again. This time, he answered.

"Is this an emergency?" he demanded with no greeting.

"Yes. Where is my child support?"

He sighed. "If this isn't an emergency, then I need to get back to work."

"Don't you dare hang up on me!"

She surprised herself with the venom in her voice. Her arms were shaking, and she was struggling to keep the phone to her ear. Her eyes pricked and quivered, but she held back the tears – she would not give him the satisfaction.

"Are you mad?" he said. "Are you completely unhinged?"

"Unhinged?"

"This is why I couldn't deal with you anymore. You're insane."

The fury flooded her body until it leaked out of her pores. She could not believe this was how he was choosing to do this.

"You haven't paid me full child support for months! What the hell is going through your mind?"

"I've paid you full child support."

"No, you have not!"

"Yes, I have. I've paid full child support for the child that I see."

She went to retort, then didn't. Finally, she understood what he was saying, and the audacity of this poor excuse for a father was too much for her to process.

"I see," she said, nodding, a hand on her hip. She turned around and yelped as she stepped on an action figure. She kicked the figure across the room and its arm came off as it hit the wall. "So you've completely disowned him now?"

"I have done no such thing!"

"But you don't see him as your child that you need to pay for?"

"He chooses not to come over at the weekend – why should I pay for a child I don't see?"

"That you don't see? What, with all the quality time they spend with you while they're there?"

"Nala takes good care when I'm not there. She's not inept."

"But they don't go to see her, they go to see *you*!"

Empty silence raged. The moment passed without words, and the fury seeped out of her, replaced with searing disappointment. How could she have ever seen anything in this man? He was abhorrent. No, worse. He was monstrous.

"Are you going to pay full child support for your kids or not?" she asked.

"I'll pay full child support for the child I see."

"You..." She shook her head, struggling to find the words. "You are such an arsehole."

"Goodbye, Delilah."

He hung up.

She bit her lip. Twisted her head. Gripped her phone so hard it slid across the sweat of her palm.

The rage became too much, and she threw the phone across the room, aware she couldn't afford a new one but not caring. She kicked another toy across the room, threw her wineglass against the wall, smashing it into pieces, then screamed with her mouth closed against her fist as she squatted and held her head in her arms.

She stayed there. Aware that if she was to move, she would damage more things. Maybe even herself.

But would that be so bad?

Would it really matter if she weren't here?

Without her, her kids could live in a mansion. Massive garden. Brian and Nala as their parents.

What did Delilah offer the kids that Nala couldn't?

"Mum?"

She lifted her head from her arms. Strands of sweaty hair covered her face. Her body felt greasy, even though she'd showered an hour ago. But it would have to stay that way – she couldn't afford the water for another.

"Mum, what's going on?"

Dayton's innocent voice matched his innocent posture. He stood in the doorway, his arms wrapped around himself, slouched, timid and unsure. How did she raise a boy with such little self-confidence?

"Have you brushed your teeth?" she asked.

"No."

"Go on then, get them brushed."

His body turned to go, but his head didn't. He paused, with his gaze set on his mother. Then, finally, in what Delilah accepted as a grand act of mercy, he turned away and went to the bathroom. She listened to how long he poured the tap, thinking of the water bill, urging him not to use too much. Then she bowed her head and hated herself for the thought.

She could no longer afford to live here without full child support.

The next day, she broke the news to Cassidy and Dayton that they had to move. Dayton's face initially lit up, until Delilah explained they were downsizing to an even smaller flat. The following week, they packed their things in cardboard boxes she'd persuaded the local supermarket to give to her. At least, she and Cassidy packed their boxes.

Dayton remained still and silent, and she ended up packing his stuff while he played on his games console.

Cassidy didn't seem bothered when they arrived at their new home. She was excited at the prospect of something new. But the flat was an even graver disappointment to Delilah than the previous one. Groups of teenagers in hoodies watched them as they approached the estate like they were stalking potential prey. A car parked on the street was blacked out, the result of a fire, and another was missing its wheels. The flat was on the top floor, up five flights of stairs as the lift wasn't working. The woman in the flat next to theirs stood outside her door in her dressing gown, with a cigarette in her mouth and curlers in her hair, and didn't say a word to them as they carried in their boxes. Inside the flat, the kitchen and living room were all one room, and there was no dining room. Cassidy and Dayton had their own rooms, but only because Delilah slept on the sofa bed.

Dayton didn't make any comments on the new flat, and Delilah was grateful for that. She was treating him like a mine that might go off as soon as she approached it. But he didn't explode, for which Delilah was grateful.

But she still felt it.

His disappointment at their life. At their family. At her.

This wasn't the life she planned on giving him when she'd conceived him with a loving husband, in a loving home, with an acting career her husband would help her pursue. She was disappointed with this life too.

But she never showed this to the children. She waited until they were too busy to notice her crying, and until they were asleep to cut herself. Only on her thigh, where no one would notice. It was hardly like she had time to be intimate enough with someone for them to see the wound.

She was as kind as she could be to her son. She never

disciplined him as she felt she didn't deserve to. She never snapped at him for fear that this might set him off. But she could feel his resentment. And she knew he had pictures of his father's house on his phone so that, when his peers asked him where he lived, he would have something to brag about.

She was supposed to be rich, and she wasn't, and that was something he could never forgive her for.

Chapter Twelve

AT THIRTEEN-YEARS-OLD, THE TEENAGE YEARS BEGAN, bringing with them rebellion and insubordination – but with Dayton, they also brought apathy and isolation. He cared little for friends and spent much of his time alone – though don't be mistaken for believing this was Dayton's choice, as much as Dayton convinced himself it was. It was just easier. He hated the anxiety of trying to engage others in conversation, and he hated the way his peers laughed at him when he spoke, and he hated the way he resented them for having fun without him. His apathy wasn't a choice; it was a way to cope – though his mother didn't understand this, and often worried about his lack of desire for social interaction.

Despite his protestations that he was happy enough alone, he still yearned for acceptance. He'd watch from afar as the boys strutted around and showed off to make the girls laugh, wondering why the nastiest people always had the most friends. His solitude left a gap in his world that he needed to fill, and he did the only thing he could – he turned to his computer.

Delilah, like many parents of teenagers from a time

when technology was developing too quickly for them to keep up, was absolute in her belief that she knew everything he was doing on the computer. But, also like many parents from such a time, she didn't realise that her child now knew more about technology than she did. She'd check up on the websites he'd visited without realising how easy it was for Dayton to open the history tab, right click on *today,* and click delete. So when Delilah did her checks, she would be fooled by what she saw, and would continue her day in the peaceful belief that he was not up to anything nefarious, and was being perfectly safe.

Meanwhile, he searched online for the social interactions he craved – and he did this with chat rooms. There were lots of them. Websites that offered teen chat, loneliness chat, and even a chat roulette where he clicked a button, a wheel on the screen span, and he would be placed in a random room.

Such websites had a liberating feel, and he had some wonderful exchanges where he learned a lot. He spoke to a shaman in Japan and learned about the religion of Shinto. He spoke to an American kid who found it amazing that Dayton used the word arse instead of ass. He spoke to a boy in Mexico who feared that his dad would soon be home, as he wasn't allowed on the computer, but needed to talk to someone about how he was feeling.

Each interaction was amazing, and connected Dayton to a world of people in different situations to him. But, as with any online activity that isn't ruthlessly monitored, not everyone had the best intentions.

There was a teenage boy who lived in Edinburgh called Simon. He had three cats, a dead mum, and two younger sisters. His father was rarely there, and Dayton related to this, so shared his own experiences. Dayton talked little about his feelings, but Simon was happy to do most of the talking, so Dayton let him.

Then Simon asked how old Dayton was.

Thirteen, he replied.

I'm seventeen. A bit older.

Yeah.

Do girls like you Dayton?

I'm not really interested in girls.

It was a lie. And a bad one. But it was also true, in a way. He felt like he should be kissing girls as it was what all the other boys seemed to be doing, but he didn't yet have the desire to do such a thing. Whilst puberty had already settled into the lives of his male peers, Dayton had only just seen his first pubic hair, his shoulders hadn't broadened yet, and his voice was still too high.

But he felt he could be honest with Simon, as Simon had already shared so much already.

Not interested in girls? Simon retorted. *What's wrong with you? You gay?*

NO.

Dayton took this as an insult and considered shutting the chat down immediately.

OK OK OK, Simon responded. *My bad. Won't call you it again.*

Okay.

Dayton was satisfied. No one had ever apologised to him for anything before. It felt nice.

You are into girls tho aren't you?

Dayton stared at the question. He'd been honest with Simon, but Simon seemed to need further clarification. In fear of what Simon might say if he did not give the expected reply, Dayton responded, *Of course.*

Good. Where do you watch your porn?

Dunno.

You dunno? Surely you know where you watch your porn?

Not really. Don't watch it.

You've never watched porn? Ah mate, you are in for a treat...

Dayton was confused. He didn't understand why he'd want to watch other people have sex. What was the point? He knew all his peers kept going on about it, but he just wasn't interested.

Then Simon posted an image.

At first, the image appeared pixelated. Unclear and fuzzy. Dayton squinted to make out what it was, but he couldn't, so he waited as it loaded.

With every second, another grain of truth emerged in the image, and it became clearer. The outline of a person with a bedroom behind them, which turned into a bed. The person's outline turned into skin. The skin became clearer. The woman's facial expression gained some clarity. She was pouting, with smouldering eyes that made him feel like she was staring at him.

The last few blobs of fuzziness left, and a huge pair of breasts with large nipples became clearer, and Dayton could do nothing but stare.

What do you think? Simon asked.

Good, Dayton replied. Because that was what he was supposed to say.

She's got fuckin crackin knockers ain't she?

Yes. Big. Full.

You ever seen a girl's cunt?

Her what?

Dayton had a vague recollection of this word. He'd seen it scribbled on the walls of the school toilets when referring to a teacher, and he'd heard boys calling other boys it. But he had never actually learned what it meant.

No, he replied. *I haven't.*

Simon sent another image. Again, it appeared in pixels, which shrunk with every second as the image became clearer.

At first, he thought it was roadkill. Or a dying animal. Or a monster pouting.

When it became clearer, Dayton gagged. It was repulsive. What was that?

What do you think of THAT? ;)

Dayton didn't know what to say. He'd had enough. He left the chatroom.

But that was not his only experience of pornography. It was everywhere. Sex was all the boys at school ever spoke about. Bragging about who was doing it, how they were doing it, and how they were 'pounding birds' or causing pain or humiliation to the person they were doing it to. In lessons where they had a cover teacher, he'd see boys a few seats across from him at the back of the classroom showing each other naked pictures on their phone. He saw one boy sell another boy a picture of page three from a newspaper for 50p. At break time, he saw a group of boys watching a video of a woman on all fours with an angry man behind her, shoving himself into her, hard – then their girlfriends came along and were horrified. The boys found it hilarious.

Dayton didn't understand what the video was of, so he made a note of the website they were on, and that evening, when his mother was reading Cassidy a story, he logged on and looked. There were many videos, and they all seemed to be the same. Every man appeared angry and aggressive. Every woman looked submissive, either like they really wanted to be hurt, or like they really didn't. Everything was being done with such hostility, and such force, that Dayton struggled to understand what pleasure was being gained from it.

Was this what sex was?

Was it meant to hurt?

Did these women enjoy being hurt?

When his mum finished telling Cassidy the story, he closed the window and deleted the history. He went to bed and thought about those women.

What was wrong with them? Why did they want a man to do that to them? Why did they choose to have sex with men who hurt them so badly?

The next day after school, Dayton didn't go back to the chat room. Instead, he went on his new role-playing game, *Maze of Magic,* where he created a character and explored the digital environment. He spoke over the microphone, and everyone seemed nice, and no one spoke about porn.

But the thought, and the images, would not leave him.

He'd watch girls in his class, staring at the back of their head, trying to figure out why that girl would want a guy to throttle her, and spit on her, and hurt her. Those boys who bragged about how they treated girls, and laughed about those horrible videos – why were they the boys those girls chose?

The more he thought about it, the more he couldn't help but feel that these girls had something severely wrong with them. He daydreamed about guiding them on the right path, and showing them how a nice guy like him could help, and how he could treat them better than any of those other boys.

But when they passed him in the corridor, and he smiled at them, they scoffed and called him a freak.

He grew wary of them. Careful about what he said and

what he did. About what he revealed. They didn't seem to want to be respected, and he couldn't understand this.

With every interaction he had, every name he was called, and every instance they shunned him, he trusted them less and less.

Eventually, he didn't trust any of them at all.

Chapter Thirteen

THE NEXT FEW YEARS ARRIVED WITH ARMPIT HAIR AND hormones. Dayton grew taller, though he was still not tall, but at least his peers weren't towering over him like before. His interest in girls grew, but by this time, so had his hatred, and there was little point in him pursuing his feelings. This loathing was exacerbated by a group of girls with bottle blond hair, fake nails, and fake eyelashes, who tended to laugh at Dayton or call him a freak when they passed him in the corridor.

There was one girl, however, called Susan, who was part of the group, but said nothing of the sort. She didn't join in the laughter, though she didn't discourage it, and Dayton assumed this meant she liked him. In his logic, if she wasn't being mean like everyone else, then she must have feelings.

His fantasies of her grew stronger. He was still reluctant to access aggressive pornography, and searched vigorously for the few videos available that were just straight-forward lovemaking between a man and a woman. He would watch the way they moved sensually, and he would picture looking through the man's eyes and seeing Susan in the woman's face. He masturbated into handkerchiefs and kept them under his bed, and they crusted and stiffened, but his mother became upset if they went through toilet paper too quickly and he didn't want to upset her – which was why he was apoplectic on the day he came home and found that his mother had tidied his room.

At first, this was out of fear that she'd found the hand-kerchiefs, then he became enraged by the way she'd organised his stuff – she had placed everything into neat piles, but they were the wrong piles. He'd arranged everything on his desk so that it was symmetrical with its length and width, and not touching any other items; now the items were on top of one another! His clothes, which were assorted into two piles over his chair – clean and worn-but-not-dirty-yet – were now folded into one neat pile. He stared at this in horror, despairing at the thought that all his clean clothes were now becoming contaminated by the other clothes – every single one of them would have to be washed, despite how much his mother would moan about the amount of water the washing machine was using! And, when he peered under the bed, he could not find the handkerchiefs. He stretched his arm into the darkness, hoping they had just been nudged further in, but he could not find them. Which meant his mother must know what he'd been doing.

"What the hell did you do!" Dayton demanded the moment his mother stepped through the front door.

She appeared perplexed as she removed her coat and placed it on the back of the chair, before taking off the tabard that Dayton hated her wearing. It was what cleaners wore, and whilst he knew her job was cleaning, he hated people being able to see that.

"Excuse me?" she asked, putting the kettle on.

"What the hell did you do!" He gesticulated wildly,

remonstrating with his hands as he aimed them toward his bedroom. "You messed everything up!"

"What did I mess up?" She kept her voice gentle and kind; she loved her son, and knew the best way to deal with his outbursts was not to rise to them.

"You messed up everything in my room! *Everything!*"

"Darling, I tidied it." She tilted her head to the side and aimed a kind smile in his direction – as if she was innocent and had done nothing wrong. "I thought you might appreciate it."

"Appreciate it? You've ruined everything!"

"Well then I won't help again."

"Good! Don't!" He turned to go, then, much to his future regret, added, "Slag!"

He marched back to his room, and his mother hotly pursued him. "Excuse me?"

She paused in his doorway. He sat on his bed and folded his arms, refusing to turn and look at her.

"What did you call me, Dayton?"

He didn't reply. He was fuming. He was justified. She was not.

"That's it," she said. "I'm booking you a session with a psychotherapist. I want you to talk to someone."

"I'm not talking to anyone!"

He marched to his door, slammed it, and waited for his mother to protest. She wouldn't let that go, and in a way, her angry response would validate him, even if it was negative.

But there was no response.

She only spoke again when she knocked on his door an hour later to say that dinner was ready. He declared he wasn't hungry, even though he was, and waited for her to come back. Her persistence was a sign of her love, but it was not forthcoming. She gave him space – though, when he went to the toilet later, after everyone had gone to bed, he found a plate of food waiting for him outside his room.

With his bedroom in disarray, he needed something else to obsess over – if he let his mind rest, his thoughts would berate him until he cried – so he aimed all his attention toward Susan, and his fixation on her grew and grew. He would watch her during class as she tossed her hair back and forth, admiring her long curls as they glided down her shoulders with angelic excellence; the way her lips pouted when she concentrated; the way her foot made circles in the air when she crossed her legs; the way she made her notes in different colour pens; the way she raised an eyebrow when she was lost in thought. At the end of the lesson, he'd shuffle past her friends, and they would snigger at him. But not her. And he'd glance back, and he'd catch her eye, then leave, assuming that her returning gaze meant she liked him too.

He thought of all the things he could say to her. He wrote letters but never sent them. Even came up with poems but threw them in the bin. Masturbated over her several times a day, now using tissue to spite his mother.

Eventually, he took action. It took all the bravery he had, but he psyched himself up, and even though he was shaking, he wrote the note – *I like you. Would you like to see me sometime?* – added his number to the bottom and folded it up.

He watched her as she left school, leaning against the school fence, gathering the courage to do it. She left her friends, waved goodbye, and directed herself toward the bus. This was his chance. He ran, hard as he could, and almost knocked her over. When he reached her, he looked at the floor, held out the note, and waited. She reluctantly took it, then he sprinted away again, high on a feeling of accomplishment.

He waited all weekend by his phone. He took it everywhere. Into the bathroom. To the tea table. To the newsagents. He spent all Friday night, Saturday morning and Saturday night playing *Maze and Magic,* but kept his phone propped up against the monitor, watching it. After each hour had passed, he'd unlock it and check that he didn't have any missed calls that hadn't appeared on the lock screen. He checked he had full signal, and that he still had data. He checked his messages were empty, and that she hadn't texted instead.

Nothing.

Sunday night arrived, and he wondered if something horrible had happened. Had she died? Been in an accident? Lost her phone? Lost the paper? Had she been in some terrible tragedy and was lying in the hospital?

He didn't sleep much that night, panicked that she was hurt. But when he arrived on Monday morning, she was there, and she didn't pay a bit of attention to him.

But her friends did.

Every opportunity they had, they'd walk past him and say, "Hey Dayton, I like you," then laugh. The boys would walk past him and say, "Would you like to see me sometime?" then high five each other.

This happened over and over, every lesson, every break time, every lunchtime, for days. Then when he went home, he'd receive messages from numbers he didn't know saying the same thing.

But not once did Susan look at him.

She chose to be with the boys who made fun of Dayton. And the girls who chose those boys. And then came the day when she saw Susan holding hands with one of the boys who'd teased him.

He ran home crying and refused to leave his bedroom.

He played *Maze of Magic* for hours and hours, speaking to the people he'd got to know on there, doing raids and building his avatar. It was the only thing that distracted his mind, because if he sat still for too long, he would fill with hate, and he would ruminate on Susan and the girls and the boys and the messages and the comments and the utter humiliation of losing out to nasty pricks like them.

When summer came, he took his GCSEs, and begged his mother to send him to a college at a different school. He didn't want to be near those people. In fact, he wanted to go to the all-boys sixth form college on the other side of town. Reluctantly, she agreed, thinking she was helping.

Because his exams ended in June, Dayton had an extra month in his summer holiday, and he spent it in front of his computer, only emerging for water or toilet breaks. *Maze of Magic* became his life – more so than his real life. He was fully immersed in the game, and he refused to turn it off.

So when Delilah informed Dayton that he would go on holiday with his dad for a few weeks, it crushed him. But she was keen for him to go. This was an attempt by Brian to re-establish a relationship. Even though he'd been coerced by Delilah, and even Nala, he'd offered to pay for Dayton's accommodation, and take him with him.

Dayton lasted two days before his father sent him home. He threw a tantrum when there wasn't any Wi-Fi in the hotel for him to play his game and refused to leave the room. Brian didn't know how to deal with Dayton's outbursts. He hadn't been a regular feature of his son's life for a while, and this behaviour was new to him. He decided his son was being difficult and, if he was making more effort to connect, so should Dayton.

When Dayton returned, his computer was missing.

"Where is it?" he demanded, charging into the living

room where his mother was watching a game show hosted by a man with too much fake tan.

Delilah considered playing the fool, but she didn't.

"I have it," she answered blankly, not taking her eyes away from the screen.

"Well give it back!"

She muted the television. Twisted her body toward him. Leant her head on her fist and surveyed her son, who was slowly becoming a young man. His voice was deeper now, but although he was sixteen in a few weeks, it still felt like she had a toddler.

"I'll give it back," she said. "But on one condition."

"What?" he snapped.

"I've booked you a session to speak to someone."

"Who?"

"His name is Doctor Sherman."

"A doctor?"

"Yes. If you go, and you answer his questions, and speak to him politely, then I will give you your computer back."

The dilemma was clear on Dayton's face. The impudence of his mother's actions was unjust and unfair. How dare she take the only thing he enjoyed? He resented the injustice of it, and considered protesting, demanding that she give his computer back, shouting at her for being so horrible, and for putting him through such an ordeal by sending him on holiday with his father.

But he'd also learned that his tantrums didn't make his mother change her mind. And he was desperate. So he agreed.

"Good," she said, and stood up. "I'll get my coat."

She said goodbye to Cassidy. They wouldn't see her until tomorrow – Cassidy was going to the cinema with her friends, then sleeping over at their house. She did that often.

Then, at the weekend, she'd see the friends who lived near her father, and Nala would prepare snacks for them when they came over.

Dayton barely noticed she was gone. To do that, he'd have to leave his game and emerge from the darkness of his room. Something he hated doing.

He sat in the passenger seat of his mother's car, watching the world go by whilst covering his face. The car chugged, and it was small, and the air-conditioning didn't work, and he didn't want people to see him in it. It wasn't the right car for him. It wasn't the right life.

They arrived at the children's hospital. There were railings painted blue and signposts to different wards. A man stood outside the entrance smoking a cigarette, and Dayton, who hated the smell, gave him a wide berth.

The corridors were beige and stale, and the strip lights overhead were too bright, and it made his body tense. His mother spoke to someone at reception, then they went to the waiting room, which smelt like body odour and cooked vegetables. There was a giant fern in the corner hanging over one of the seats, and Dayton took the seat furthest away from it. A mother talked on the phone whilst pushing a pram back and forth even though her toddler was on the floor playing with wooden blocks. There was a pile of magazines, but they all seemed to be aimed at women. He hated the child, he hated the mother, and he hated the magazines.

After a few minutes, a man came to the entrance and said, "Dayton Dankworth." He was too tall, wore an ugly brown sweater, and had a patchy moustache. His head looked too long, and his hair sprouted out of it like a cabbage doll.

"Come on then," Delilah said as she stood. Dayton, remembering how much he wanted his computer back, reluctantly followed. The man led them to a room and introduced himself as Doctor Sherman.

There were three small armchairs in the room. One was grey, one was yellow, and one was green. Doctor Sherman invited Dayton to pick his chair, and it felt like a test. He chose the grey one.

"So how are you, Dayton?" Doctor Sherman asked. His voice was too posh. There were certificates on the wall behind him, and Dayton scanned them for the man's qualifications; he had a degree in Child and Adolescent Psychology. There was also a bookcase full of children's books against the far wall, displaying a model sun with a face on the top shelf, and a poster further along that said *Thoughts Aren't Facts*.

Delilah nudged her son.

"Fine," Dayton said.

"Are you happy with your mother here?" Doctor Sherman asked.

Dayton shrugged.

"I'd like to get to know you a little, Dayton," Doctor Sherman said. "If that is okay with you?"

Doctor Sherman put on a pair of glasses, crossed his legs, and placed an A4 pad over his knee. He didn't seem bothered by Dayton's lack of response.

"Tell me about school," Doctor Sherman asked.

Dayton felt his mother's stare so intensely that he became highly aware of it.

"What about it?" Dayton asked.

"Do you get on with your peers?"

"Not really."

"Why not?"

"Because they are all dicks."

Delilah gasped and went to apologise, but Doctor Sherman raised his hand to halt her.

"Why are they dicks, Dayton?" he asked.

Dayton shrugged. "They all think they are so great. They think they are better than everyone else. But they are not. They are fools. Especially the girls."

"Do you have any friends?"

"Yes."

"At school?"

"No. On my game."

"Are they real friends?"

"Why wouldn't they be real friends?"

"Because the internet is just a fantasy, isn't it?"

Dayton frowned.

"Do you have any friends in real life?"

Dayton didn't answer.

"Or is it just pretend friends in this game?"

Dayton's scowl intensified. "Fuck you," he said.

Then he said nothing else.

Doctor Sherman tried asking more questions. He asked a lot of them. Over and over. In many different ways. Interrogatives about his family, about girls, about how he feels about himself, about how he handles stress, about how he feels his mother supports him.

Dayton could not stop thinking about how this revolting man had the audacity to insult him. To insinuate that his friends online were only 'pretend.' Like he was making fun of Dayton. Which was especially impudent when this man was such a joke himself – how could someone so pathetic teach Dayton anything about how to live his life? What wisdom could this man impart on how to live one's life better, when he was nothing like the man Dayton dreamt of becoming?

When they arrived home, Dayton was expecting an argument with his mother over whether she'd give his computer back due to his lack of cooperation. But she didn't argue. She took it out of the cupboard without a word and handed it to him. He received it with the same silence and carried it through to his room.

Within ten minutes, he had his headset on, and was laughing with those he played the game with.

Delilah watched through the crack in the door, listening to the conversations her son had, wondering where she'd gone wrong. What did she do to make him this way? How had Cassidy turned out so well, and Dayton had not? Was this her father's fault? Was it hers?

When it came to his bedtime, she didn't bother telling him to turn the game off. It wasn't worth the fight. She was exhausted, and she had a twelve-hour shift the next day. So she unfolded her sofa bed, stretched her arms and legs out into the empty space, and went to sleep.

When she awoke the next morning, Dayton was still playing the game. She got dressed, said nothing, and went to work.

Chapter Fourteen

DAYTON LASTED LESS THAN A WEEK AT THE ALL-BOYS sixth form college.

He was convinced it would be different. There were no girls there, so the boys wouldn't need to show off. They would be older, so they would be more mature. Most of all, he had a chance to reinvent himself and show everyone that he wasn't the weirdo he'd previously been known as. It was within walking distance, so his mum wouldn't embarrass him by showing up in the old, small, loud car she drove, meaning he could hide the fact his mother was poor and tell everyone about how his dad was rich.

But he hated the flexibility and the lack of routine. In his previous school, every lesson was scheduled, meaning he could study his timetable the night before and know every movement he was going to make, such as which corridors he'd need to take, which teachers he'd have, and which students would be present. Now, he had study periods. He could go wherever he felt it was best to study. But where would that be? The common room? Study hall? The library? And what if people weren't quiet when he needed to concentrate? What if there weren't enough spaces? What if he couldn't find a seat with the right cushion, or next to the right window with the right amount of light? There were too many unknowns, and it made him dread every morning, and his mother had to coerce him out of the bed for the first week.

And, when it came to his peers, if anything, the mixture of testosterone and bragging and toxic masculinity and crowd mentality and aversion to Dayton's strange eccentricities was worse. The instant he sat down in his registration room, the boy next to him, who had been talking to a large group of boys on the other side of Dayton, turned around and shouted, "Fuck me, you're small!"

The group marvelled at Dayton's short stature, and the familiar sniggers spread through them like a plague that caused hysteria.

"Are you one of those fucking midgets or something?"

"Did you get stepped on at birth or what?"

"My little sister is bigger than you."

He'd spent the previous night noting down all the things he could say when he met someone new. He had questions prepared – What school have you come from? What subjects are you doing? Are you excited about the new term? – but every one of those questions fell out of his mind like water through a sieve. He stayed in his seat, hands gripping the side, remaining dead to the laughter until the bell rang and he could hurry out as fast as he could without actually running.

At lunchtime, he warily took his first steps into the canteen, surveying the faces of the rowdy hall. He'd promised himself he'd be a new person; he'd introduce himself differently; create a new persona – but everyone was already in a group, and they were all so noisy it made him panic. But it was fine. He'd sit on his own and survey the area, then he'd find a group to join, and he'd tell them how he was rich and how he was too cool to skateboard and how he had loads of friends at his old school.

He took a seat toward the back and took out his lunch, but he'd barely eaten half his sandwich when he felt something splat against the back of his head.

He didn't turn around to see what it was. He didn't want to know. He could feel something wet sliding down his hair, and this alone was enough to bring tears to his eyes. The laughter spread through the canteen and filled him with rage; all he ever heard was people laughing at him. He picked up his lunchbox, his lip quivering, and strode out, eating on a bench outside instead.

When he walked home, the laughter was back again, following him down the street, the taunts pursuing him like a predator after prey.

After that, he never walked home again.

He used the key his mother had cut for him to enter the flat block and climbed the many stairs to the top. With his legs aching, he entered the flat, pleased it was empty, and ran into the kitchen. With no intention or thought of doing so, he leant against the corner of the room and slid down, the knob of a cupboard door prompting a throb of pain, and remained slumped on the floor. He had a new view of the flat from this level; he could see old food between the washing machine and oven, and a thick layer of dust beneath the edge of the kitchen side. He stayed there anyway. If he kept himself on the floor, they wouldn't be able to get to him.

The spaces between the dim grey blinds of the far window exposed the late afternoon light. It gradually faded, and the shadow extended until it shrouded the room in darkness.

People were evil. Nasty. Horrible.

It was their nature.

There were no good people. No kind people. Just monsters.

No one wanted to hear about his father's house, or his views on skateboarding, or his old school. There were just pricks and bastards eager to taunt him and mess with him for their own selfish entertainment.

This was what the human race amounted to, and they did not deserve their place on this planet.

When Delilah arrived home, she didn't notice Dayton at first. She dropped her bag on the sofa and sifted through the mail, scowling at more bills, before jumping at Dayton's silhouette in the corner of the kitchen.

"Dayton, what are you doing there?" she asked, but as she approached her son, she didn't ask anymore. His cheeks were red and the bags under his eyes were moist. There was a painful absence in his eyes that she'd seen before, but never this strong.

Instead of interrogating him further, she leant against the cupboards and slid down beside him. She tucked an arm around his shoulder and held him close to her chest. He didn't fight it, as much as she expected him to. In fact, he embraced it, and nestled his head into the curve of her neck.

They stayed there for a while. No words were exchanged, but they weren't needed. Delilah would have sat in silence with him all night if she needed to.

Eventually, he spoke.

"How could you send me there, Mum?"

She was about to remind him that the all-boys sixth form

centre was his choice, but she didn't. Instead, she told him she was sorry, and she wouldn't send him back.

"Would you like to go back to your old school instead?" she asked. "They have a pretty good sixth form college, and they may still have spaces."

He shook his head. "No."

He didn't give further explanation, and she didn't ask for one.

"Okay," she said, stroking his hair. "We'll find you somewhere else."

Dayton didn't want somewhere else, but he didn't protest. He would never admit it, but he was relishing the moment. His mother was often absent, either working late or picking up extra shifts in the evening, and when she was there, she was sitting in front of the television, too consumed by fatigue to engage in deep conversation. Cassidy was always busy with her friends, and she rarely spoke to her brother when she was there, so it wasn't like she was around to keep him company. This kind of interaction happened so rarely.

Eventually, however, it had to end, and Dayton stood up. He declined the offer of dinner, returned to his room, and a few minutes later, Delilah heard the familiar sound of *Maze of Magic* starting.

She still made him spaghetti bolognaise and placed it beside his computer, though he didn't acknowledge it.

She spent the rest of her evening in front of the television, though she didn't pay any attention to what was on. She was on her computer, determined to find somewhere that was right for him. She disregarded all the other local sixth forms and colleges until she found one further away that seemed more appropriate. They specialised in high-functioning children with special educational needs, and

they endeavoured to help their students recognise and overcome their barriers to learning. Over 70% of their previous
year's cohort achieved A Levels or vocational qualifications,
despite their difficulties, and this impressed her. She was
resolute that her son would go to university and wouldn't
end up with a life like hers. But this school was costly, which
led her to the last resort.

She checked the corridor for Dayton. His door was ajar,
but the sound of him talking to people he'd never met, along
with the sound of make-believe characters shooting
weapons, made it clear he could not hear her. Even so, she
took her phone to the far side of the room – which was only
a few steps away – and stood by the window, one hand on
her hip, gazing down at the teenagers loitering in the car
park, and waited to speak to the last man she wanted to
speak to.

"Delilah, is it important?" he said once he answered.

She sighed. "Yes. I promise I'll only take a minute."

"What is it?"

She looked down at her feet. There was a hole in her
sock, and it revealed a broken toenail. She smoothed her
sock over the hole with the heel of her other foot to cover
it up.

"I need to send Dayton to a new school," she said. "It
costs money."

"What's wrong with the school he's at now?"

"They aren't meeting his needs."

"His needs?"

"Yes, his needs. They aren't providing him with enough
support."

"And this new one will?"

She sighed again, though this time it was more of a huff.

She closed her eyes for a moment and ignored the sting of pride she felt when asking him for help. "Yes."

"I don't get it. What's wrong with—"

"He's being bullied, Brian. Badly bullied."

"So? All kids get bullied. He needs to learn to toughen up."

"Thing is, he's really struggling in his school. There's another one a bit further away that specialises in children like him. I can drive him if need be, but—"

"I'm not paying for some pansy-ass school he doesn't need."

"But you'd pay for Nala to have another holiday in Majorca, and another extension on your house with, what, eight bedrooms, is it?"

"Don't fucking try to guilt trip me Delilah."

"I'm not guilt tripping you. I'm just pointing out that you have enough money to do this. More than I do at least."

"And how much is the school?"

"Three grand a term."

He cracked a loud, audible, "Hah!"

She held her hand over her face. Oh, how much she regretted ever meeting this man.

"He needs this, Brian," she insisted. "Please."

She glanced back at the corridor to ensure Dayton hadn't heard a word. The same noises continued.

"Fine," Brian said. "If it gets you off my back – I'll pay half."

"Half?"

"Yes. Half. That's fair as a co-parent, isn't it?"

"I can barely find the money for the life we have already, how am I supposed to—"

"Half, Delilah. That's it."

He hung up. She was becoming used to the sound of the phone clicking when he decided the conversation was over.

She paced back and forth, mulling the situation over, going over her options. Then she opened her laptop again and navigated to her bank's website.

Within a few minutes, and after a bit of fibbing on the application form, she had a loan for ten-thousand pounds. The repayments were excessive, as the interest rate was ridiculously high, but she'd find a way to pay it. If she didn't have breakfasts, and she picked up some more night shifts, maybe she could do it. Or maybe she'd get into more debt. Who cared? She had the loan. She had what she needed.

She filled in the online form and enrolled him in the school. It took a few reminders and further coercing, but Brian transferred his portion of the money. And, with the fees paid and her anxiety over the repayments high, she showed nothing but smiles to Dayton, and took him to look around the school.

He felt insulted at first. Then he saw how much routine there was, and how there was a room especially for him to release his emotions, and how there was a quiet room where no one was allowed to speak for when he had auditory over-stimulation, and that there were only a few people in a class – and he agreed.

He did mainly vocational courses, and whilst Delilah was sceptical, as she'd learned to place more emphasis on academic subjects, they reassured her that these courses would still give him the UCAS points he needed for university. She didn't know how he would manage university, but that was the next step – for now, she would just get him there.

No matter what it took.

The Day of the Twenty-First

Chapter Fifteen

THE BMW WAS BLACK AND SHINY. THE SEATS WERE immaculate. The engine purred in response to pressure on the pedal.

Dayton had it cleaned a few days ago. When he hadn't been sure it would come to this. There was still time. Still hope. Still room for the world to change. But fate had intervened, and here he was, in a freshly waxed, new smelling, flashy car that was sure to attract the women he needed.

He'd spent all day cruising around town with no destination in mind. When there were women, he'd slow down, hoping they'd turn and look. Why wouldn't they? It was a cool car, and it had a smooth, suave guy driving it. He even wore shades. And a clean shirt he'd ironed the previous morning. Smart jeans, even though he found jeans too restrictive. He was a damn good catch, and he just needed one woman to be attracted by his car, and his fresh demeanour, and he would have his first target for Torture Palace.

There was a huge flaw to the logic to this perfectly formed plan, however.

Dayton's rage had developed through an inability to attract a woman. His car, and his image, and his kind personality had not yet attracted a woman. And he'd made many attempts. So how was this going to change today?

But no, the delusion was too grand, and he was fully confident that, with the extra effort he'd made, a woman was sure to turn her head and find herself attracted to the prospect of a guy who drove such a car.

He turned down one of the less busy streets of the city. Although it was now early evening, and the nighttime revellers and partygoers hadn't quite emerged from their pre-drinking at their homes, there were still enough women setting out early, which meant there were plenty of women to choose from. The time of waiting was now over, and the time to select his first targets had arrived. And, as he cruised at a slow, smooth speed down this street, he came across a group of women who attracted his attention.

There were three of them. Their legs were magnificent. At first, Dayton only saw them from behind, so he did not know what their faces or tits were like, but he was attracted to the way their outfits hugged their curves.

The first wore a red dress that finished a few inches below her crotch. It squeezed against her arse, which was large, but in an enticing way. She had long, black hair and a handbag over her shoulder. She struggled to walk in high heels; she was petering a bit from side to side and walking top-heavy. He saw too many women trying too hard with high heels like this, and he wished he could advise them to stop. The second wore a dress that flowed a bit more, and bounced off the roundness of her arse, and if he watched well enough, and waited for the just the right time, he could see the tip of her black panties. She was blond, as was the third – but the third was evidently a fake blond, and she wore a tacky silver dress that would look more suited on an old lady at a disco, and struggled even harder to walk in her heels.

He was willing to be the man who taught them to have more self-respect.

He cruised past them, slow enough to attract their attention, and stopped a few steps ahead of their route. He wound down his window, draped his arm over it, and sat there, waiting for them to saunter past and notice him.

Their conversation grew louder as they approached. They were talking about a guy. Of course they were. And, by the sound of it, it was a guy who'd cheated on one of them with some girl called Becks. They were becoming more and more impassioned in what they said, talking about how she should have seen the signs, or should have listened to him better, or should have confronted him.

They were all wrong, and Dayton knew it.

The solution? They shouldn't have dated an arsehole in the first place. Not when there were men like Dayton in the world. Why go for a pent-up, macho doofus of a bloke, when there were nice, gentle souls like Dayton?

Because they were idiots. All of them. And Dayton was going to teach them a lesson.

They were almost at his car. This was it. Be cool. Be uncaring. They seemed to like men who didn't care.

He didn't make eye contact, but looked around, like he was waiting for someone else, his face cold and menacing, but in what Dayton believed to be a smouldering way.

The women walked past and didn't even glance in his direction.

If anything, they gave him a wider berth.

Dayton watched them leave in utter disbelief. His jaw dropped as they remained engrossed in ardent, heated conversation. They hadn't even noticed the nice-looking guy in the car. This was what was wrong with them. There they were, moaning about the bad guys, and they didn't even notice the good one.

He felt tempted to grab his knife and go after them. He even placed his hand around the handle, ready to do so – then they turned the corner, and walked up the path to a pub, and his chance was gone.

The bouncer let them in, then eyed up Dayton, and he decided it was best to leave.

He spent another hour cruising around town, spotting groups of women, but finding that they were either with men, approaching pubs, or joining even more women to form bigger groups.

Evening became night, and dim light became dark, and more groups of women emerged. He lit up his phone screen to check the time, but didn't register it, as he was too distracted by a large number of missed calls and text messages from his mother.

Dayton what's going on?
What is this manifesto?
Is the video a joke?
I don't understand.
Please contact me.
Please don't do anything stupid.
I'm here if you need me.
Just call.
Please Dayton.
Please.

He turned his phone off. He didn't need it.

He realised why his plan hadn't worked yet; he'd been cruising around the busy and semi-busy streets – instead, he needed to try a backstreet, full of darkness and evil deeds.

Drug deals happened here, and if he really couldn't lure a woman into his car, he'd solicit a prostitute from one of these backstreets and take her back to Torture Palace. This night would not be wasted.

It turned out to be a good idea; he found a woman fairly quickly. She wore a cotton white vest and a black leather skirt, and was more modest than the others, though there was still a considerable amount of leg on show, as well as a clear line of cleavage above her top. Her blond hair bounced off her shoulders, and he overheard her on the phone, discussing with friends where they were going to meet.

She was perfect.

She didn't seem as prissy and stuck up as the others. She seemed nice. Kind. A woman who would offer a man like Dayton more of her time. Someone who was better than her friends.

She hung up and he parked a few steps ahead of her. Anticipating the moment she passed, he turned to look at her. She looked back. Their eyes met, and the moment between them became a profound moment of destiny. He waited for her to be intrigued by his slick style and approach him.

But she frowned. Looked a little freaked out. Then averted her gaze. And walked on.

Dayton took a large intake of breath, held it, and let it out. Rage was pushing at his skin, like fists of a demon desperate to escape. His teeth ground, his fists balled, his leg shook.

How dare she.

How fucking dare she.

To snub him?

And to look at him like that?

Like he was the freak? The weirdo?

Like there was something wrong with *him?*

Without another thought, he leapt out of the car and charged at her. His face curled into a snarl, something ugly and fierce, and he envisioned doing to her what he'd done to his housemates – and he anticipated liking it.

She noticed him running toward her, and she turned to flee, but she was wearing stupid heels that only granted her the ability to commence a modest trot. He barged into her shoulder, knocked her to the floor, and went to lift the knife above his head–

But the knife wasn't in his hands.

Where was it?

He glanced over his shoulder at the open car door of his BMW.

He'd left it in the car.

Shit.

She kicked him in the crotch and he fell onto his side. He intended to go after her, but she was gone too quickly, and the pain was too intense.

He scalded himself for being so reckless – how could he forget his fucking weapon? – and glared at the route she took before she disappeared around the corner.

She'd not only rejected him, and given him side-eye, and run away – she'd also kicked him in the bollocks.

The fury was unlike anything many of us experience.

We all experience anger, yes, but most of us have the self-control to leave the situation before the anger drives us to the moment of murder. Dayton did not.

Many people were going to pay for this woman's audacity.Men and women.

Chads and Staceys.

Pricks and bitches.

He returned to his car. He'd had enough of the city

centre. He knew of a house that usually had house parties on a Friday night. There'd be plenty of people there.

He felt the handle of the knife on the seat beside him. His faithful passenger he'd forgotten. His duty demanded better. He must be better.

He drove away, determined that three pathetic house-mates would not be the extent of the blood he was to shed this night.

Before the Twenty-First

Chapter Sixteen

MASTURBATION BEGAN AS A SMALL HOBBY.

It was something to do. A way to pass the time. Something to kill ten minutes.

Then it became a compulsion. Something that needed to be fitted into the day. Something that needed planning and arrangement.

Then it became a fixation. It was always on Dayton's mind; he was searching for fantasies at all opportunities, scanning the surroundings for what excited him, scrutinising the nearby women for which pieces he'd like to add to the Frankenstein's Woman he'd put together in his imagination for when he touched himself later.

Even at seventeen, pornography still scared him. It was easy to access, and he did so frequently, usually before he began playing *Maze of Magic* so he was not interrupted by any urges or desires. But it was still as aggressive as it was when he first saw it, and he despised the knowledge that women craved this level of violence in their sexual interaction. It showed him that women were just animals, and that they weren't sensible enough to decide what they wanted, and that they needed someone to dictate to them what their fantasies should be.

For Dayton, he stuck to the vanilla stuff, though this was something one had to search for on a pornography website. He mainly watched the amateur category because it mostly consisted of couples making love and treating each other with more tenderness. There was something real to these videos – they weren't created on a sound stage or a set up bedroom, and the women's breasts weren't fake, and the men weren't constantly demanding that the woman shares how much she loved being pounded. Instead, he could find genuine couples having a genuine exploration of each other's body.

It was what Dayton dreamt of doing.

It was a wild dream. It shouldn't be, but it felt like it. An unattainable notion that lay somewhere beyond the realm of possibility.

He'd watch the same videos most evenings, but his imagination would feed the images he'd logged throughout the day. Sometimes, when his mum texted and said she'd picked up another shift and he needed to get the bus home, he'd walk home instead, searching the local talent for excitable flesh he could store for later. Besides, Dayton hated the bus – it was too rowdy, and there were always loud teenagers at the back playing music on their phones, and it intimidated him. And, although it was a four-mile walk and took well over an hour, his route went past the local girl's sixth form college – and this was where they all hung out in their groups.

He resented how hard they tried to show off, whilst admiring and fantasising about the sexuality they showed off about. When a woman bent down to tie her shoelace and gave Dayton's prying, passing eyes a full view of the entirety of her cleavage, he would both judge her and desire her. He'd want to tell her how she should dress appropriately, whilst also wanting to caress that cleavage with both hands. He'd yearn to teach her how to behave in a way that wouldn't attract such negative attention from boys, whilst imagining what her nipples might look like.

He knew other boys liked these girls' promiscuous behaviour, but he was the exception. Yes, he had sexual thoughts, but he never desired hurting any of these women. While he might crave what he saw, if he was granted access to it, he would treat it well, and cover it up so it was all his, and no woman he took care of would ever feel mistreated.

As was inevitable, those girls wouldn't be alone for long – soon enough, a group of meat-headed, imbecilic, male adolescent miscreants would peter over from the local boy's school and place their lecherous hands all over the girl's flesh, and they'd laugh it off like it was a joke.

One day, as he walked home after staring at these girls from across the street, he decided he would not do this again. It was pointless. He was never actually going to get a girl to notice him, or talk to him, or want to be with him. He didn't exist in their world. His peers might boast about the girls they had sex with, and Dayton was unsure whether it was true, but he still hated them for it. Why did they get to be with a girl, and he didn't?

The final time he detoured past this school, he found himself walking home behind a solitary girl from the group of girls he often marvelled at, though he'd had no intention of doing so. She had a leather satchel over her back, and her ponytail bounced and bobbed as she walked, as did her skirt that danced around her posterior. Her legs were smooth and curved. Her waist was slim and tight. Her body was perfect in every way, and he couldn't help but think about–

"What are you staring at?"

She halted and turned around. Dayton said nothing.

"I said, what are you staring at?"

Dayton looked around. For what, he wasn't sure – help, maybe? Words? An answer?

"I've been looking at my reflection as I've been walking," she continued, indicating the shop window. "You've been staring at me. What are you, a perve?"

Dayton panicked, turned around, and ran away. He was going back on himself, and it added another mile to his journey, and he'd arrive home even later, but he didn't care. He was terrified. It was the first time one of these girls had acknowledged him, and it was to abuse him.

Yet she didn't abuse the guys who treated them so badly. Why did she choose to be so nasty to someone as nice as him, and not those blokes who behaved so lecherously around her?

He arrived home, dumped his school bag down, went into his room, and furiously masturbated to work out the frustration. Then he began *Maze of Magic* and tried to forget about the ordeal.

Delilah arrived home a few hours later, and she paused outside Dayton's bedroom as she always did. She asked about his day, what he'd learned at school, and what he'd done afterwards, and he grunted as he did every day. But she still asked.

She brought him his dinner and placed it on the computer desk. She'd given up long ago trying to coerce him away from his computer game to eat with her and Cassidy in the kitchen.

Delilah mostly found out how Dayton was doing from his teachers. Since parents were paying for the school and it catered to special educational needs, they received biweekly updates via email about what their child had been doing and the progress they were making. Although Dayton didn't do any of the little amount of homework that was set, he was making good progress. Most of his courses were assessed through coursework, but they had sent some resources through for the few exams he was going to have to sit.

There was one common piece of feedback she received, however, that troubled her. The teachers shared that Dayton required constant reassurance from his teachers. That he would often resent or snap at his peers for being weird, despite his own eccentricities. And whilst he presented as someone uninterested in social interactions, he evidently craved it – it was just easier to convince himself he didn't feel the need for friendship, than to admit he wasn't alone by choice.

There were only a few weeks left of the school year, and Dayton would go to university soon, but Delilah was concerned about how he would get on with other students, especially without her there. So she organised a dinner at one of her friend's houses and took Dayton straight there after school so she didn't have to drag him away from his computer game.

The friends were a couple who lived an hour away. Delilah had lost track of them after her divorce – it's a lot easier to remain friends with other couples when you're in a couple yourself. The woman was a writer who'd just won an award for Best New British African Voice, and her husband was a neuroscientist. Their home was grand and welcoming, and Delilah could tell Dayton was impressed by the way his eyes widened and he kept looking at every wall, and every painting, and every picture.

At dinner, Delilah asked Dayton if he remembered the boy who sat opposite him. Dayton said no. The boy was a well-dressed young man who could easily pass as a mini-politician. Delilah told Dayton that they'd played together when they were toddlers; Dayton asked why she thought he'd remember him if they hadn't seen each other since they were toddlers when he was too young to form solid memories, and it made everyone laugh except Dayton.

But there was also a spare place next to the boy. And, after they'd all sat down, the doorbell rang. The boy asked everyone if they minded, but he'd asked his girlfriend if she'd come along.

Dayton didn't say another word. He barely ate any of the food. And he didn't take his glare away from the smug couple sat opposite him. She was pretty and perfect, and he probably played rugby, and it sickened him.

On the way home, he could tell his mother was angry. The car had a furious silence that its metal casing struggled to contain.

"You really upset me tonight, Dayton," she eventually said. It felt abrupt. Dayton said nothing, but turned to look at his mother. "Those were nice people, and that was a nice boy. You could have made an effort."

She drove with one hand and rested her chin on her fist with the other. The silence continued, suffocating them both, and occasionally she would shake her head as if she was arguing with someone in her thoughts.

Dayton, in an action that was both abrupt and unexpected, cried.

Delilah wasn't sure what to do at first. She barely saw her son show emotion, never mind cry, yet here he was, covering his eyes, turning away, and looking like he was squeezing his face together to contain his despair.

She pulled the car over to the side of the road and put the hazard lights on.

"I'm sorry, Mum," he said. "I don't mean to cry. I know it's pathetic."

"Oh, of course it's not," she said with complete sincerity. "What is it that's upset you?"

"It's just..." He looked down at his hands, the fingers of his right hand fiddling with the fingers of his left.

"What?"

He shook his head and wiped his eyes. "Why does he get to have a girlfriend, and I don't?"

Delilah frowned. It wasn't that she had an issue with this, she was just surprised – he'd never expressed a desire for a girlfriend before.

"I hate it," Dayton said. "It makes me want to kill myself."

Delilah grabbed her son and, not caring for the force she used, pulled him in close to her. She wrapped her arms around him, held him tight to her neck, and whispered in his ear, "Don't you ever say that. You hear me? Don't you ever say that again."

He sniffed, but said nothing.

She lifted his face and held his red cheeks in her cupped hands.

"Do you know what I would do if I lost you?" she asked. "Do you know?"

He shrugged.

"I could not go on, do you hear me? You are my every-thing. My *everything*."

He nodded.

She pulled him close again and held him there.

Traffic built up behind the car, a line of vehicles with impatient drivers aiming angry glances at them as they passed.

Delilah held her son close without caring for any of them.

Chapter Seventeen

Much to Delilah's delight, Dayton achieved the grades he needed. University beckoned after the summer months, and the moment she returned from results day with an envelope of grades, she insisted he stopped playing his game immediately and opened them.

This irked Dayton. He was in the middle of a raid, and didn't want to be disturbed, but he found a place where he could pause, and he opened the envelope to appease his mother. He announced the grades, and she threw her arms in the air and shrieked – a howl of glee – before throwing her arms around Dayton and kissing him on the cheek.

Dayton frowned and said, "Can I finish my raid now?"

Delilah left him to it, practically dancing to the kitchen, where she pumped her fist and wiped away a few happy tears. He'd done it. She'd done it. They'd done it. All the money she'd had to scrimp and save and coerce out of her ex-husband, all the nights where she'd lost sleep as she worried for her son's future, all the arduous attempts at getting him to engage with his education – it had been for this; he had the grades he needed. He'd chosen to study creative writing after her suggestion, and she was so excited to see what kind of writing he came out with. He would be brilliant.

She had a glass of wine and celebrated by herself, not wishing to interrupt the sounds of artificial fighting coming from Dayton's room.

Dayton had little interest for grades, or university, or creative writing. He went with it because it was how his life was unrolling – his existence was like a raft being taken along the river, guided by the waves with no proper care for where the water took him. Unfortunately, none of them knew rapids were ahead, and a waterfall would soon sink the raft, and the water would claim it for its own.

For Dayton, he only cared about two things – *Maze of Magic,* and his hatred toward humanity.

He found opportunities to quietly seethe at those around him whenever he could. He rarely ventured out of the flat that summer, too occupied by his game, but his mother made some final attempts at family time before he was to leave, and it became easier to appease her than protest. The final of these was a trip to the cinema with his sister and mother, and whilst Delilah's intentions were good, the trip gave him further fire to add to his rage.

As they walked to the bus stop – Delilah had been forced to sell her car, and even though she'd only received £500 for it, she'd needed that money – Cassidy talked aimlessly about her summer plans. She had a boyfriend of seven months. His name was David, and even though Dayton had never met him, he hated the guy. And he hated how she blathered on about meeting his parents, regaling them with stories of her politeness and efforts to get on with them. Dayton could be polite and make an effort with parents, so why didn't he have a girlfriend?

She spoke of holding hands in school and helping each other with homework – but Dayton could help someone with homework, so why didn't he have a girlfriend?

And she spoke of how happy he made her, and how happy she made him – but Dayton could make someone happy, so why didn't he have a girlfriend?

On the bus, Delilah and Cassidy sat together, and Dayton sat on the seat beside them. A couple sat on the seats in front of him with their faces attached; they barely took their lips apart for the entire bus journey. The bus was full, but no one said anything. They even made sloppy noises, and he could see their tongues leaving the other's mouth when they briefly pulled apart to smile before resuming. He thought this was uncouth behaviour on her part, and she should have better standards than such public indecency.

Then came the film they had dragged him to the cinema to watch. It was about a woman with a busy job who didn't have time for love – then a man entered her life and showed her that love was the answer to all her worries. Dayton despised that man. If this man could be her answer, why couldn't he?

His mother bought him his gaming magazine, and he read it on the bus home while Cassidy kept nattering on about her boyfriend again. Dayton ignored them as he became engrossed in his magazine. Then he came across a perfume advert. It was in black and white, and the man was muscular and topless, and the woman was scantily clad, draping her hands across his chest. Dayton ripped up the magazine and dumped it on the floor. The bus driver complained about the mess, so Delilah apologised and picked it up.

Dayton just didn't get it. Why were so many unworthy, sickening men having sex, and he wasn't? What was so defunct about a woman's logic that they gave their time to horrible men, but not to him? These men were lemmings, and he was one-of-a-kind, so why weren't women after something special?

When he returned home, he went straight back to his game, but every time his character shot at something, he missed. He usually led their raids, but he kept going into the wrong rooms, messing up, and leading them astray.

"What are you doing?" said one who called himself Felix. "Your aim is shit."

"I'm just pissed off."

"It's all right man, just use your focus button."

"No, I'm not pissed off about the game."

"What is it?"

Dayton sighed. "Can we go into a private chat?"

They finished the raid and went into a private online room. He told his unknown friend about his sister, the couple on the bus, the film, and the magazine. Felix sympathised, and Dayton's rant progressed into a tirade of thoughts about newly developed philosophies. Saying them aloud was something new – until now, they had just been thoughts, and he hadn't given them any greater precedence than that – but in verbalising his beliefs, they made even more sense, and he realised just how passionate he felt about the perspective he was developing.

"I think sex should be a crime," he blurted out.

"A crime?" Felix echoed. "Shit, man. But I want to have sex. At least someday."

"If I can't have it, then why should anyone else?"

"Then why don't you have it?"

"Because no one will..." His voice faded away, not wanting to ruin the cool image he felt he had with these people he'd never met. "You know, maybe it shouldn't be illegal," he decided. "But it should be compulsory for all women to have sex with at least one person who doesn't already have it. Like, if they are going to keep picking the wrong men, they should have to spend a night with the right one to make up for it."

"Like compulsory prostitution?"

"No. Because we shouldn't have to pay for it. It should be a duty, like national service. Sex should be the man's choice, not the woman's."

"That sounds sweet."

"Women make too many bad choices. It's time that someone like me intervened."

Felix seemed to fall silent for a moment, and Dayton wondered if he'd gone too far. Then Felix spoke in a voice a little quieter than usual, with an eager wariness that felt alien in his tone, like he was cautiously unveiling an excitement he'd previously kept concealed. "You know, there's a website you should really look at."

"Oh yeah?"

"It's an online forum. I post in it a lot – I think you'd really like it there."

A link dropped into the chat. Dayton clicked on it, and the website loaded quickly. It was a basic forum with a list of threads, each with their own replies and discussions, and a tag that categorised the original post such as *Blackpill, Suicide Fuel, Cope, Brutal* or *It's Over*.

He scrolled past the first few headlines:

Made a Foid Cry Today.

This bitch blocked me for being honest.

Is ascension easier for blacks or whites?

Not wanting to fuck an ugly abomination isn't fakecell.

Big dicked incels are a waste.

I got an F for this assignment cuz I told the truth to an ugly foid slut teacher.

I look like a child is that why no girl wants me?

20 reasons I hate foidwhores

I saw a slutty curry foid try to fuck chad and fail LOL.

Thank you for this forum and all of you.

He read a few of the posts, and briefly scanned the content in the discussion, and one thing stuck out in all of them – each and every post was written by men as equally frustrated as him.

There are moments in one's life that, when reflecting in years to come, one recalls as a moment of significance; a monumental event where one's existence changes immeasurably, and an alternative course of events is put into motion, and a new level of awareness and thinking occurs.

One day, Dayton would look back on this as his moment.

Before this, his beliefs were just thoughts. Musings. Solutions most would consider taboo.

But not now.

This website validated his thoughts. His opinions. His desires.

He'd never found a space where he fit in before, or where he was appreciated, or where he could speak his mind. But here, in this forum, on this website, he had finally discovered his people.

He spent the next few days reading every post, and he learned so much. He'd read about blue pill and red pill ideology created by conspiracy theorists before, and he'd dismissed them as ridiculous – but now he learned of the black pill principle. This was new. People wrote about how feminism was the cancer of this country, and that only twenty per cent of men got to sleep with eighty per cent of women, and that the entire social status situation of society needed to change; that the status of men should stop being settled on looks, muscle and brawn, and should be settled on those with the intelligence to guide women's desires toward the men who they should procreate with. These people asserted that intelligent, polite, kind men, like Dayton, should be the ones who spread their genes, and not the animals women always went for.

After a week or so of reading and watching, Dayton made his first post. It took a lot of courage, and a lot of mental fortitude, but he had ideas, and he wished to relay them. He spent all day writing an article, then posted it.

It was called *Why Rape Should Be Legal – But Only for the Right Men.*

He highlighted the facts as he knew them. That women often orgasm during rape, so they must like it. That rape fantasies are hugely common, so women must want it. He pointed out that even the bible condones rape, and he even quoted the verse in Deuteronomy 28:30 when it states that, once a man has raped a woman, that man should pay the woman's father to marry her. If God approves this ideology, then how can one argue with it? After all, this solution would solve the crisis shared by the men on this forum. Women were the gatekeepers to sex, and they constantly flaunted this with their short skirts and cleavage and long hair – if they persisted in perpetuating this unfairness by dressing and acting provocatively, were they not responsible for the reaction it provoked? If they were deliberately making men sexually frustrated, surely it was their responsibility to solve that frustration?

He didn't tell his mother about the forum, but she did comment on how he suddenly seemed happier. She attributed it to him looking forward to university, and concluded that he would be fine living away from home as a result – after all, look at the change in him. He was like a different man. He even spoke to her with a smile – something she couldn't remember him doing since he was a child.

In the week before he left, she took him out to buy clothes. When Dayton walked past couples, he no longer looked at them with resentment, but with a sense of awareness, content that he possessed knowledge that they didn't, optimistic about a future where that couple's world would be shattered.

Delilah bought him a new jacket, new trousers, new shirts, and even took him for a haircut.

Dayton created a new social media profile. He uploaded pictures of himself looking at the camera with a cool grimace and posted quotes from philosophers that made him appear to be a deep thinker. He'd redone his image before, but never with this newfound outlook on life, and this time it would be different. The prospect of renewal excited him, and university was going to be a perfect opportunity to be the man he truly was. He was even going to have sex and get a girlfriend. Of course he was. Look at him now. How could any woman resist?

He kept checking his article every few hours over the weeks before he left. At first, there were only a few comments praising the ideas. Then a few more. Then a hundred. Then thousands. A mass of men all saying that he was spot on – that he was saying what they had been thinking, and he had articulated it brilliantly.

His words were praised by many, and that was how he knew he was right.

Chapter Eighteen

DAYTON WENT TO UNIVERSITY WITH LITTLE INTEREST in the actual learning part; the prospect of more education didn't excite him. He was at university for the experience – for the interaction, the living with new people, but mostly, for the women; for the girlfriend he hadn't met yet, but knew he would.

He attended lectures for the first few weeks with no interest in what the stuffy lecturer was waffling on about. He'd sit toward the back, like the lecture theatre was a bus – the back was where the cool kids sat.

He'd never been the cool kid at the back of the bus before, but here was his chance. His reinvention. His opportunity to be the person he really was.

Twenty minutes before the lecture was due to start, he'd be there, nonchalantly draped over the chair, watching the women saunter in – usually in their groups, sometimes alone – and he'd wear the coolest, most smouldering look he could, waiting for them to approach him and ask if they could take the seat beside him, inevitably intrigued by his intellectual curiosity and his handsome magnetism. His new shirt looked great, his hair was short and trim in a way it never had been before, and he rested one of his feet on the back of the chair in front as if to show how little he cared for what people thought.

But despite his clear attractive features, several lectures went by with none of these women approaching him.

They sat in their groups, giggling and talking, animated and engrossed in conversation, delighted to be nattering away to each other, but never to him. At first, he thought they must only be interested in conversation with friends, and not interested in talking to men – so imagine his horror as he watched, gobsmacked and with savage bemusement, as other men, even groups of them, approached these women, sat down, and engaged them in conversation. And not just general chitchat, either – electric, engaging, delightful conversation. These women would toss their heads back and laugh, tittering and snickering at what these men said, placing an apparently innocent hand on the male suitor's arm, and Dayton would wonder – do these women not have any pride? Is this really the kind of men they want? Are they so easily seduced that they would cackle and laugh at men with such little intelligence?

And all of this while Dayton was sat at the back, on his own, with empty, untouched seats surrounding him, week after week. He'd look smart and cool, but remain unapproached by the same women who flaunted their exposed necks and lines of cleavage and easy laughter at these repugnant brutes.

Eventually, he stopped going to lectures. What was the point? Evidently, the women who went there were too stuck up. Too disinterested. Had poor taste, much like those disgraceful women he knew at school.

He didn't tell his mother he'd stopped going. Of course

he didn't. Since Cassidy spent most nights at her boyfriend's house, and was due to leave for university the following year anyway, Delilah had downsized to a one-bedroom council flat so she could send the money she saved to Dayton to support him, and he couldn't tell her for fear she'd cut off this payment. With this money, and his student loan, and the interest free student overdraft, and the grant he received due to his mother's low income, he had plenty of money to flash around and make himself look good. Women loved rich guys. But university was evidently not the right place to meet the kind of women who would be interested in a cool, kind, rich guy. Campus was full of arrogant feminists who were too stuck up to be interested in him. The environment was the issue, and he needed to find somewhere else.

Consequently, he spent his empty evenings strolling around the neighbourhood, wandering with no destination in mind. Sometimes he'd stop at a bench, or lean on a fence, and sit back, his arms draped over the wood, waiting for the right woman to approach. But they never did. In fact, a few times, he was sure they crossed the road to avoid him. Which infuriated him. Why were they so willing to throw their heads back and push their perky tits at those other guys, yet saw *him* as the creep?

Fucking bitches, he told himself. Fucking bitches, the lot of them.

Again, the environment was the problem. The women near his house had no taste. He started gravitating closer to the city centre, where people no longer crossed the street to avoid him. In fact, on the first time he tried this new setting, he noticed two women approaching him, arm in arm, deep in conversation. He expected them to veer away at any moment, but they didn't – they were coming toward him, and they weren't breaking stride.

He became giddy. Nervous. Sweaty. This was his chance. He sat back, rested his right foot on his left knee, and tried to look tough and pensive as he assessed their potential. They looked like smart women, both wearing backpacks that sagged like they were full of books. He'd be a gentleman and offer to carry those bags – women love chivalry, don't they? It's what men do in all those romcoms. They were pretty as well, but they weren't in-your-face pretty – they both had jackets on, and wore jeans; there was no sluttiness, which made them far more respectable than the women in his lectures who wore skirts then crossed their legs so they rode up their thighs and teased all the men in the room. Like they didn't know what they were doing.

The women approached. This was it. Ooh, this was it! It was actually happening!

He braced himself. Ready. Looking cool. Looking nice. Smart. Smouldering expression. And...

And they walked straight on past.

Didn't even look at Dayton. Didn't even glance down to see who they were leading on. Too engrossed in conversation, amid discussion, not even averting their gaze from each other – as if they didn't know what they were doing! As if that wasn't all done entirely to taunt him.

He glared at them as they walked away. Their buttocks in their tight jeans wiggled back and forth. Shoving it in his face. How dare they tease him like that!

With a throw of the fist and a mumble of anger, he marched in the opposite direction. These women were stupid. They did not know who he was, and how great he would be for them. They had a potentially perfect boyfriend waiting for them, and they didn't care. He was going to be a millionaire someday, and they were missing out on the opportunity to live the lifestyle they dreamt of. This was the worst part – their own poor choices were getting in their way.

The next day, he tried a coffee shop. Maybe he'd find a sophisticated woman reading a book, who might raise her eyes from her paperback and spot this handsome man across the cafe; or a business woman taking a break from her busy day who might find what she's looking for in another lonely soul, sitting with his coffee. He wore a different shirt to try a slightly different image – this one had a pattern on, with squares of different shades of red and brown, and he did the buttons up all the way apart from the top one. It made him look casual, but not too casual. He sat in the window with a latte, waiting for women to walk past the window and notice him, and direct themselves in.

After half an hour, he grew impatient. There weren't many women, and these few that had come in hadn't so much as glanced in his direction. Then came a possibility; a group of three women walked in, removed their coats, and joined the queue to be served. They had their hair tied back. Modest dress. Smiling and laughing with each other, mumbling about what they were going to drink. They weren't nerdy, but weren't bimbos. They didn't look stupid, but didn't look stuck up either. They were the kind he'd attract, and he knew it.

He approached the counter. Finished his coffee. Built up the courage to smile at them. It took all he had to conjure the bravery for this small social interaction, and in doing so, he conquered terrors that no one knew, battling nerves that waged war inside his belly, anxieties bashing against his insides like a mosh pit – but he did it. He smiled. He was proud of himself. And he waited for their smile in return.

The first one looked at him. She wore a beret, a patterned dress, and dark green tights, which gave her a unique, intriguing look. He made eye contact. Widened his smile. She noticed it.

He held her gaze, a bead of sweat trickling down his forehead, feeling suddenly hot.

After a few seconds, her hands started fidgeting, and she turned around, searching for who he was looking at. She turned back, locked eyes with him, and realised it was her.

His eyes were wide and he wasn't blinking.

She frowned. Turned back to her friends. Whispered something. They looked at him and frowned too. Turned away, disgusted. Pulling horrible faces at the awkward situation, even laughing a little.

It was too much for Dayton to take. His face curled into a snarl, his arms shook, and those butterflies in his belly bore weapons and waged war in his gut.

His expression morphed into something fierce, his fist collapsed his disposable cup, and the rage rose through him, up his dry throat, filling his mind with poisonous fantasies.

He threw the remaining contents of his coffee cup over the woman.

It was only a little coffee, and she leapt back, meaning that most of it landed on the floor, and a little on the exposed toes in one of her sandals. Still, she was shocked, and her friend's arms wrapped around her and pulled her close as they gaped at him, waiting for an apology and an explanation.

The tension in the cafe rose. The man behind the counter stopped serving. A few other men stopped drinking and looked his way. Even a child in the far corner stopped crying, and its mother rose from her seat.

He shoved his hands in his pockets and strode out with as much pace as he could.

He charged through town. Stomping endlessly forward.

Curling up his face to fight the tears. He wouldn't give them the satisfaction. How dare she? How fucking dare she? Who did that bitch think she was?

A smile. That was all it was – a smile. And she'd made him into the bad guy.

How the hell was he the arsehole in this situation?

He imagined the woman going home to her boyfriend, with his big biceps and chunky pectorals, regaling the story of the freak in the coffee shop who lost his temper over a smile. He'd laugh, and then they'd fuck, and they'd forget about the kind man who smiled. Then he'd leave her, and she'd moan to her friends about how all men are arseholes, and never realise she'd missed the chance to be with someone who would have respected her.

But so what? He didn't want her anyway. She was arrogant. And the coffee shop was stupid. Why would he go there if someone like that went there?

After twenty minutes of walking, he'd convinced himself he'd left because the cafe was shit – not because he was afraid.

Perhaps he needed to make even more improvements to his image. His new dress sense was great, and his haircut was slick, but his body was small and gangly. His limbs were thin and loose. He wanted to look good with his top off for when the day arrived that a woman might remove it.

So he joined a gym. Why not? He had free time. Even if a bit more muscle didn't help his image, it would help him pack a punch should he need to. Next time, he wouldn't need to run out of the coffee shop, scared away by strangers – he could stand up to all the people glaring at him.

But the free weights were heavy. The machines were uncomfortable. The treadmills made him out of breath. And he was sure people were looking at him. It wasn't as easy as those fitness videos online made it look.

He focused on the really big weights – that was how he'd build his muscle. The gym kept them in the far corner, on low shelves beneath mirrors and gym benches. It was full of men, all much bigger than him, wearing vests that exposed their large, sculpted biceps. They wore expensive headphones and spent a lot of time looking at themselves in the mirror. They also walked a certain way – it was more of a strut, like a peacock showing off its colours, and he tried copying them; though he quickly turned away when they noticed.

Unfortunately, he only used the free weights once. As he tried lifting a set of 20kg weights, watching his face tighten in his reflection as he struggled to raise his arm, he could see them behind him. He could hear them too. They were sniggering at him.

He tried even heavier weights to show he wasn't weak, but they strained his arms too much, and he toppled over, collapsing on his knees.

Their sniggers became a lot louder.

Except one man, who placed his weights down, removed his headphones, and approached Dayton with a kind smile. "Are you okay?" he asked. "Here, these are too heavy, why don't you try these? I'll show you how to use them."

Dayton stood, scowled at the stranger, and marched straight out of the gym without looking back.

He didn't need anyone's help. What did they think he was? A weakling? Pathetic? *They* were the ones who were pathetic. *They* were the ones acting like animals, puffing their chests out, ambling around with their bulging arms, parading themselves in front of women they'd later subjugate and treat like whores they could use then discard.

Dayton was better than them. All of them.

And he was sure he felt buffer after that first gym session.

He tried going out at night instead. He'd overheard students talking about a house party. It was going to be a big affair; so big they wouldn't notice a stranger. It was to be at a house he'd passed a few times on a Friday night; one that was always busy, with people hanging outside the front, smoking and kissing and chatting. Maybe the women there would be drunk, and he could show up and be the nice guy who takes them home.

When he approached the house, however, he filled with dread. He felt like an imposter. Like he didn't belong there. And, as he crossed the lawn, he waited for one of the smokers to tell him to get lost. But none of them did, and he opened the front door, entering like he was walking out on stage without knowing his lines.

The inside of the house was loud. Music was blaring from speakers, and it felt like the speakers were inside his head, pumping his brain, and he tried not to panic. It was crowded too, and the house wasn't that big, and the walls felt like they were closing in on him. Everyone seemed to know each other, and they were all talking, and they were so boisterous, and so confident, and he didn't fit in.

This was a bad idea.

He turned to leave as some bloke shouted across the room to him.

"Who the fuck are you?" he said.

Dayton turned back around. The man wore a Hawaiian shirt, with hair down to his shoulders, and held a spliff between his fingers. His eyelids drooped, and he had a knowing smirk that put Dayton on edge. His friends were staring at Dayton expectantly, with half-smiles like they were waiting for the punchline.

"I don't know you," the man said. "Who are you?"

Dayton scanned the faces. They were all watching him. His mouth opened, but only a few stutters came out. The music was too loud, and there were too many people, and they were talking too much.

"Eh, come here," the man waved Dayton closer. "Come on, come here."

Dayton edged forward.

"Closer, come on."

Dayton edged forward again, until he was next to the man. The man put his arm around Dayton's neck and pulled him closer.

"I don't know who you are," he said, his breath smelling like cigarettes and whisky. He left a dramatic pause, then concluded, "But your shirt looks fucking stupid."

The man's friends burst into hysterics. Dayton gaped at the shirt this man was wearing, full of palm trees and bright colours, and was about to object to the audacity of someone wearing a shirt like *that* criticising his.

No words came out.

Instead, Dayton released himself from the man's grasp and pushed him away with all the weight of his body behind it, expecting him to fall off his sofa and howl in pain.

The man barely moved.

But his expression changed. He stood, wearing his grimace like a mask, and smacked Dayton around the back of the head.

"Get the fuck out of here," the man said.

Dayton, shaking from the hostile manner of this stranger, did as he was told, and shuffled out of the house to the sound of group laughter.

Dayton learned a big lesson that day.

Not about his shirt, that he promptly removed when he arrived home and put in the bin, but about the nature of people, and the need to defend himself.

If he was going to go to parties, and other places where he might meet women, he was liable to encounter ingrates like that, and he needed protection.

From that day on, he never left home without his Stanley knife again.

The Day of the Twenty-First

Chapter Nineteen

THERE WAS ALWAYS A PARTY AT THIS HOUSE.

Every Friday and Saturday night, as relief at the end of another workweek arrived, and plans were made for what to do over a few days off, the house at the dead-end of the street boasted loud music, and noisy crowds, and flashing lights. It was part of the routine of the street, and however much the residents were prepared for it, it must have enraged the neighbours.

But these students didn't have children to put to bed, or families to spend time with, or fatigue from middle-age and a nine-to-five, so why would they care? And besides, the young adults who lived here loved that their house was known as the party house; it was where pre-drinks started, and the drunken nights ended.

But not for Dayton.

For Dayton, it was the place of a onetime humiliation by a bastard with long hair and a loud shirt. He hadn't returned since, but here he was now, almost three years later. It wasn't even term time, yet the parties persisted, and it made

Dayton sick – not for the inconvenience to the neighbours, but for what he wasn't part of.

Everyone inside that house was a sycophantic, sanctimonious, arrogant narcissist. He loathed them with a contempt one rarely has for strangers they'd never met – it was almost feral, the way his instinct was to treat them all like prey. He was just excited to finally become the predator.

This was the Beta Uprising, and the alphas were about to understand why they should not be in charge.

Dayton parked his BMW a few doors down. It was early evening, and whilst the other houses were still, with curtains drawn, families inside, and a quiet serenity descending over them, the house at the end of the street was not. Boisterous characters shouted and joked with each other as they stumbled across the lawn, hanging around the exterior with spliffs and beer bottles and cigarettes and poor attitudes and rowdy anecdotes.

There were several women loitering as he pulled up, all dressed for the occasion; some wore shorts, some wore dresses, and some wore skirts, but they all had something in common – they were all too short to be worn whilst retaining their dignity. One sat on the edge of a plant pot by the front door, her frilly skirt draped over her legs, the top of her thighs visible; another sat on the ground, legs apart, occasionally hinting the frill of her panties, a cigarette in her mouth making her prettiness become ugly; and another had her arms around a man who leant against the wall of the house, on her tiptoes so her mouth could reach his, with her vest and shorts revealing more skin than she had covered up.

Dayton considered them to be a disgrace. And infuriating. They were the kind of women who would moan about the horrible men they kept dating, but what did they expect when they dressed for sex? Did they think such an outfit would attract a good man like him? This was why they needed his guidance; if he had control of their clothing decisions, and their mating decisions, and their actions, he guaranteed they'd make better choices – choices that would result in them being far more content than they were getting drunk, stoned, smoking dirty nicotine sticks, and shoving their tongue down the face of future regret.

Just as Dayton's seething reached its climax, and his sweaty grip tightened over the handle of the hunter's knife he kept on the passenger seat, perched on the leather with its alluring beauty – Dayton saw *him*. Leaving the house, arm around a woman's shoulders, showing off with his loud jokes that probably weren't even funny. He had more stubble on his beard, and his hair was a little longer, but his Hawaiian shirt was just as repugnant and noticeable.

This was Dayton's opportunity – he would not waste it.

He sniffed inwards, held his breath, and pushed it out of his mouth. He collected his knife and stepped out of the car, clutching his weapon like he was dragging his whore, and locked his vehicle. Keeping the blade behind his back with his right hand, he strode forward, his eyes dead set on his target.

It would have been easy for someone to look outside their window and see the weapon he was carrying – but this was the beauty of middle-class suburbia. Everyone locked their doors and closed their curtains to keep the baddies out, hiding themselves away from the dark deeds of night-time.

The street felt long, and with every stride, Dayton felt his fury surge, his determination compelling each movement forward. The annoying man kept his arm around the woman's shoulders, and she laughed at his pathetic jokes, and Dayton knew, as he walked through the gate, leering at his target, that each of those women would die for the injustice they perpetuated; the loneliness they induced; the poor decisions they made at the detriment of his happiness. It was a day for retribution, and his vengeance would be his justice.

"Hey," the annoying man said as Dayton approached. "What's with this guy?"

Dayton didn't wait to be taunted – he unleashed his knife and swung it haphazardly. The man dodged it instinctively, but Dayton didn't hang around to bemoan his mistake – he swiped the knife again and sunk it into the braggart's neck.

The annoying prick fell to his knees, clutching his throat, blood squirting like a broken faucet, before collapsing on his front.

The women screamed. They fled like weaklings, but Dayton didn't wait for his targets to disperse. There were plenty of directions for them to run should they get through the gate, but he was blocking it, and they could not flee without passing his bloody blade.

He launched himself at the woman the annoying man had previously had his arm around and swiped the blade. His aim and execution were poor, the result of bad coordination, so he just kept swinging until it landed – which it did, right in her belly, and he held it there, scorching her eyes with his searing glare, watching her suffer, watching his justice, watching the way that, in her dying moments, she saw that he would no longer be ignored.

He pulled the blade out and ran after another fleeing woman. Most of them had used their friend's death as an opportunity to escape – a few into the street, but most back into the house; even the man who'd been snogging someone minutes ago had betrayed his apparent alpha status by running away and leaving the women to fight on their own – but there was one straggler, left behind by the others, who hadn't been able to run quickly enough in her ridiculously large heels, and had been further delayed in her attempts to kick them off. In an oddly satisfying turn of events, the arrogant décor of her feet had turned her into the runt of the pack, and Dayton ran up behind her and kicked her legs out. Her legs flew into the air and she landed on her face, causing an audible crack as her teeth collided with the pavement. It felt good; he'd never taken someone out like this before unless it was a computer game, and exerting such dominance over another person made him feel supreme, especially against a scantily clad woman making poor decisions in mate choice and dressing like she deserved it.

He mounted her as she drearily rolled herself over. Her skirt rode up. He was closer to a woman's underwear than he'd ever been in his life, and it sent a tingle through him, and he became hard. *I could have this girl if I wanted,* he thought, then scalded himself for the hesitation as she fought back, throwing her arms at his face, pushing at his body, and attempting to wriggle out from beneath him. He smacked her nose with the butt of his weapon, causing a dribble of blood to trickle down to her lip. The disorientation quelled her fight, and she began begging instead.

"Please don't hurt me, please let me go..."

Oh, how things change. She'd have frowned at him a day ago, or mocked him, or ignored him – now she was begging him. In this moment, he felt like he ruled the world; like it was all his. He had never felt power like it.

He lifted her top and held it around her neck. Her bra was red with a lace trim and a frilly flower pattern. His feelings of arousal were overtaken by his fury at the situation. Why had it taken him until twenty-one-years-old to see this for the first time? Why had women persistently denied him this opportunity? Why had it taken him attacking her to finally get her to reveal what so many men take for granted?

She struggled again. He stopped wasting time. She deserved all the death in the world.

He grabbed her hair, held her head in place, and drove the blade into her neck.

Just as he did, he felt a large weight collide with his body, and he fell to the ground beside her, and his knife fell away from him.

He looked up. A big, beefy guy had barged him to the ground. Dayton acted quickly, and wriggled away from his opponent's reach, pushed himself up, grabbed his knife, and swung it aimlessly in the direction the man had come from.

The man backed away. But he wasn't alone. They were streaming out of the house, alpha after alpha, Chad after Chad, emerging to protect the women. How disgraceful – these women were feminists, were they not? Couldn't they protect themselves?

Regardless, they flooded out of the house, charging after him, and he didn't have time to think about what further havoc he could wreck here. His time was done.

He turned and ran.

They were behind him, and they were faster than him, and they were gaining on him.

He sprinted with all he had, pushing himself across the street toward his car, feeling wind against his back as they swiped to grab him.

He took the key from his pocket and unlocked his car from a few steps away.

One of them grabbed him, but he waved his knife at the arm, sliced some skin, and the guy quickly retracted it.

Dayton opened his car door, dived inside, and hit the lock button.

They surrounded his car like a horde of zombies trying to get in, hands clattering the exterior. When they couldn't open the door, they tried punching the windows. Typical brutish males, always aggressive, trying to bash their way into a confrontation.

Dayton didn't have time to dwell on his contempt; if he didn't flee, his day would be over before it even started.

His arm shook as he shoved the key into the ignition. He shifted into first gear, dropped the handbrake, and accelerated away.

Once he was out of reach of the clamouring fists and angry men in pursuit, he stopped. Watched them loiter in his rear-view mirror. When they realised he'd halted, they charged after him again, and Dayton had an idea.

He shifted into reverse, and took off quickly, aiming for all of them, sure that he could hit at least two or three.

But he didn't hit any of them; they all stepped out of the way, and he punched the steering wheel in frustration.

They approached the car again, and he didn't wait around this time. He sped away, demonstrating to these pumped-up pricks that his car was far faster than they were. He skidded around the corner and zoomed through the estate until he turned onto the main road.

He slowed down once he was clear. The adrenaline was charging through him and he was shaking, but as his heart rate settled, he couldn't help but smile.

What he'd just achieved was magnificent. It sent a message. He was thrilled with his accomplishment.

The day was finally getting going.

Before the Twenty-First

Chapter Twenty

SHORTLY AFTER HIS NINETEENTH BIRTHDAY, DAYTON admitted to his mother that he didn't wish to go back to university. He'd been home for the summer, spending most of his time on *Maze of Magic* and the online forums where he could speak to people who felt the same as him, and didn't see the point of returning. What was the purpose of university if he wasn't having sex? He'd heard this was part of the student experience – studying, partying, and casual encounters – yet Dayton spent most of his time hanging around on his own, never approached by women, and locked in his room on his computer. He could go on his computer and be ignored by women whilst not at university.

"Okay then," Delilah said, sitting back on her cheap sofa, sipping from a glass of cheap wine. "If that's what you want, you can quit university."

Dayton's face lit up; he wasn't expecting this to be so easy. "Really?"

"Sure." She left a beat, then added, "If you are going to get a job."

Dayton frowned. "What?"

"If you're not studying, you're working – after all, you won't be living here for free."

"What? You'll charge me?"

"Absolutely. If you stop university, I won't be giving you any more money, and if you wish to stay here, you'll need to pay rent. Why don't you go on the computer and see what jobs you can find?"

Dayton slumped back on the sofa and folded his arms. He shook his head and glared at the television where the host of some pointless daytime show was shouting at his guests. Then he figured, fine, he'd do that – he'd find a job he could do.

He loved his computer games, so he thought of being a games designer. That would be a cool job where he'd get to create the graphics and write the scripts for awesome games. But when he looked at the first job, they required a degree of at least a 2:1, a year's industry experience, and knowledge of how to use the appropriate software. Not only this, but the website indicated that over a hundred people had already applied for this job. He looked over the rest of the jobs, and they were much the same.

Fine. He'd try something else. He spent a lot of time on his computer, so he could be a computer engineer. He looked up those jobs, and once again, they demanded a degree, experience, and had hundreds of applicants.

He wiped his brow, feeling a little sweaty, and quelled his anger. How dare they say he wasn't good enough just because he didn't have the fancy qualifications other people had; how would they know that meant he wasn't good enough?

Trying a different tack, he adjusted the filters to his qualification level, and looked over the potential jobs that came up. Most of them were in retail. A few shops looking for people to sit at tills. A supermarket looking for someone to stack shelves. A pub looking for a night porter to take deliveries. Dayton felt insulted. He was above such menial jobs. He was destined for great things – *amazing* things – and the idea of him working for some shitty retail company on minimum wage infuriated him. When someone is destined for greatness, they do not lower themselves to insignificant acts. This just would not do.

He told his mother he'd changed his mind. He'd go back to university. And when she said goodbye to him at the beginning of September, as he left to stay in his new student accommodation, his mother was unaware that he was being asked to redo his first year due to lack of assignments. She assumed his desire to drop out had blown over. Meanwhile, Dayton planned to continue snubbing lectures, ignore letters about his attendance, and not tell his mother for fear that she would stop his funding.

But the notion of a minimum wage job had scared him. He was meant to be rich, but he wasn't, and this perturbed him. One afternoon, as he played *Maze of Magic,* executing a raid with his online friends, his mind dwelled on other thoughts. How could he become rich? If he was rich, he'd have no problem getting a girlfriend – women would love to be with a man who had an endless stream of money.

The next day, as he took his afternoon walk, wearing his smart shirt and waiting for a woman to approach him as he often did after a few hours on the computer, he walked past a shop and saw a poster for the lottery in the window. They were boasting a jackpot of millions. In fact, not just millions – tens of millions. It would be money he could only dream of.

He went in and bought a ticket. A lucky dip – the numbers didn't matter, they all had an equal chance of coming up. Then he thought, how was he meant to win the lottery with one ticket? So he bought another. And another. Still, it wasn't enough – he checked how much money he had in his bank through an app on his phone. He had enough to buy fifty tickets. That would put him in a great position to win – so that was how many he bought.

When he arrived home, he blu tacked them all to the wall behind his computer, then stood back and marvelled at them. This was his opportunity – his ticket to greatness. He had fifty tickets – *fifty* – which meant he stood fifty times as much chance as anyone who'd just bought one. The fools.

The lottery numbers wouldn't be announced until later that evening, so he logged onto the forums and spent the afternoon reading and responding to posts. Since he'd posted his article on legalising rape, he'd gained a lot of admirers. When someone saw his name next to a post, they would reply about how much they loved him, how great his thoughts were, and how wonderful he was. But it wasn't enough for Dayton. There were militant members who were far more involved than he, and they were talking about taking action.

Dayton had to outdo them.

So, with the impetus and excitement at his imminent victory in the lottery spurring him on, he increased his presence.

Someone posted about how their brother's girlfriend pretended to come onto him only so they could laugh at him. Other people sympathised and responded that this woman was a bitch. To Dayton, it wasn't enough.

Then why don't you do anything? he wrote.

What can I do? came the reply.

Dayton sat back. Spun a little on his chair. Grinned at his lottery tickets and his imminent riches, then responded.

Nothing will change if we don't take action. She humiliated you. He humiliated you. And you just took it? Fuck that.
DO SOMETHING.

He didn't need to reply further – other people filled the space beneath his comment with their own eager suggestions, providing instructions on how to poison them, on how to acquire a gun, on which knife would cause the most damage, on which parts he should chop off, on how he could make their humiliation public – Dayton had sparked something, and it made him proud to see how people listened.

Another man posted about how he was fed up with being a virgin. Dayton responded.

You have been a virgin for too long. Stop complaining.
DO SOMETHING. *Nothing will change if you don't make a stand – if she won't fuck you, make her. What's she going to do? If you're alone, it's your word against her's. Fucking do it.*

Finally, fed up with reading pathetic complaints, he posted a new thread to convey his anger over how many people were moaning but doing nothing:

DO SOMETHING.

That's what I keep saying – but how many of us do?

We need to take a stand. The alphas have run the world for too long, and it's time for The Beta Uprising.

We must take control, and we must make things how we want them.

And how do we do that? Here's what I propose:

1/ Legalise rape. But not for everyone. The Chads can fuck right off. They get enough, and they don't deserve it – they just take these women and fuck them over. Make it legal for the INTELLIGENT twenty per cent of the population who know what's best for women who never make the right decisions. Which leads me onto:

2/ *Control who women spread their genes with. If Stacey keeps fucking Chad, they will keep having little ChadStacey babies, and the world will be full of them. They are reproducing at a far higher rate, and if we're not careful, evolution will kill off the better part of the population. Women should not copulate with fucking alphas who are just going to produce more fuckboys. We know better, so we should make the decisions.*

3/ *Educate women about which men they should put their energy into. The fucking Chads can sit at the side line for once and watch us fuck their birds. Tell them what they are doing in a way that makes them understand. Beat it into them if we need to. I'm fucking fed up with bitches who fuck fuckboys then complain about being fucked over by fuckboys. Like, bitch, what did you expect?*

So enough with your fucking words. We need to take action.

DO SOMETHING.

Dayton sat back and waited. Within seconds, the first reply came in:

This is why you're A FUCKING LEGEND.

Then the next few:

You speak so much sense it hurts.

YES – FUCKING YES!

You're right. I'm fed up of waiting and being the beta. It's time for our time.

The comments continued much the same, and Dayton sat back with his validation, wearing a smug smile. It felt real – these people were with him, and in their numbers, they would find strength.

He would not have to be a virgin forever. And, even better, he was about to win the lottery and become rich. Life was becoming sweet.

He left the house with extra energy and paraded through town. Women still didn't look at him, but that didn't matter – they would soon. He would be rich, and they would have no choice. He could fund a militant uprising with his money, and he would sit in his mansion and watch the chaos, waiting for them to come begging for help.

He paused outside the window of the jewellery store. A fancy gold watch sat in the window, with a price tag of thousands beside it. Tomorrow, once he had his money, he'd come back and buy it. Women would see that watch and know he was rich.

He passed several car dealerships, drooling over the Jaguars and BMWs and Bugattis, knowing he would own a shitload of them soon.

He put the television on when he returned to his room, almost shaking with giddiness, excited to see his numbers come up on the screen. He sat back in his chair, relaxing, knowing he was going to be filthy rich soon. He even had a beer, though he didn't like them – it just felt like something he should have.

When the first number came up – a three – it wasn't on forty-five of his tickets. This was annoying, but he reminded himself it didn't matter. He still had five left over. He just had to relax.

Then the next came up.

It wasn't on any of those five.

He checked them all again. This couldn't be right. He checked the other forty-five again, looking for the mistake. He must have read them wrong.

Another number came up, and it was wrong again.

All wrong.

It didn't match any of his tickets.

Nor did the next one. Or the next one. Or the final one.

How could this be? He'd bought fifty tickets. *Fifty* tickets! He was going to be rich. He was going to buy that watch, buy a fancy car, fund the uprising, buy a mansion, and have his choice of all the women.

He ripped up the first ticket. Then the next. Then the next. Then he put them all into one wad and ripped them in half – at least, he tried, but they were too thick to tear, so he split them up into groups of ten and ripped them in half. His fury rose, and in his rage, he left the tickets all over his room, pieces of torn paper decorating the floor and furniture, displaying numbers that meant nothing.

Fuck the lottery. Fuck the numbers. And fuck those people in the car shops and the jewellery store and the mansions.

Didn't they know he was meant to be rich?

This would not do.

It truly would not do.

Chapter Twenty-One

DESPITE HAVING MOVED TO AN EVEN SMALLER, ONE-bedroom flat, the space felt too big. Delilah had waved goodbye to both of her children as they boarded the train for university, and felt an odd loneliness in the walk home, and in her empty residence.

She'd been used to being on her own for so long now that solitude had become normal, but with both her children away, the feeling of loneliness grew larger, like an ominous shadow growing over her, and she felt isolated in a way she hadn't before. She reluctantly, despite her initial resistance to the thought, found herself wanting company. She'd had a few casual relationships in the years since her divorce, but never anything serious; she'd hadn't had time – she had a son with many needs to take care of and they had taken over her life. But now he wasn't there, and she wasn't constantly taking food to him, pestering him to do homework, and ensuring he had some sleep instead of playing his game all night, she felt an emptiness on the sofa beside her, and an unwelcome silence throughout the flat. Cassidy called her most evenings to talk about her lectures and the good times she was having, but aside from this, Delilah went for weeks without talking to someone outside of work.

Eventually, it became too much, and she wanted companionship. And she felt guilty for it. But why?

For so long, her son had been her priority; she had obsessed over his welfare, and there wasn't room left in her life for romantic love. She kept those few brief affairs she'd had away from her children, and often lost track of potential suitors amid the bustle of working several jobs. But she didn't need to care for Dayton all the time anymore – so why did she feel so unsettled about the idea of having someone else to share her life with? Had her love for her children grown so large that there was nothing left for a man? Or did she worry about the effect the change would have on Dayton if she pursued someone long term?

She only had to recall the issues he'd endured with Nala to know how Dayton felt about his father's new spouse. But that was different. His father was absent, and Nala was hostile, and there was a neglect in that household that exacerbated Dayton's issues. She hoped Dayton would understand a new fella in her life wouldn't be his replacement, she just wasn't sure.

Cassidy would be fine with it. She'd find it a little strange, of course – they'd gone almost two decades of their lives having their mother entirely to themselves – but, in time, Cassidy would come to appreciate her mother being happy.

Happy.

Huh.

She laughed at the thought and changed the television channel to something else she didn't want to watch. Delilah saw happiness in the same way she saw her boss's holiday pictures – she'd look at the photos of their family on a cruise, or on a safari, or on a beach getting a tan, resolute in the knowledge that these were things other people had, but not her.

But she was happy. Wasn't she? Her son was thriving, doing well in his studies, and coping with being away from home far better than she thought he would. Perhaps she wasn't giving him enough credit – perhaps her trepidation was the problem.

She sighed. She was happy, but it wasn't enough. Her happiness was a selfless type of happiness, and she craved the selfish kind – the kind where she was happy for herself, and for no one else.

But did she have time? With all the extra shifts she was taking to fund Dayton and Cassidy's studies, could she fit a man in?

Screw it. She decided to go for it. She couldn't just sit around on her worn-out sofa all evening, in her pyjamas within ten minutes of being home, eating cold pasta she made in batches on Monday to save money.

But where would she even start? She didn't have friends to go out with. She had no hobbies. But people used online dating nowadays, didn't they?

She searched online for dating services. They all charged money. She couldn't afford it – she was already hard up from the money she gave to her children and the loan she was still paying back for Dayton's school. There was a free one, though she was a little wary – she'd heard of this platform's sleazy reputation. But she considered herself to be a good judge of character, and decided she could figure out the good from the bad.

She took a picture of herself. Created a profile. Wrote her name. The difficulty came when it asked her for interests. What were her interests? Her children? Television?

Work? She asked herself what she would like her hobbies to be. What would she like to share with someone else? She put down long walks and reading. Men started messaging her within hours, but she kept looking back at her profile, concerned that she would make these men think she was better than she really was. She never went for walks, and she hadn't had the energy to read a book in years; was she selling a lie?

Screw it, she figured. If she went in with no expectations, she wouldn't be let down when they realised she wasn't that great.

Her first date was with a man older than her. He was balding, wore a shirt tucked too tightly into his jeans, and occasionally made a strange mumbling noise before she spoke. He was nice enough, but she felt no spark, and bid him a good night after he asked if she wanted to come back to his flat afterwards.

The next guy was much the same, but a little younger. Too young, in fact. He was full of energy, excited about a film script he'd written, which he was trying to sell to a producer his uncle knew. He was nice, but too innocent. He could have been her son.

It wasn't until the fifth guy, a gentleman by the name of Patrick, that she found a connection. She showed up at the fancy restaurant he'd invited her to, scared that she was underdressed and that she couldn't afford the prices. He showed up in a suit, hair neatly parted, and with a kind smile. As he took her coat and hung it on a coat hanger next to the bar, she felt like everyone was watching her; that people were looking up from their meals and scowling, knowing that she didn't belong here.

He ordered expensive wine, and it tasted exquisite. She was used to supermarket value stuff that had a nasty kick and a sour, vinegary taste, but this wine went down naturally. They spoke about their children – he had three daughters, all of which were at university, and was on great terms with his ex who he co-parented with. He owned several businesses, some overseas, and lived in a fancy apartment in a building with a doorman.

She went back to his flat for a drink after their fifth date. He hadn't pushed her, which she appreciated, but she had wanted to. She didn't want to seem easy, but she had missed intimacy, and she craved this man's hands on her skin. He gave her the tour of his apartment, and everything was so shiny and expensive. He had digital albums of his children that changed picture every few minutes, paintings that cost more than her monthly wage, and antiques with vast backstories she found fascinating. They made love on his king size bed beside a large window that looked over the city. She caught her reflection in it and felt self-conscious; her skin wobbled as she shifted back and forth on top of him, and her breasts drooped a little lower than they used to, and there were stretch marks on her belly, and her sex face looked like she was somewhere between pain and tears.

Patrick didn't seem to care. She loved the way he looked at her. Like her body amazed him; like every part of her skin was a wonder that he was fascinated by. He'd stroke her hair and whisper in her ear that she was beautiful, and though she hated being defined by her looks, it made her feel as valuable and expensive as the items in this flat.

She was hesitant to show him where she lived and put it off for quite a while. But the day came when he was running late from work, and he said he'd pick her up instead of meeting her in town. She tried to insist he needn't, but he said it was no problem, and she felt rude for saying no. She paced back and forth in her living room, biting her nails, thinking their relationship was going to end that evening.

But he didn't say a word, and when they arrived back at his flat, he said she may as well move in with him. He assured her she wouldn't have to pay rent, he'd just enjoy having her company to come home to. She considered it, and thought about how lovely it would be, living in a place like this, with a perfect view, and a doorman, and items of luxury.

But she said no.

It was too surreal. It felt like it wasn't her. Like it was moving too fast, even though she wanted it to move fast; in fact, she wanted to move even faster. But her flat belonged to her, and Cassidy, and Dayton. It was where her children would stay if they ever came down to visit, even though they never did. She wanted to keep their home so her children had somewhere to come back to, and though Patrick insisted they'd be welcome at his flat, and that he had spare rooms for them, she couldn't bring herself to move out. It just felt so wrong. Like she'd be putting herself before her children. And whilst they were nineteen and eighteen now, both adults who could take care of themselves, she felt like she'd be abandoning them.

She invited them to meet him at Christmas. She was terrified. This wasn't something she'd done before, and she imagined Dayton having a meltdown, storming out of the flat, or saying something rude, or throwing a tantrum.

Patrick was great. Even though she insisted on having it at her flat, he insisted on cooking, and he made a delectable Christmas lunch using her small oven. Cassidy was delighted to meet Patrick, and overcame any trepidation she felt. Dayton, however, was standoffish, and wouldn't look

Patrick in the eyes. That was, until Patrick tried talking to Dayton over lunch.

"So how are you finding university, Dayton?"

Dayton said nothing.

"What did you say you were studying? I think your mother said creative writing."

Dayton nodded.

"She said you like computer games too."

Dayton nodded again and shoved a forkful of stuffing into his mouth.

"I own a computer games company," Patrick said. "I'm sure I can get you some work experience there if you like – if that's something you'd be interested in."

Dayton's head rose. He glanced at his mother, then at Patrick. "Seriously?"

"Yes. They make a lot of role-playing action games. Do you like role-playing action games?"

Dayton furiously nodded. "Yes."

"What's your favourite?"

"Maze of Magic."

"I love Maze of Magic! Have you downloaded the new expansion pack?"

"Yes! Yes, I have!"

"What did you think?"

"The orcs are weird."

"They are, aren't they? Their heads are a little too egg-shaped."

"That's what I thought!"

From there, they spent the entire afternoon and evening discussing computer games. Dayton kept asking every question he thought of – *What character do you like best in Maze of Magic? Have you done many raids? What level are you? What does your avatar look like? What's your favourite monster to fight?* – Delilah was concerned the interrogation might put Patrick off, but it didn't seem to faze him at all. He engaged with her son with a warm smile and spoke elaborately in response to all his questions. It was like a dream.

Later in the evening, shortly before Patrick was to leave, Dayton told his mother he'd decided what he wanted for his next birthday in August.

"Have you?" she said.

"Yes! I want a car."

She laughed, then quelled it when she saw he was serious. "That's a little expensive, don't you think?"

Dayton shrugged. "It's what I want."

"Why don't we just see about getting you lessons first?"

"I can teach you if you like," Patrick interjected. "If you're staying for another week or two, we could go out a few hours each day, do a crash course."

"Patrick..." Delilah said, caution in her voice. "That's very nice of you, but I can't afford to insure him, or pay for his test."

"Don't worry about it." Patrick finished his drink. "I'll put him on one of my cars. And I have a friend at the driver's school who owes me a favour, he can do the last few lessons and the test."

"But I can't afford to put him on one of your cars."

"It's nothing, really. It'll cost me barely anything."

Delilah was about to protest again, but Dayton shouted over her. "That's amazing! Thank you!"

She looked at her son and saw genuine delight in his expression. She'd seen such genuine happiness in him so few times that it took her by surprise. She wished she could give him the things he wanted that would illicit such a smile and, while she wouldn't admit it, she was a little hurt by how someone else could provide for him in a way she couldn't.

Even so, true to his word, he gave Dayton lessons, each one lasting hours, and Dayton returned at the end of each day full of vigour, giddy with enthusiasm. At the end of the Christmas break, Dayton took his test and returned to university with a driver's license. It was remarkable.

But it wasn't real.

This entire life she was living, the world Patrick was giving her, the opportunities he was providing for her children... it wasn't real. And she was scared that, one day, he would take it away, and Dayton would be devastated. She could see him becoming too attached to him. He phoned her some evenings, which he hadn't done before, and she was pleased to hear his voice – but he always asked to speak to Patrick. Then Patrick would ask what Dayton was up to on *Maze of Magic,* and they would talk about this world that Delilah wasn't part of.

Then came the day, in the thick heat of summer, where Patrick took her for a meal out in the fanciest restaurant yet. He bought her a gown for the occasion, but she felt like she was in fancy dress imitating a rich person. The waiters tended to her every need, bringing her drinks and food as soon as she wanted it, but she knew how it felt to be one of those people appeasing the wealthy to pay for their child's education, and she felt guilty for accepting their help. And when they took a walk along a private beach afterwards, and he went down to one knee and presented an engagement ring, the diamond gleamed far too much. That ring probably cost almost as much as she'd paid for Dayton's school, and it felt wrong to receive it.

"I... I can't," she said, suddenly feeling stupid to be holding a shawl around her fancy frock.

"You can't?" He didn't rise from his knee, hoping she would realise her mistake.

"No, it... It's all wrong. I'm sorry."

"What's all wrong?" He stood and placed his hands gently on her arms. They were covered in goose pimples. "Have I done something wrong?"

"No. No, you've been perfect."

"Then what's the matter? I get on with your children, so that's okay. I'm offering you a life where you don't have to work – if you don't want to, that is. Where you can live in a big house that belongs to both of us. Where we can dine in the best restaurants, take holidays wherever we like – isn't this what you want?"

She hesitated. Wiped a tear away. She hated herself for saying this. "I thought it might be."

"Then what's the issue?"

"It just isn't real, is it?"

"What do you mean? Of course it is."

"No, it isn't. You're not real, and this dress isn't real, and what you have with Dayton isn't real."

"I – I don't understand, Delilah. If I've done something wrong–"

"No. You've been perfect."

"Then what is it?"

She looked away. What was she saying? And why was she saying it? She had no awareness of forming these words, yet they were coming out.

But she had only one image in her mind – the day Dayton's father left, and the day he refused to pay child support, and dropping him off to spend a weekend with his wife while he was absent. She couldn't do that to Dayton again. She couldn't let him get attached, only to have it ripped away when Patrick realised she wasn't as perfect as he thought.

Why would this man love her, anyway? She was a

vulnerable wreck. A cracked piece of China. Barely even a woman.

"I'm sorry," she said.

He didn't push it. He was a nice guy, so he respected her decision, though he spent the silent drive home hoping she would realise she'd made a mistake and tell him to turn around.

Instead, he dropped her off at her council flat, and she never saw him again.

When she told Dayton, he was apoplectic. He shouted at her and hung up the phone. But she knew it was the best thing she could have done – he was hurt now, but he'd be even more hurt when Patrick left in a few years.

For Dayton, this was an insult to his ambitions. An affront to his aspirations. Patrick was rich, and was to be Dayton's way out of this pitiful life, his path to greatness. She'd taken away his opportunity to live a superior life, along with the prospect of attracting all the women he could with his new status. Whilst most people would understand this decision wasn't personal, for Dayton, it very much was.

For the rest of his life, he never forgave his mother for doing this to him.

The Day of the Twenty-First

Chapter Twenty-Two

It had started with messages while she was at work. A few texts from people she hadn't spoken to for some time, which she saw as nothing important. Then someone sent her the video. Then the mum's WhatsApp group started pinging her phone:

Have you seen this?
Delilah is this your kid?
Delilah have you spoken to him?

Once someone mentioned her child, she instantly diverted her attention from the floor she was mopping to the notifications on her phone. She was halfway across the marble corridor of an office building where people passed her without acknowledgement, so no one noticed when she stood still, mop resting in one hand, and her phone in the other.

He wrote an entire manifesto.
Doesn't he go to uni where the attack was?
Have you seen the video too?
Total nutcase.

Always thought he was a weirdo, never thought he was a killer.

A killer? Her Dayton? Delilah shook her head and tried to wipe away her bemused expression – what were they talking about?

She'd seen that he'd posted a video that morning. She'd watched the first few seconds on mute when she was on the bus, just to see his face. She even sent him a message to say how well he looked. But she knew, considering the terrible things they were saying, she needed to see the rest.

If only so she could understand.

She clicked the link, and Dayton's face filled the screen. Not wanting to attract anyone's attention, she turned the volume down – she needed this job after all – and she held the phone to her ear.

"I am Dayton Dankworth."

It was his voice, all right. But it sounded different. Twisted, somehow. Like he was telling a joke, but not. Sadistic, but innocently so.

She glanced at the screen. It was still him. She returned it to her ear.

"I am a kind, gentle man. I am a loving soul who would make a woman very happy."

Her boss walked past, a collection of papers in his hand, and shot her a perplexed expression.

"I am better than every one of you who cannot see this."

Her boss stopped in front of her. Raised his eyebrows to feign curiosity. Tilted his head to await a response.

"And today, you are going to learn your lesson."

She paused the video and put it in her pocket. Her boss was talking to her, but she didn't hear a word; it was like she was underwater, sinking further and further away from him.

She had a deep-rooted fear of someday drowning; she didn't realise that she already had.

"Delilah?" he snapped.

She shook herself out of it. "Yes?"

"Is everything okay? You look pale. Who was on the phone?"

She opened her mouth to speak but stuttered over syllables.

Was that really her son? What had he done? Why were people talking about him?

Her phone vibrated in her pocket, over and over. She imagined it was either the mums' chat picking up the fever of their conversation, or more people sending her concerned messages, eager to collect the gossip so they could spread the news like a game of Chinese Whispers.

"Delilah!"

She snapped out of it again. "It was my son," she blurted out.

"Your son?"

"Yes. He's ill."

"Isn't he at university?"

"Yes, but he's unwell, and they've just phoned me." The words were coming out of her so robotically that she wasn't even aware she was lying.

"Do you need to go?"

She looked down at the half-mopped floor and realised she was clutching the mop. She stretched her fingers and it fell from her hand, clattered to the ground, and echoed around the corridor. A few people slowed down as they passed, but her boss waved them on. Her hands rose to her mouth, and she held them there. She was struggling to breathe.

"Oh, Dayton..." The words passed out of her mouth in a whisper only she could hear.

"Look, go home," her boss said. "We can get someone to cover you."

She never went off sick. Ever. She couldn't afford to. She needed her meaningless jobs, so she always turned up and did the best she could, ensuring she was more valuable than anyone else, fearing for the day when redundancies would be required and decisions would be made. But today she couldn't care less about her job, or redundancies, or who would mop a floor people were walking over anyway.

She could only think of the video. And the messages. And her son.

"Delilah." Her boss's hands were gently gripping her shoulders. "Go home."

She looked up at him, her arms hugging her chest, her body curling in on itself, like she was visibly shrinking and would soon disappear, and only her tabard and cheap jeans would remain.

"O-okay," she stuttered.

"Do you need any help?" he asked. "Are you able to get to your car?"

"I... I'm walking..."

"Shall I call you a taxi?"

A taxi. She couldn't afford a taxi. "No thank you," she said, and looked up to him, suddenly aware of how weak she must look; she portrayed a fragility that made men want to take care of her. "I will be fine."

"Here," her boss said, pushing a ten-pound note in her hand. "There's a taxi bay outside."

She nodded vacantly, turned around, and walked away, her muscles cramping. Somehow, she made her way out of the building and meandered to the taxi bay with no conscious acknowledgement of moving. She realised she was clinging to the ten-pound note. She climbed into a taxi, passed it to the driver, and stated her address.

She looked out of the window as he drove, watching the world pass. Couples holding hands. A man in a suit eating a sandwich on a bench. Mothers pushing prams. The sun was shining and it all seemed so perfect.

She hadn't realised that the radio was playing, but the chimes for the news began, and she tuned in to the reporter.

"Further reports on the attack that have taken place outside a student house in the South West of England today," he said. "A man and two women, who were both stabbed and taken to ICU in critical condition, have now been declared dead. Onlookers reported that the suspect fled the scene in a black car. Police are hunting for the suspect and have warned the public to be vigilant. When asked whether this may be the actions of a spree killer, they refused to comment."

She bowed her head. A spree killer? Not Dayton. Not her baby. Not him.

"It's awful, isn't it?" the taxi driver said in a foreign accent she couldn't place.

"What is?"

"This guy they say is going around killing people. They are saying it's some nerd online – an incel, they call them."

"An incel?"

Delilah had never heard this word before, but it felt like an important one. She mulled it over, inspecting its vowels, interrogating its consonants, repeating its syllables.

"Yeah, I think it stands for involuntary celibate," the driver continued. "They are basically a bunch of blokes who can't get a woman to have sex with them, so they bitch about women on the internet. I had a friend who worked for the government, and he was saying incels are becoming an actual terrorism threat." The driver stifled a yawn. "Just a bunch of weird virgins if you ask me. How much harm can they do?"

Delilah didn't respond. She didn't want to talk. She didn't want to hear anymore.

She realised her phone was still vibrating. She took it out and lit up the screen. She had over four hundred notifications.

The taxi driver came to a stop. She looked around, panicking, wondering why, then realised she was home. She stepped out of the car, staring wide-eyed at nothing, her muscles weak, as she scuffled across the grass. A few men loitered in the outside corridor, smoking with dead expressions, and they glared at her as she passed. She passed a few teenage girls on the stairs who did the same. When she approached her flat, two women were engaged in heated discussion outside their doors, they stopped immediately as they saw her.

She entered her flat, closed the door, locked it, and bolted it.

She removed her coat, dropped it on the back of the sofa, placed her splayed fingers in the curls of her hair, and paced back and forth, shaking her head, panicking about what might be happening – then she realised she still had more of the video to watch.

Something told her not to watch it. A feeling inside that grew, infecting her like a deadly sickness. But she couldn't not see it. This was her son. She must.

She retrieved her phone, ignored the messages, and opened the video again.

Her trembling thumb hit play.

He rambled on about red pills and black pills, and

women in society, and inferiors, and she didn't understand any of it, until he added, "I am a charming, friendly, kind man."

She nodded. Yes, you are, Dayton. You are charming. You are friendly. You are kind. Please let everyone know this.

"Yet I have learned that no amount of charm, friendliness or kindness, will have any effect on women who only want mindless men with beefed up bodies with vacuous, empty heads."

What did this mean? What did any of it mean? Why were there so many horrible comments below the video?

"You are too inferior to choose your mate, and you need someone with higher intelligence to dictate this to you – this much is evidently clear."

He took a large inhale through the nose, then lowered his head, creating a partial shadow on his face, and she recognised the expression he wore when he didn't get his way.

"Your Chads and Staceys have put the Betas away for too long, and now we are coming out to play."

Chads? Staceys? Betas? What was he on about?

"By the time this day is through, you will understand that we will not take this anymore."

She stopped pacing. Her legs stiffened and fixed to the ground. All her hope sunk down through her chest, her hips, her legs, and into the floorboards.

A message came through at the top of her screen. It was from Patrick – *Is everything all right with Dayton?*

"I attach my manifesto to this video," Dayton continued. "Read it well and understand my reasons."

She was on her knees with no recollection of descending

to them. She held the phone high, the screen above her head like she was crying out to God with it.

"Once the Beta Uprising has started, there will be no turning back."

The Beta Uprising?

"I call on all my comrades to join me. You know what to do."

The video ended.

She returned to her messages. Scanned them. They were full of questions, so many questions – *Have you seen the news? Do you know where Dayton is? Is Dayton at university? Is that video serious? Did he actually write that manifesto?*

The worst messages were in the mums' group, who had started out as concerned, but had since devolved into gossip and speculation.

The video had a PDF attached to it. The manifesto. She told herself not to read it, but her thumb found its way to the icon, and she knew she couldn't help but open it.

She read some of it but stopped after a page – just after the bit where he justified legalising rape.

She shook her head. Sweat trickling down her cheeks. There was commotion outside her flat – this was a small community, and people were militant on this estate, and they were gathering, eager to be involved in a stranger's lives. Like they were responsible for implementing justice, or for finding out the truth. They were only murmuring hushed voices, but they would soon turn to anarchy.

All she could think about was getting in touch with her son.

She selected his name and put her phone to her ear.

It rang until the answerphone answered.

She hung up, selected his name again, put her phone to her ear, and paced back and forth. She beseeched her son to answer; as if he could hear her thoughts from far away.

Ring Ring. Ring ring. Ring ring. Answerphone.

Hang up. Select his name. Phone to ear.

Ring ring. Ring ring. Ring ring.

"This is Dayton, I can't answer the phone, leave the message."

"Answer your phone Dayton! Please, just answer your phone! I am your mother, and I need you to answer your phone!"

She hung up. Waited a few seconds. As if he would return her call. She messaged him as well. Panic encapsulated in capital letters – *CALL ME*.

She ended up on the floor, rocking back and forth, grabbing her hair, tearing a clump out, hyperventilating.

She considered checking her news app for updates, but didn't. She tried ringing him again instead.

Ring ring. Ring ring. Ring ring. Answerphone.

Ring ring. Ring ring. Ring ring. Answerphone.

Ring ring. Ring ring. Ring ring. Answerphone.

"Please, Dayton, please..."

She tried again, and again, and again, listening to the irritating rhythmic pulse of the rings as they preceded the same answer from a voice she struggled to recognise.

Ring ring.

Come on, Dayton.

Ring ring.

Come on, please.

Ring ring.

Please.

Ring.

Ring.
Ring.
...Ring.

Before the Twenty-First

Chapter Twenty-Three

A FEW WEEKS AFTER HE TURNED TWENTY, DAYTON returned to university – or so he told his mother. The truth was that, shortly after he moved into his accommodation, he received a letter from the university terminating his place.

The only surprise was how direct the letter was. *Following your lack of attendance and failure to hand in assignments for your modules, we have attempted to contact you several times. As we have not had a response, we are terminating your place with immediate effect.* It finished with *We wish you the best of luck for the future* before the dean's signature, which made Dayton snort out a burst of ironic laughter. He ripped the letter up and put it in the bin before his mother returned from work, then accepted her offer of payment for a train ticket back to university.

The student house he was moving into was located toward the end of a large row of semi-detached houses with small gardens and cars half parked on the pavement. The street was full of large families stuffed into small houses, and Dayton noticed immediately how many of his neighbours looked like immigrants. There was a mosque on the adjacent street, an off-licence run by Pakistani men a short walk away, and a park where black hooded teenagers loitered. Dayton wondered why the shittiest of places also attracted the most foreigners.

Regardless, the house had everything he needed. Upon entering, there was a small corridor, with a bedroom immediately on the left, stairs straight ahead, and a living room that led to a kitchen. The living room was small, occupied by a non-functional fire place with cracked wood, a coffee table so small it was practically useless, and a worn-out cream sofa on frayed carpet. The back of the sofa was quite low, and Dayton knew he would find it uncomfortable with nothing to rest his head against. There was a bookcase in the corner of the room with a few books that appeared to be gradually sliding downwards; the floor at the edge of the room was on a slight slope, meaning furniture placed against the wall was somewhat tilted.

The kitchen felt more like a thin corridor with an oven. There was a microwave, with a sink on one side and cupboards on the other, leaving enough space for only one person to fit between them. The oven was a gas oven that needed to be lit by a match; it looked old and had stains marked on its exterior that no amount of scrubbing could remove.

Dayton surveyed his surroundings with his hands on his hips and a large huff. This was not the life he was meant to be living. It was insulting to suggest that it was. He was waiting for greatness to arrive, but it kept being delayed.

Perhaps he needed to stop waiting for greatness to be thrust upon him, and search for it himself. He kept telling his friends on the forums to DO SOMETHING, yet he was not heeding his own advice.

He made himself at home in the first bedroom at the top

of the stairs, putting his own duvet on the bed and setting up his computer on the desk. He opened his suitcase and placed it in the corner of the room, but didn't unpack his clothes – the wardrobe's interior smelt damp, and he dreaded the thought of smelling bad; it was a sure way to end his chances with any prospective women. Thankfully, the internet was already set up, and he found himself absorbed in a game of *Maze of Magic* within minutes. When he was hungry, he put on a microwave pasta, then scrolled through the forums as he ate, feeling high on the affirmation his posts were receiving.

He was the first housemate to arrive as he'd travelled down a week before university began, eager to be free of his mother's persistent need to mother him and regain his independence, whilst also keen to scope the local area for the best places to find women. He sat in coffee shops, and the student union bar, and the park, scrolling through the online forum on his phone as he waited for a woman to approach. He had bought some smart leather shoes to go with his neat jeans and tidy shirt. He hated wearing jeans, as they felt so constrictive, but he wore them to look smart, and was incensed with women didn't seem to appreciate it.

Over the next week, his new housemates arrived. The first was Samuel, who chose the bedroom across the landing from Dayton's. He strode in, instantly filling the space with his grand movements and loud voice, thrusting his open palm at Dayton for him to shake. He spoke a lot, and Dayton spoke little, and Dayton appreciated this at first – he wasn't much of a talker and preferred it when others spoke – but Samuel's conversation quickly became unnecessarily vulgar. He'd just finished asking Dayton how his journey was, what course he was doing (Dayton lied and said he was still at university), and which cupboard he'd picked in the kitchen, when Simon blurted out, "So where's the pussy at?"

Dayton frowned. This was the kind of guy he hated, yet women were attracted to. Vulgar and coarse, treating women like shit, and making them think less of all men as a result.

Although, if Dayton was to be honest, he also felt a little optimistic about this man's companionship; if this guy could attract women, maybe he could attract one for Dayton. Like a wing man.

But no such friendship formed. Simon left the house on the first evening he arrived, and came home at one a.m. with his arm draped around a woman who wore a small, black leather dress, stumbled over nothing, and laughed when there wasn't anything to laugh at. Simon helped the inebriated woman up the stairs, winked at Dayton as they passed his room (Dayton had momentarily lifted his head up from a raid to see what the commotion was), then shut them both away in his room. Shortly after, sex noises overcame the house, the volume of which rose above anything Dayton did on *Maze of Magic*.

At first, it was Samuel; deep, manly grunts so rhythmic you could have timed it with a metronome. Then came hers, even louder, like someone exaggerating it for porn, almost screeching, bellowing an "Uh!" after each of his grunts.

This continued for half an hour.

Fury rose through Dayton like water through a broken dam. At no point did he entertain the notion that Simon and this woman were making the noise to exacerbate or demonstrate their pleasure to each other. It could only be as an insult to Dayton. To abuse him. For Simon to show off what he could do, and Dayton couldn't; to demonstrate how Simon was the alpha who fucked random drunk women, and that she was the easy slut that even Dayton couldn't get.

It was an intentional display of sexual dominance for Dayton's benefit, and he would not consider it to be anything else.

His resentment for Simon grew. Although Simon went out on his own and returned alone the next night, the following night he returned with a woman again. This time, the woman could barely stand. She was falling over on her high heels, her top was halfway down her chest, and she had to crawl up the stairs, such was the state of her drunkenness. Simon ended up dragging her up, gave the same wink at Dayton, and made the same grunts as before.

This time, the woman did not make any noise, but Simon seemed to be louder to compensate.

Dayton became distracted from his game and daydreamed about what he could do to his new housemate; he could take his laptop and slam it against Simon's head over and over, or he could take a knife from the kitchen and slit Simon's throat, or he could wait until Simon was sleeping and smother him with his pillow. He entertained each fantasy for a while, acting it out in his mind, his hatred growing with each murder his thoughts committed.

By the time his next housemate arrived, Dayton wasn't interested. He assumed it would just be another show-off, ready to rub his status with the opposite sex in his face. Even so, Clark knocked on Dayton's door and introduced himself, offering a hand which Dayton reluctantly shook. Clark seemed kinder and engaged in polite conversation, though Dayton still resented Clark's handsome looks. He was effortlessly good-looking, with neat hair swept over his head, and a chiselled chin at the base of a symmetrical face.

Marcus arrived last. He seemed studious and polite like Clark, but he was well-built and part of the rugby team, and Dayton did not relate to him either.

One night, however, they were in the living room whilst Dayton was upstairs replying to comments on the forum, when Clark knocked on his door.

"Hey mate, how's it going?" Clark asked.

Dayton minimised the window on his computer and turned around. "Fine."

"We're having a few drinks downstairs and getting to know each other. Fancy joining us?"

Dayton turned back to his computer. He was reluctant. The idea of sitting downstairs and talking to three blokes provoked an anxiety in his gut he struggled to quell.

"Come on, mate," Clark insisted, offering a pretty-boy smile. "We want to get to know you."

With a sigh of hesitation, Dayton closed his laptop lid and followed Clark downstairs.

There was another guy in the sitting room Dayton didn't recognise. A cool-looking black guy with a wide smile who introduced himself as one of Simon's friends called Tom, and he shook Dayton's hand. All the seats were taken, so Dayton leant against the arm of the sofa, and they carried on with whatever it was they were discussing before Clark had collected him.

Dayton said little. He responded to questions when asked, but with short sentences. Even so, he quite liked the company, even if he didn't admit it to himself – he'd never been part of a friendship group, or had real life friends, and he felt included in the jokes and conversation they were having. They offered him beer, and though he didn't like it that much, he accepted, and drank straight from the can like they did. They spoke about sports, and their courses, and their dissertations, and where they came from, and what they hoped to do after university. Dayton found himself smiling, feeling part of it.

Then came the topic of women.

"So what's your deal?" Simon asked his housemates. "Who's hitched up, and who's a free man?"

Clark smiled widely. "Been with my girlfriend for just over two years."

"Two years? Jesus... I struggle with two minutes."

"She's really sweet. Her parents have given us the money for a house deposit after we finish uni, so I'm looking forward to that."

"To each their own... Marcus?"

Marcus tilted his head and shrugged. "Just broke up with my bird of three years."

Simon pursed his lips and released an "ooh" as if he'd just witnessed something painful. "Harsh. Did she dump you?"

Marcus chuckled. "Amiable. We both weren't happy."

"Amiable? So she dumped you, yeah?"

They all laughed. Dayton didn't get the joke.

"What about you?" Simon asked Dayton. "You got a bird or what?"

All eyes turned to Dayton, and an uncomfortable silence descended. They waited, and he felt like there was a spotlight on him, and he was in the middle of a police interrogation. He wondered what to say – the truth? A lie? Nothing?

Did he tell them exactly what he thought of their attitudes toward the opposite sex?

"I'm single," Dayton eventually replied.

"You got any birds on the go?" Simon asked. Every time he said *bird* it made Dayton shudder.

"Not at the moment." They kept staring at him; they were expecting more. "I just like to keep my options open, you know?"

Simon raised his beer. "I hear that!"

They chuckled. Again, Dayton didn't get the joke.

"I've been single all my life," Simon said. "And there ain't no way I'm going to give up that shit for no one. Not unless they are something really special." He took a large swig of beer, swashed it around his mouth like mouthwash, then turned to Tom. "What about you, my friend?"

"Ah, well, you know," Tom said. "A man doesn't kiss and tell."

"Ooh, this sounds good!" Simon leant forward. "Come on mate, spill the beans."

"Well, I always have a few projects on the go, if you know what I mean."

"I bet you got one hell of a body count."

"I do all right."

"I bet you lost your virginity young too?"

Tom gave a cocky laugh and finished his can of beer. "Thirteen."

"Thirteen?" Simon looked agape. "You fucking kidding me?"

"To my babysitter – this seventeen-year-old blond chick who lived down the street my parents trusted way too much."

"Shit me..."

"So, you know, I'm not big on monogamy. I have a few women I go to, but none of them are good enough to give up the game for."

"I hear that." Simon raised his beer and tapped it against Marcus's empty can.

Talk continued in this vein for a while longer, each regaling their story of how they lost their virginity. Marcus at nineteen, Clark at eighteen, Simon at sixteen. When it came to Dayton, he said eighteen, not wanting to elaborate on why he still hadn't had sex whilst they seemed to have so much of it.

Conversation then turned back to sports, and football, and whoever was winning the Premier League, and Dayton tuned out of it. He was aware of the talking going on but had nothing to contribute when it came to football, so allowed it to continue as he festered on his loathing; he despised his housemates already, and this established how the rest of the year would go. He would shun every social interaction, reject any invitations to dinner, and shut himself away in his room and try to ignore Simon's sex noises.

For this evening, however, he focussed on Tom. He didn't realise he was staring, but he was, and Tom occasionally tried to appease Dayton with a smile or nod, but nothing averted his gaze. Dayton saw Tom as yet another insult to his superiority. To lose his virginity, at thirteen, to a white girl who would lower herself to this black man, whilst all the white girls snubbed Dayton, was a thought that inspired levels of revulsion that made his arms shake and his throat close up.

And although he never saw Tom again, it was yet another reason to resent the choices women made; that they would choose someone like *him*, instead of Dayton, was an affront of epic proportions.

He didn't consciously decide that he would kill his housemates on that night, but he knew something had to happen; that, should he take the stand he was trying to invoke in others, it would begin here, with these people, in this house.

In less than a year, those three housemates would be dead – and their demise had just begun.

Chapter Twenty-Four

No matter how much Dayton wandered, or loitered, or sat in the windows of coffee shops, or sat with an intensely stern expression at a bar, or sat on a bench with a book, he was learning that no woman was going to approach him.

At the same time, he witnessed these women's mate choices, and it reaffirmed everything he thought – and it *incensed* him.

Sitting in the window of a coffee shop, he watched a couple pass, the man's heavy arm draped around her dainty shoulders while he used the other arm to text. She would speak animatedly about something she was evidently passionate about, and he would grunt or, if she was really lucky, glance up for a moment. Dayton just couldn't fathom why this woman chose this man when there was a gentleman like him sat so close. He would never text someone else while she was instigating conversation; he would listen, keenly and eagerly to hear what she had to say.

Sitting in a bar, he'd watch women on the dance floor mere yards away, in their groups like baby animals congregating together for safety, their bags over their shoulders and their gin and tonic in their hand, moving from foot to foot, sometimes raising their arm or doing a little twirl. It was adorable, and he wished he could protect them from the lecherous groups of blokes that circulated them, spilling the contents of their beer as they shimmied from side to side. Most women didn't fall into their trap, but there'd always be one – and, as the night grew longer, and the women's dance moves became a little more extravagant and their gin and tonics became a little emptier, the success rate of these narcissistic blokes would increase.

Dayton would watch from his place at the bar, nursing his drink, glaring at this interaction with a loathing he felt churning inside of him.

All of this only affirmed his conclusion that women had inferior minds.

They were not attracted to gentlemanliness, or intellectual supremacy, or the money he'd convinced himself he would soon fall into, but to yobs, hellbent on wrecking their lives, only interested in which hole they could slither their way into first.

He'd trudge back to the taxi rank alone, mumbling and muttering about another unsuccessful night. His house was less than a mile away, but he felt too scared to walk home late at night, despite keeping his Stanley knife in his pocket, and that was why he took a taxi – and he resented how other men made him feel so unsafe; the kind of men these women were willingly fornicating with.

One day, shortly after the new year, as Dayton lazed away the days in his room, living off the money his mother gave him and the student loan he still received, having not informed them he'd left university, he received a call. It was from his father.

He did not answer it. Instead, he called his mother.

"Dayton, how lovely to hear from you. How is university?"

"Dad called," he declared, ignoring the warm greeting.

"Did he?"

Delilah knew that he'd called. It had been her constant berating of Brian that he should phone his son that led him to call. Her intimate encounter with Patrick had made her realise how desperate their son was for a father figure. She needed Brian to share the care of their son.

Of course, Brian had responded how she'd expected, barking at her in response that "The boy is twenty-one soon. He's a man. He can manage his own needs."

"He's still our son, Brian."

"But he's not our responsibility anymore."

"He will *always* be our responsibility."

"Yes, but you mother him like he's still a child–"

"Mentally, he is still a child–"

"Not this again."

"Brian, you visit Cassidy, you take her out to dinner, you even tell her about your and Nala's plans – would it hurt to do that with your son?"

"It's not that!"

"Then what is it?"

There was a grave silence, then Brian said, "It's just..." and his sentence faded away.

Delilah had never understood why Brian was so obtuse when it came to Dayton; why he was so hesitant to engage like he did with his daughter. But, in the silence that Brian left in refusing to finish his sentence, Delilah finally understood.

Brian didn't actually like Dayton.

Regardless of whether Dayton was his son, or whether

he held obligatory love, or whether he feigned interest when Dayton's welfare came up in conversation, or whether he shoved money at the situation so it could go away – he didn't like his son. In fact, Brian hated him; he could not understand how his son turned out to be such a weirdo.

But Dayton wasn't a weirdo. He had needs. He had issues. And he deserved a father who made as much of an effort with his son as he did with his daughter.

"Fine," Brian reluctantly said after Delilah had let the silence fester. "Fine, I'll call him."

Of course, as Delilah spoke to her son on the phone, she did not reveal that Brian's effort was a begrudging one that had taken much coercing.

"What did your father want?" Delilah asked Dayton.

"Dunno," Dayton said as he loaded *Maze of Magic* on his computer. "Didn't answer it."

"Well, perhaps he wishes to take you out to dinner."

"Take me out to dinner?" The words sounded like Dayton had a foul taste in his mouth, and Delilah hated how alien the concept was to him.

"It might be a good idea," she said.

Dayton considered this – but not for the reasons Delilah believed. Delilah assumed Dayton was considering the benefits of a relationship with his father, but honestly, Dayton's logic went as thus: *My father is wealthy. I should be wealthy. It might not hurt to use this to help me be wealthy.*

"All right," Dayton concluded. "I'll do it."

He rang his father back and arranged for him to visit for dinner in a few weeks' time. They went to a fancy Chinese restaurant on the other side of town – the side where the houses were bigger and people looked healthier. It was the end of town Dayton believed he belonged.

Brian and Nala went through the routine formalities of

asking how Dayton was, and if Dayton was more astute, he might have picked up on his mother-in-law's distaste for being there, and the way she never looked him in the eyes. He may have even noticed how she rarely instigated conversation and spent most of the time with her chin rested on her fist and her gaze aimed at the door. Fortunately for Dayton, he rarely picked up on such social cues, and spent the entire evening caring little for how much enjoyment Nala was having.

"So how are your studies?" Brian asked.

Dayton shrugged. "Fine," he lied as he scoffed down his starter.

Nala didn't finish hers, and Brian would usually have finished it for her, but it felt too formal to do so.

"Do you have any idea what you want to do after you finish?" Brian asked.

This stumped Dayton. As far as his family was concerned, he was in his final year, but Dayton hadn't thought that far ahead. Honestly, he'd expected to be rich by now, and getting a job after university wasn't something he'd expected to have to do.

But he still had time. A few months should be enough.

"I have another film in the line," Brian said to fill the silence. "We start in a few weeks. We're going away before... Having a nice holiday, you know. Before..."

Brian's eyes fell on his wife's belly, which Dayton didn't notice. Instead, Dayton was glaring at the family across the restaurant. The two children were colouring in the activity sheets the restaurant provided to help keep kids occupied, whilst the couple were holding hands and staring at each other across their table with such intense loving Dayton almost envied it.

Except, he didn't envy it. It repulsed him. Because this

woman was white, with neat, long hair, a pretty dress, a slim figure, and everything going for her. The man, however, had brown skin – Asian or Indian, Dayton didn't know, and didn't really care – and this infuriated him. To him, this white woman was lowering herself to an immigrant, while he still hadn't even kissed a girl. It was sickening. The man was wearing a cheap shirt and cheap jeans, and didn't even look that rich.

Their mains arrived, and it brought him out of his trance, and he realised his father had been watching him.

"Thank you," Brian said to the waiter. Nala and Dayton remained silent.

They began eating.

"Nala and I have something we wish to tell you, Dayton," Brian announced after a few mouthfuls.

Dayton lifted his gaze from his noodles and looked from Brian to Nala, then back to Brian. Nala was still not returning his gaze, and his dad looked nervous. Brian reached his arm across the table, placed his hand on Nala's, and forced a smile.

"We're having a baby," Brian said.

Dayton looked at Nala, as if waiting for her to confirm it.

"We've been trying for quite a few years," Brian admitted. "And we've finally got there, so we're happy."

Dayton didn't continue eating. His fork remained in his hand, noodles wrapped around its end, but he didn't move.

"We're having a daughter, Dayton. You're going to have a little sister."

All Dayton could mumble was, "*Half*-sister."

"Okay, half-sister," Brian said, forcing another fake smile. "How does that make you feel?"

Dayton frowned. What kind of question was that? It sounded like something a therapist might say. Why did it matter how he felt? When did it ever matter how he felt? His dad had left regardless of how it might make him feel, and he was hardly going to care now.

Nala sighed. A long, exaggerated huff out of her nose. She put her fork down and left the rest of her meal.

When he arrived home later, he had a text message from his mother. *How did it go?*

It made him wonder... did his mother know about this? Had they spoken about it before? Did she know this was going to happen; that this forced meal had been to cover up what his father and his mother-in-law were doing to him?

This wasn't how it was meant to be.

Dayton was meant to have been raised by both his parents, in a big house, like the one they lived in when he was little, and they were meant to love each other, and they were meant to love him.

Not... this.

This empty, forced space that sat between him and his father, waiting to be poked and prodded at every few years when Brian made some random attempt to reconcile with his son.

And Dayton was meant to be rich. And have a girlfriend. And have a life.

Instead, he was this pathetic mess of a man who lived in his room, masturbating then going on his game then going on his forum then repeating this over and over and over and over.

This was not who he was.

He *refused* to let this be who he was.

Something had to change. And if he would not change, and the world would not change, then he would have to change it.

Chapter Twenty-Five

"You *WHAT*?"

Delilah knew her neighbours could hear her. Her reaction came out as more of an impassioned shriek than an audible shout. But she didn't care. This was ludicrous.

"Delilah, calm down," came her ex-husband's voice on the phone, speaking with a stillness that made *her* sound like the unreasonable one.

She hated it when he told her to calm down. He was always so patronising, and it was one of the many things that had made her fall out of love with him. When did telling someone to calm down ever work? And why was it always *her* that needed to calm down? If one of his male friends became irate and angry, he'd listen and provide sound advice; if Delilah was angry, he would inform her she was being irrational and she needed to monitor her reaction.

"No, Brian," she spat, enunciating every syllable. "Why don't you repeat to me what you just said?"

"I don't need to repeat what—"

"Yes, you do. Maybe so you can hear it as well as me."

"You know what, Delilah? Maybe this wouldn't have

happened if you'd actually treated him like an adult, or like a capable human, and not this bomb that will explode at any minute."

"You're questioning *my* parenting?"

"Why do you think he's like this? It's because you molly-coddled him! You were overbearing, meddling all the time, switching his schools at the first sign of difficulty. He'd be far more competent if you'd treated him like he was competent."

"And what about your parenting, Brian?"

He sighed so audibly he could almost have been standing next to her. Delilah didn't care for his dismissal; she'd been filling with resentment for over fifteen years, and she was finally about to burst.

"You know what?" she continued, jabbing her finger as if his smug face was right in front of her. "Maybe I didn't get everything right. Maybe I made a few fuck ups. But at least I was there."

"I tried to be there–"

"How? You left him with your wife on weekends! You couldn't even be bothered to be there!"

"Delilah–"

"No, do not do that!" She bit her lip. "Do not *dare* do that!"

She hated how he said her name.

How he uttered it like he was speaking to a child; like he was about to reprimand her or put her on the naughty step. She was sick of this shit, and it was time he heard it.

"I worked night and day and weekends," she said, her voice breaking, menacing in its slow pace; her anger was being slowly replaced by tears and despair, and she was making no effort to fight it. "Non-stop working my arse off in dead-end jobs while you had the money to change every-thing, and you couldn't even do that."

"I paid half for his school–"

"Oh, well done!" She placed the phone between her cheek and her shoulder so she could give him a few sarcastic claps. "Aren't you father of the year?"

Another sigh. Always the martyr. "Are we done?" Brian said. "Because my wife is pregnant, and I need to make sure she's okay."

"Oh, fuck you, Brian – fuck you and your wife." She huffed and made a concerted effort to think clearly. "So have you told him?"

"Told who?"

"Dayton. Have you told him of your decision?"

More silence.

She could sum up Brian's entire relationship with his son in a moment of silence.

"I'm not telling him," she said quietly, her voice fading. "I'm not doing your dirty work."

"Do we need to tell him?" Brian said. "Will he even notice?"

She laughed a pitiful, sorry laugh.

"No," she said, shaking her head. "I guess he won't. And that's the saddest part of this, isn't it? His father has decided that he no longer wants a relationship with him, and he won't even notice that such a decision has been made."

More silence resumed. It lasted longer than the previous one. She could hear him breathing, so she knew he was there, but his words were not forthcoming. There were no more apologies, no more excuses, just resolve. There was no changing his mind, and if she was honest, Delilah felt no reason to try.

"I'm going to go now," Brian said.

"Okay," Delilah replied, filling her voice with all her spite.

"I tried, Delilah," he said. "I really did."

"Did you?" she asked. "When?"

More silence.

"When did you try?" she asked again.

Even more silence.

"When did you try, Brian? Please, I want to know."

More silence, long and arduous, painful and empty.

Eventually, he said, "Goodbye Delilah," and the phone call concluded with a click. His name left her phone screen, which returned to a background image of her, Cassidy and Dayton together at Christmas.

She leant against the kitchen counter. Lowered her eyes and placed a hand over her face. She felt like throwing her phone across the room, but she saw no point in damaging her belongings. In fact, she saw no point in hurting herself or her family over that man anymore.

Perhaps she should be impressed. It took him far longer to abandon his son than it took him to abandon her.

She couldn't help but think of Brian and Nala's daughter, who was due around the same time as Dayton's birthday. Every year, August would come around, and only one of Brian's children would receive presents. Perhaps he'd have a cake specially made, whilst Dayton ate whatever she could afford from the local budget supermarket.

She found Dayton's name in her phone contacts and traced her thumb over the outline of the letters. She dreaded phoning this number nowadays, aware she would be met with an answer phone message, and she hated how much it hurt when he didn't pick up his phone. But she didn't care. Right now, she needed to hear his voice, and she needed him to know that he was loved. So she pressed his name, put her phone to her ear, and let her mind wander as she listened to the rings.

She'd tried so hard to give Dayton a better life. Cassidy had been content, and understood Delilah's limitations, and had appreciated the effort she saw her mother making to provide for them. But Dayton had been different. He hadn't been able to see it, and she didn't blame him for that; he had his difficulties. This just wasn't what she'd imagined when she'd shown Brian that positive pregnancy test and they'd hugged, and cheered, and celebrated, and planned, and bought the cot, and painted the nursery.

She felt like she'd let Dayton down. He'd wanted so much, and all she could offer him was her love.

"This is Dayton, I'm unable to get the phone, leave a message."

She dropped her phone by her side, standing alone in the living room, staring at the space her son used to occupy, in her small flat that felt so large. She wiped away a tear and refused to let herself cry another one over her ex-husband.

She just hoped that she alone could be enough for her son – she was, after all, all he had.

The Day of the Twenty-First

Chapter Twenty-Six

ANOTHER CALL ENDED, A FEW SECONDS PASSED, AND her name popped up on Dayton's lock screen again.

Mum 68 Missed Calls.

There were more messages too. They were much the same, and they melded into one.

Please call me Dayton.

Know that I'm here if you need to talk.

I love you so much Dayton please just don't do anything stupid.

He'd silenced his phone a while ago, and now he considered turning it off. He had no intention of answering his phone. And he'd only listened to one of her voicemail messages – a teary message where half the words were indecipherable due to her inability to form syllables whilst her face was contorting into tears. He could imagine the ugly way her face twisted when she cried so hard. That face was once so pretty. He remembered when he was a young child, and his mother's hair would flow down over her shoulders, and her smile would make men's eyes linger over her a little too long, and her clear skin highlighted a prettiness that only natural beauty could attain. Now, her hair was grey, her skin had formed wrinkled lines like cracks in hard dirt, and her arms sometimes shook when she stood still. Dayton could never figure out how she had aged so quickly. What had life done that had managed to destroy her body before it had destroyed her soul?

His phone rang again. He rolled his eyes. Perhaps he should look up how to block numbers, it couldn't be that difficult. Did she not realise she was responsible for this? If she'd created a stronger man, or a more sociable man, or given him two parents, maybe things would have been different. If she hadn't moved her children out of the large, lavish home where they'd belonged, perhaps he would have grown up feeling like he hadn't been betrayed by the two people who were meant to love him. Oh, how he resented her failures, and the woman she had become.

He intended to address this resentment, and her part in the shoddy life she'd provided for him – but not yet. That would come later. The Grand Finale.

For now, he sat at the window of the only coffee shop that stayed open late, nursing his paper cup with half a latte left. They had apparently run out of normal cups, and now everyone had to use a recyclable paper cup, which was odd – surely, if they were going to run out of cups, it would be the ones they could reuse, not the disposable ones. Still, he didn't question it – he'd learned not to question the illogic of humans. People so rarely saw the folly in what they thought, did and said. It was why they were stupid, petty, pathetic little creatures, and he was the immense, superior, intelligent being who was required to point out their follies.

A group of women walked in and shuffled to the counter. They ordered without looking in Dayton's direction. Today, it didn't bother him. He wasn't here to attract the attention of a potential girlfriend anymore. He was past that. Today, he was here for something else.

A news alert came up on his phone, the sound of which prompted a fleeting glance from a few people on nearby tables who were absorbed in their own phone screens. They didn't look up long enough to see Dayton scowling at them. People are self-centred that way.

The headline read *Three People Murdered Outside House Party*. A jolt of giddiness shot through him and his leg started shaking. He quickly plugged his earphones into his phone, placed them in his ears, and listened to audio in the breaking news report.

"The police have revealed that a man has attacked a group of students who were standing outside their home, fatally wounding two women and one man, before residents came out of the house and chased him away. The attacker is still unidentified, but residents of the house said they recognised him as another student at their university. He left in a car, and as it was dark they could not get the make, but said it looked like an expensive black sports car. Police have assured the public that they are using all means necessary to track this car and to identify the culprit. They have made a clear warning to the public that this attacker is still at large, is considered highly dangerous, and is not to be approached. Today, we spoke to psychiatrist Professor Daniel Humphrey who speculated that this may well be the beginning of a spree killing."

Dayton mulled over those last few words, chewing them like a tasty piece of gum.

This may well be the beginning of a spree killing.

Maybe that was correct, in a way. Serial killers murdered their victims over an extended period of time, whilst spree killers do it all within a small period of time, like over a day or two. This was accurate enough, he supposed, but he resented the implication of the word *killer*.

Because he wasn't just a *killer*.

He was a goddamn revolutionary.

He was the instigator of the Beta Uprising.

He was Sergeant General of his army, and once those comrades on the forums saw he had finally decided to DO SOMETHING, he knew they would all follow.

A spree killer? He scoffed. Hardly. This was so much more than a nutter knocking off a few strangers. This was a genius taking down the establishment that had served the alphas for far too long.

Another few women walked in, hooking arms and laughing, clearly having had a few cocktails. Their movement was loose and free in the way that Staceys often were, and he imagined they'd placed those delicate hands on many muscular biceps this evening, flirting and taunting men with their weaponised sexuality.

Usually, he would be overcome with hate at the sight of them. And he was. But today, he thought clearly. In this moment, he saw what he must do.

The three of them ordered coffees to go. Two of them kept talking whilst the loosest of them leant over the counter, far enough that the young male barista could see down her top at her pink bra (Dayton could tell it was pink by the straps that showed through the back of her white vest) and asked him how his night was going.

If anyone asked her why she was leading him on, Dayton was certain she would accuse them of gaslighting her. He'd seen women like that do such things before. He could hear her excuses now:

Leaning over the counter? I was trying to see his name tag!

Showing him my bra? He was looking!

Asking him how his night was going? I was being friendly!

But Dayton saw it for what it was – the only way this woman could feel powerful. She could not physically overpower this man, nor could she outwit him in intelligence, and nor could she outdo him in a competition of kindness. The only authority she held was in her tits, in her body, and in her cunt. And she used each and every one to her advantage, making sure she delivered her performance on the line between clear flirtation and naïve innocence.

He gave them their coffees. He told her he'd put an extra squirt of cream on her mocha, and put the chocolate shot in for free – and he winked at her while he did it.

"Thanks, stud," she said, smiling at him in a way that made him think he had a chance.

This was what Staceys did. They used their sexuality to get what they wanted, and they never cared how it made a man feel.

And that was why Dayton was going to do what he did next.

As they left the coffee shop, he downed the last few drops of his latte. The milk had gone cold, but he didn't like leaving any. He took his paper cup to the counter and asked if they had a bin.

"I can take it for you," said the barista, still smitten by his previous interaction. Dayton would feel sorry for the guy, but he pitied him instead. Only idiots could think that a woman like that would ever like them.

A quiet chime over the door announced his departure, and he zipped up his hoodie as he stood outside the doorway. Across the street, the three women were walking away, falling over each other with their giggles, sipping from their coffee cups, the slut enjoying the extra mocha shot and the cream she hadn't asked for.

Dayton pressed the button on his keys to unlock his BMW and climbed in. He took his time, in no rush, turning the key in the ignition and switching on the radio. They were playing the mindless, repetitive electronic nonsense they usually played on a weekend night, but Dayton tolerated it as he waited for another update in the news about his apparent spree killing.

He pitied the news reporter for being so foolish as to think this was a menial, mindless set of killings. Once, he would have been angry – now he felt sorry for those who were not armed with the greater level of awareness he had.

Down the street, the women turned the corner and walked down a darker road. This was perfect. There were fewer shops and more residences on that street – but there were also fewer street lamps. Now the authorities were tracking him, he needed to be aware of being captured on CCTV cameras in the street. He didn't want to be caught before he finished.

He indicated, checked his blind spot, and manoeuvred onto the road. His lights came on automatically, and he drove slowly forward, finding no other cars coming toward him or behind him. He turned onto the street the women had walked down.

There they were. Sauntering down the street. Not caring about what they had done. Already forgotten about the barista. Keen to keep laughing and being happy. Ignorant to the destruction their bodies left behind.

Dayton shifted into first, found the biting point, then hit the accelerator. The car revved, lurching forward, and he discovered just how quickly he could take off.

The women turned and looked at him but, at the

moment they realised what was happening, they fled – caring little for each other – they realised it was too late.

Dayton drove through them like a bowling ball through a set of pins.

The clatter of their bodies over the body of his car was heavy and loud, but brief. His instinct was to worry about the damage done to the BMW, but he remembered that, in the long term, it didn't matter.

He screeched to a halt and looked in his rear-view mirror.

Two of the women lay on the ground. Their limbs skewwhiff from the rest of their body. Face down in the wet street. Not moving or twitching whatsoever.

The third woman, however, wasn't still.

She wasn't particularly spritely, either, but she wasn't inanimate like the others. She pushed herself up, slightly, falling down again, and trying to push herself up once more. Her legs were flat, but her arms were allowing her vague movement, and she was aware enough to look around and see the blood in the street.

Dayton shifted the car into reverse and accelerated hard.

The car thudded her head, and when he brought it to a stop, she wasn't moving anymore.

Dayton shifted the car back into first gear, drove forward, his car rising as his wheels drove over them again, and sped away.

It rained a little as he left the town centre. He put on the windscreen wipers, and it wasn't long before the rain had cleaned his car's body of blood. He drove on into the night, with his final two destinations in mind.

Before the Twenty-First

Chapter Twenty-Seven

A PERSON'S TWENTY-FIRST IS A SIGNIFICANT milestone, though it's not clear why. They aren't turning into an adult, they aren't entering a new decade, and they aren't able to do anything they weren't previously legally able to do – not in the United Kingdom, anyway – but Dayton did not see it this way.

He saw his twenty-first birthday as a huge milestone. A potentially cataclysmic event. A world-changing moment where the follies of his youthful perceptions were over, and it was time to be an adult who took action.

And this huge milestone was only a few weeks away.

For Dayton, twenty-one felt old in the way it does when one is so young. And he was in disbelief that the date was approaching, and he was still a virgin.

Nay, more than a virgin.

He had never kissed a woman. Never been on a date with a woman. Never even held hands with a woman.

He saw men using women all the time, and he resented how much they took it for granted. He'd wonder what it was like to interlock his fingers with the woman such men would ignore until it was time to fuck her. Sometimes, he imagined the feel of her skin, the hand smaller than his, the sweat of their palms sticking together, the daintiness of the hand making him feel rugged and firm. Simple acts of affection were not something he'd ever experienced and, back when these thoughts began to fester, he'd hated himself for feeling so upset. Now, he didn't hate himself. It wasn't his fault. It was the world he lived in. He hated society – it was the fault of *the way things are*; the perpetually low standards of a superficial civilisation. Everyone was an animal, and they pretended they weren't, and it sickened him.

And, as he sat in his room, staring at the end of a pornographic movie with the remnants of brief masturbation sticking to his belly, he didn't clean himself off. Instead, he watched the two people making love on screen and felt pathetic. Truly pathetic. Constantly doing this, several times a day, over movies that just demonstrated some kind of love, or affection, or a connection between two people, was not conducive to where he wanted to be in life.

He decided there and then – if he had not lost his virginity by his twenty-first birthday, then his twenty-first birthday would be the day he took action; the day he would DO SOMETHING.

Twenty-one years was too long for anyone to be deprived of love, and it wasn't good enough.

If that day came, and he still hadn't encountered the woman's touch he sorely felt he was due, then the human race would suffer for what it had done to him.

He cleaned himself up and, hearing silence downstairs, took the opportunity to make his dinner without his housemates present. He despised their conversations – they were mostly brags with vulgar language and insults disguised as banter.

Relishing the quiet, he leant against the kitchen counter while his readymade dinner span slowly around in the microwave's light. With his arms folded, he allowed himself a sigh, and a gaze at the floor, digesting this life he'd never wanted. Where was the wealth? The wonder? The greatness?

As his food reached two minutes to go, the sound of the front door opening forced an eyeroll from Dayton, and he bemoaned his luck as his housemates entered in the midst of irksome conversation.

"Mate, they are not winning the league this season."

"It's a sure thing bruv."

"You got more chance of me fucking your mother."

"I'll take those odds."

The 'banter' was followed by a nod and a grunt in Dayton's direction. They'd asked him if he wanted to join their social occasions several times, and Dayton was relieved they had given up, and that they no longer tried to start meaningless conversations with him. Instead, they sat on the sofa and continued the menial conversation that proved what animals they were.

"You seeing that Tracy bird tonight?"

"Dunno. Kinda bored of her."

"Didn't sound bored of her the other night."

"Didn't have any other options, did I? Nah, I'm going to see what else I can get. What about you?"

"Got that Charlotte bird coming over."

"Oh, yeah? Any good?"

"Crackin' tits. I like them small."

"Small? You a fucking cuck or what?"

"How does liking small tits make me a cuck?"

"Dunno mate, I just like to have something to grab onto."

Dayton watched the clock on the microwave count down from twenty to one, unable to avoid listening to their conversation; they were so loud, there was no way to avoid it. And whilst he appeared quiet, and like he wasn't listening, and like he was focussed on the countdown, inside, his rage was festering, tremoring like the moment before a volcano erupts.

His hand was in his pocket. As was his Stanley knife. He kept it secure in his fist and, as they kept talking, his thumb ran over the side, flicking the blade slightly out, then retracting it again. Flicking it out, then retracting it in.

Out, then in.

Out, then in.

Out, then in.

He imagined using it. Subtly walking past them, pretending to trip, and bringing the knife out of his pocket before plunging it down into their neck as he did.

The microwave pinged.

He took his meal out and scraped it into a bowl. He took this through the living room, ignoring his housemate's attempts to greet him, and ignoring their sniggers as he left.

He had weeks until his twenty-first – then they'd see who the butt of the joke was.

But he couldn't be reckless. He shouldn't make this decision lightly. He knew this. And that was why he was going to make one last concerted effort – a final attempt to be a man that women flock to – to enhance his superiority – to be the gentleman who could fix the problems the alpha had created.

The first step was wealth. He'd watched a few seminars by wealthy people online, and had noted down a few pieces of their advice, hoping to emulate it and create his path to riches. They consistently spoke of mindset – that you need to believe you are something, then you will become it.

So he believed he was rich. Therefore he was rich.

The next day, he bought a BMW on finance. Brand new, shiny and clean, with a rev that sounded like a proud lion. The car firm did a credit check, which came back fine, and he told them he worked for a local finance firm – he'd searched online for names of local finance firms in preparation – and there were no more questions asked. He had enough from the money his mother sent to pay the deposit, and he trusted that his imminent wealth would take care of the monthly debt he'd incur – he believed he had that wealth, therefore he would have it.

He drove around town, cruising past groups of people his age, slowing down when there were women. Heads turned, slick alphas nodded in approval, and women nudged their friends to point it out. He felt good. Powerful, even. Like this was the turning point. Like this car portrayed the greatness he was imminently going to achieve.

He put on a posher accent too. Most people at university spoke differently to him – he grew up on a council estate, unlike most of the middle-class students who hung around the night clubs on student nights. So he spoke more eloquently to bouncers, and bar staff, and baristas, and to women he mumbled hello to when he leant against his car, trying to lure them in with his smouldering eyes.

He expected this to work. For women to approach him. For his rich mindset to instigate conversations. He leant against his fancy car in anticipation, an eagerness in his shaking arms, excited that he was finally going to get a girl-friend, and have his first kiss, and his first sexual encounter, and his first time holding hands. The women were out in great numbers, and it was only a matter of time.

Except, after a few days of loitering, leaning against his car, and a few guys complimenting him on it as they passed, there were no women who responded to his smouldering glances. In fact, they mostly averted their eyes, or crossed the road, or hurried past him.

What was wrong with these women?

What did they want?

What else could he do to make these bitches like him?

He didn't get it. He really didn't. It made no sense. He was rich – at least, he looked rich – smart, posh voice – fancy car – hanging around where all the women hung around – and nothing. Fucking nothing. At all.

What the fuck did he have to do?

He drove around in his BMW for the next few nights, glaring at the women who'd snubbed him and the men who they liked.

There was one couple in particular that filled him with hatred. He'd just been to the drive through, and was turning the wheel with one hand while sipping from a strawberry milkshake with the other when he saw them. It was a black man and a white woman, which made him especially angry. They held hands, she leant her head on his shoulder, and they meandered slowly down the street, sharing their love without a care for how public their display was.

He parked across the street. Hand in his pocket. Thumb on the side of his knife. Flicking out the blade, retracting it back in.

Out, in.

Out, in.

Out, in.

He could do it. He could run out of his car, stab him first, slice his throat, then slice her over and over and over and over. He'd leave them bleeding to death on the street. Run back to his car. Speed away. It would be so easy.

So, so easy.

For a moment, he decided he was doing it.

Fuck it – why not?

He was going to run out of the car.

He even took out the knife, unleashed the blade, and put his hand on the door handle.

But something stopped him.

Was it his conscience?

Couldn't be sure. Maybe, maybe not. He couldn't see himself regretting it; his hatred was too strong. Perhaps it was the promise of his twenty-first birthday. What he could achieve if he was patient. He could eradicate far more of them in one day than if he just did something silly now and got caught.

Instead, he wound the window down, cruised past them, and took the lid off his milkshake. They stopped to kiss as he passed, with their mouths wide open and their tongues slithering into the other's gob. He leant out of the window, ensured he didn't spill any milkshake on the plush interior of his car, then threw it at them.

It landed perfectly on their heads, and they were covered.

"Fuck you!" he shouted.

The man turned, fists clenched, and charged at the car.

Shit. Dayton panicked. This guy was well-built, and it scared him. He hit the accelerator and sped around the corner, not slowing down until miles had passed and there was considerable distance between him and them.

When he arrived home, he was panting. Grinning. A wide smile across his face. He felt high. He felt amazing. He was proud of what he'd just achieved, and his leg was bouncing up and down, a heavy giddiness overtaking his body.

"Whew!" he shouted, punching the steering wheel in celebration, repeating his hollers of joy.

It was a feeling unlike anything he'd felt before.

He strode into the house and took the stairs two at a time, feeling full of power. Fuck his housemates. They could brag about their conquests all they wanted. He'd do the same to them as he'd done to that couple. No, he'd do worse. He marched into his bedroom, eager to brag about what he'd done on the forums.

But he paused. Hovered in the doorway.

He could hear something.

He silenced his breathing, twisted his head to the side, and listened intently.

From Simon's bedroom. Across the corridor. The noises again. His vague grunting. A woman moaning in pleasure.

It wasn't as loud as it usually was, but it was clear. Another brag about what Simon could achieve, and what Dayton couldn't.

His hand was in his pocket. Fist around his knife. Thumb moving the blade out, then in.

Out, in.

Out, in.

Out, in.

He considered going into that room and slicing both their throats.

The sound infuriated him. He was so happy, on such a high, and this had brought him right back down again and reminded him of reality. The indignity of having to listen to another slut with another animalistic pleb was too much. He'd heard enough. It was time it ended.

He took his knife out. Stared at the shades of silver in the blade. Anticipated slicing them apart.

Then he retracted the blade and put the knife back in his pocket.

Not yet.

There wasn't long until his twenty-first. He'd made a promise to himself. If things didn't change, that would be the day.

He entered his room, shut the door, and put his computer on. He played *Maze of Magic,* but his mind wasn't in it. All he could think about was the feeling of throwing his milkshake over that couple, and how amplified that feeling would be if he'd used his knife instead.

He was addicted to the feeling now.

There would be no going back.

Chapter Twenty-Eight

THE KNIFE MADE DAYTON FEEL POWERFUL.

He'd never felt powerful before, and he liked it. He kept it in his pocket, often holding it, nursing it, treating it like the woman's hand his fingers lacked.

No one knew he had it but him.

Some people looked at him. Some didn't. Some avoided him, some pitied him. But none of them knew.

He could take their life at any moment.

Just one flick and a swipe. That's all it would take. A quick action, like in an action movie – he was the hero; they were the villain – he was the superstar; they were the arch nemesis – he was the winner; they were the loser. For once, they were the loser. And this was how it happened.

With this power, he felt invincible. And he felt able to do something he'd never done before.

He was going to approach *her*.

That's right – enough standing around, waiting for them to come to him. It had taken long enough, but he was going to instigate the conversation. He'd seen other men do it, and whilst he felt a woman should have enough sense to come to him first, evidently they weren't intelligent enough to take such initiative, and he needed to be the one to take action.

But with whom?

He parked his BMW in a visible spot and took his time getting out of it, wanting as many people as possible to see him with it. Then he sauntered from the car park into the town centre, past the fancy shops on the boulevard, walking with a sluggish pace that showed he had nowhere to be. His hand remained in his pocket, retracting the blade then recalling it, as he surveyed the surrounding people with a newfound awareness.

Their lives were in jeopardy, and none of them knew.

A smug smile crossed his face. No need to look smouldering if he was going to be the one to approach the woman. He didn't need to attract her to him, he just needed to show how powerful he was.

He sat on a bench and watched passing women like a hunter picking out his doe. One hung around outside an expensive bookshop, holding a paper bag displaying the shop's logo, staring at her phone. She put her phone to her ear and spoke. She seemed to enter an argument with the recipient of her call almost immediately. This put Dayton off; too intense, too nasty.

On another bench, a young woman sat forward, wearing a supermarket uniform beneath an open coat. She ate a readymade wrap from the fridge section of the supermarket and stared at the pigeons gathering in the space before her feet. She even twisted a bit of wrap from her meal and threw it to them. They fought over it, and it was a feeling she must be used to – showing something of herself to men who strut around her and letting them fight each other over who had it. At first, he thought this was kindness, but decided it was arrogance, and lost interest in her.

Finally, he watched a woman leave a clothes shop, sunglasses perched on top of her head, her black hair scraped back into a ponytail, talking on the phone. She wasn't bad to look at, but there was nothing remarkable about her either. She was plain, and Dayton liked that. Her clothes were stylish and well-fitted without being overly revealing. Her smile as she spoke was pleasant, and there was no hostility in her expression.

This was her. He knew it.

He stood. Brushed off his trousers. Took a deep breath. Panicked. Felt like backing out. Almost did.

Then he felt the blade in his hand, and he reminded himself that he was powerful, and she was not.

He walked toward her, eyes fixed on her face like the bullet from a rifle travelling toward its target. He ignored those he bumped into, focussed on what he was to achieve, and kept the knife clutched tight. He came to a halt a few steps behind her, but she didn't turn around.

He paused. Took a deep breath. Opened his mouth.

"Hi."

The word came out in a broken voice, and he felt embarrassed. But she hadn't noticed. So he tried again.

"Hi."

She was too engrossed in her phone conversation to notice he was there. He was too far away. He needed to get closer. He took a few steps toward her, reaching the boundary of her personal space.

"Hi," he said.

She turned around. Noticed him. Frowned. Turned away and said on the phone, "Sorry, there's some bloke here. What were you saying?"

The urge to cry beat his urge to take out his knife; he felt his face twisting in that ugly way a face does before one weeps, and the force was too overwhelming to fight. He fled, rushing to the public toilets across the road, and entered the gents. He barged past someone leaving, bound into the cubicle, locked the door, sat on the toilet lid, and buried his face in his hands.

He hadn't cried for years. It was a weakness he did not entertain – he was meant to be powerful. But this was something too big to contain, too devastating to put into words, too large to keep inside. His body convulsed under the weight of each sob, and he lost track of time, sitting there, crying. For the first time in a long time, he missed his mother, and thought of hearing her voice, only to dismiss it as a step too far into the realm of debilitating weakness.

There were footsteps outside the cubicle, so he silenced his tears, which meant the sobs forced his body to convulse harder. His shoulders rose and dropped with the force of his weeping, and the fingers he held around his eyes like prison bars grew wet and sticky.

He unwound some toilet paper, disposing of the first few bits, aware that someone may have touched them with dirty hands, then pulled a handful away and wiped his eyes.

He remembered the knife in his pocket, but even that didn't work. At least, temporarily. Then he reminded himself of the need to feel rich and powerful in order to be rich and powerful, and he felt embarrassed for letting some stupid woman have this effect on him.

Fuck her. Fuck all of them. He's too good for those bitches.

He stood. Ceased the tears. He refused to be pathetic. He opened the cubicle, strode out, and checked his eyes in his reflection. They were a little red, but not noticeably. He washed his hands to give the impression to a stranger at the urinal that he'd been peeing rather than crying, and left.

As he stepped out the door, he saw her. The woman. Only, she wasn't alone. She was meeting an Asian man. She kissed him and hugged him. Wrapped her arms around his waist and beamed up at him with a smile that was meant solely for him. Then they walked down the street, hand in hand, and he could tell she was smiling even from the back of her head. The way her pony tail bounced off her shoulders looked like happiness.

He followed them.

It wasn't a conscious decision. It was automatic. But he didn't stop himself.

They walked down the street at such a slow pace, forcing people to move onto the road to overtake them. They didn't notice the inconvenience they caused. No clue in the world. They only saw each other.

He put his hand in his pocket, wrapped it around his knife, and picked up his pace.

He approached them, moving faster, ready to pull out the blade, about to stab the guy first, about to take his pitiful little life, showing that if Dayton can't have it then neither can he, the bastard, the alpha, the Chad, the–

He stopped himself.

Halted, dead in the street, forcing people to divert their route around him.

What was he doing?

It wasn't his twenty-first yet. This could ruin everything.

The town centre was crowded. There were too many witnesses. Did he really want to waste his freedom on them when he could achieve glory in a week's time?

Scalding himself for how close he was to being foolish,

he diverted his route away from the couple, and deliberately chose the long way back to the car park to avoid them.

But he still felt irked. Still angry. He needed to vent. To unleash.

When he arrived home, he bypassed his roommate's open doors, scowled at Simon who stood aside so Dayton could pass, charged into his room, opened his computer, logged onto the forum, and clicked *New Post*.

This was going to be another of his brilliant articles. A magnificent one. He could feel it. He was going to introduce even more strands to the ideology of those online, and he was already excited about the praise he would receive.

He began the article with the headline: *The Dangers of Diversity*.

He leant forward and allowed his fingers to pour his thoughts out. He didn't stop writing, a continuous stream of consciousness unloading his thoughts, and he felt his anger lessen and his excitement grow as he shared his ideas.

He wrote of how close he'd come to wasting his moment on a minority. How Asian men were ugly and white women shouldn't lower themselves to mating with them. How even Asian women shouldn't lower themselves to Asian men, and they were already pretty low. How this was an example of another reason the sex life of women should be controlled, lest we end up with a country full of half-caste men fucking with women's heads.

He posted without even proofreading. But he didn't need to. The mistakes were part of his passion.

The praise was instant, and within an hour, there were thousands of comments, lauding him as a visionary, extolling him as a leader of men, commending him as the one who could lead the Beta Uprising.

The validation was all he needed. With the encouragement, he posted a new thread. A shorter one. One that put his plans into writing, and therefore made him committed to them.

It simply stated:

It is my twenty-first birthday in a week.

I refuse to be a twenty-one-year-old virgin.

If I reach that day with my virginity still intact, then that day will be our reckoning.

I've spoken many times about how we should stop the words and DO SOMETHING.

I am going to DO SOMETHING.

Watch the news. Watch the internet. You'll see my video. You'll see my reasons. I will post them before I begin.

It's time to take action.

I encourage you to do the same.

He hit post, and there it was. His commitment in words. He couldn't back down now. If he did, he'd be a coward, and those who'd heaped so much praise on him would not forgive that.

He took his knife from his pocket and held it as he refreshed the page, over and over, every few minutes, reading every word of support he received.

The replies spoke of how many people in society would see him as insane, but anyone who belonged to the forum would know he was the sane one.

How his actions would make him even more of a legend.

That, when he took the lead, they would follow in the days after.

It was decided. His determination overrode all hesitation. His twenty-first wouldn't just be a day of celebration for him – it would be a day of celebration for all of them.

All that was left was to make his plans. Put together

what he intended to do, how he intended to do it, and what the timings would look like.

He knew how he'd begin.

He knew where he'd go.

And, as he looked at his phone and saw another missed call from his mother, he knew how it would end.

Chapter Twenty-Nine

THE NEXT FEW DAYS PASSED IN A DAZE. DAYTON DIDN'T go out much. There was little point. The only way his potential targets could avoid their fate was if he lost his virginity, and he had little motivation to try.

Not anymore.

He'd tried enough. He'd been out so many days, and so many nights, waiting for someone to show some interest. His supremacy, his manners, his kindness, his handsome face, his dress sense, his kickarse car – *none* of it had been good enough, and that was unlikely to change if he left the house now.

So he stayed in his room. Simon now had a girlfriend, as shown on his social media account – *Simon is now in a relationship*; the words Dayton read with a whiny, mocking voice – and she was around most nights, and he was forced to listen to them have sex.

It was repugnant. Vile. Obscene. And for this reason, his housemates would go first. That was certain. But what of this woman? What about this girlfriend? What would he do with her?

As her overexuberant grunts began their crescendo, like a woodwind band with out-of-tune flutes, he clicked on this woman's social media profile. She was a brunette with curly hair. Pretty smile. The kind of woman who photographed well, but all her selfies were taken from above, as if she was too insecure to show an unflattering angle. He kept scrolling until he came across photos from her holiday to Magaluf three years ago, where she'd posted endless selfies of herself in a red bikini. Her body looked better then than it did now.

He chose the best three pictures, copied them onto a document, enlarged them until they filled the screen, then shoved his trousers and boxers to his ankles and masturbated over her. He listened to her eager sounds as he did, pretending they were for him. He imagined a world where a woman's mating choice was his decision, and he could command Simon to sit in the corner like a pathetic cuckold as this woman descended to her knees and saw to his pleasure. He traced the curves of her body with his eyes, staring at the unblemished skin of her legs, marvelling at the perfect indent of her navel, licking his lips at the painted red nails on her toes, and imagined what her nipple would look like; the one an inch away from the top of the bikini. He came over this final thought then deleted the document. It was his own way of saying *fuck you* to them both; an action only he would know about.

He spent the next few hours on his favourite forum. Someone had posted a link to a feminist forum and suggested they all post replies. Dayton read it, out of curiosity for what a feminist could have to say – they had the vote, didn't they? The power? The sexual dominance? – he scoured the posts and guffawed several times at the diatribe these people were posting.

One post shared thoughts of how women shouldn't feel

pressured into sexual acts. Dayton posted his reply: *Then you shouldn't lead guys on you dumb ho.*

Another shared anecdotes of how women should have equal pay. Dayton posted his reply: *Then do the same job you fucking bitch – I don't see you at a building site.*

And another individual recounted the story of how, when she was young, her older brother's friend molested her, causing her to never feel safe around men. Dayton posted his reply: *He wouldn't have had to rape you if you'd just fucked him you stupid cunt.*

His reply didn't send. He didn't understand why at first, then he realised – he'd been blocked. Removed from the forum. He grinned, cocky at how he'd pissed them off to the extent that they'd barred him, and laughed at their stupidity.

There were only two days to go, and on that day, no one would be able to block him.

Feeling it was pointless to make dinner, as people of greatness did not make their own food, he ordered a pizza online.

Then something strange happened.

His card was declined.

He didn't understand. His mother paid into his account on this day every month. There should be money. He doubled checked the date. He was right – the money should be there.

So imagine his horror when, with trembling hands at the impudence of the woman who'd raised him, he opened his bank app on his phone, signed into his account, and saw that the money wasn't there.

How dare she.

He looked at his phone. He had another bunch of missed calls from her. Was this payback for him not answering her calls? What, if he didn't want to speak to her, this was her revenge?

Fine. He'd speak to her.

Oh, they'd talk, all right.

He picked up his phone and put it to his ear.

* * *

Delilah hated herself for what she had no choice but to do.

This moment had been coming for weeks. She'd tried phoning him, tried texting, tried leaving messages, desperate for answers – but there was no response.

She knew he was okay, because his bank statements were sent to her address, and although she resented the idea of disrespecting his privacy, she'd opened them, needing to know he was okay. And, unless someone had stolen his card to pay for extra upgrades on *Maze of Magic,* he was still using it.

A big payment on the first page of the statement drew her attention. A large bill from a car financier.

Had he bought a car?

And one that cost *that* much?

She sighed. Tried to remain calm. Told herself there must be an explanation. But she still held another letter in her hands. The one that had sparked her fury. The one she'd found weeks ago, and could now recite word for word.

There was a box of Dayton's stuff in the corner of her bedroom, and though she didn't like to interfere with his stuff, she missed him, and had looked through the items for a sense of nostalgia. After her tough conversations with Brian, she'd longed to hear Dayton's voice, but with him ignoring her calls, she figured this was the next best thing. So, one evening, after a few glasses of wine and thoughts of how lovely he'd been as a child, she opened it, hoping to find some comfort from his possessions. She held a teddy bear he'd loved when he was a child, but no longer touched, and it still smelt of him. A photograph of them together that he'd never bothered hanging on the wall. And a letter from the university, dated a year ago, terminating Dayton's place on his course.

She read the letter twice. And a third time. And a fourth time. Then checked the date again. And again. Trying to convince herself she'd misread it.

There had been quite a few letters from the university addressed to Dayton over the past few months, and she'd left them in this box, ready for when Dayton came home. Delilah knew she shouldn't open them, but was too upset not to. She felt compelled to understand what Dayton had been doing for this last year if he hadn't been on his course.

The first letter was asking Dayton to return his student card and the books he'd borrowed from the library.

The second letter was making Dayton aware that he was still living in a student house despite not being a student, and this was not allowed.

The third letter was a warning that the university would take action if he continued to claim student finance for a university place he didn't have.

So what about the money she'd sent him every month? The money she'd worked extra shifts and an extra job to provide for him? The money she'd sent out of love, and out of desperation for Dayton to do something with his life?

She thought that money was helping him get a degree, and then a job, when in fact, it was helping him to laze about, doing nothing.

She tried calling him day after day but he never answered. So she cancelled the standing order of money into his account. It was less than a day after doing this that she finally saw his name appear on her phone – at last, her son was going to talk to her.

She paused before answering it, watching his name, urging herself to be strong.

"Hello Dayton," she said, trying to keep her voice as casual as possible. She wanted to be calm for this conversation, however hard it was going to be – even though she felt the urge to cry simply upon hearing his name in her voice.

"Mum, where's my money?"

"Excuse me?"

"Your money hasn't gone through."

"Hasn't it?"

"No, where is it?"

"I cancelled it, Dayton."

He said nothing, and for a moment, she wondered if he suspected she knew. Then he said, "Why the hell did you do that?"

She hesitated before responding, and wished she'd come up with more of a strategy before this call. How would she approach this? Angry? Resolute? Or would she reveal just how deeply betrayed she felt, especially after all she'd done for him?

"Mum?" he prompted. "Stop ignoring me."

"I'm not ignoring you, Dayton," she said with a wobble in her voice.

"Then why aren't you answering me?"

She took a deep breath. Tried to stay calm. This was tough, but she was going to do this. "Why don't you tell me what you're doing in student accommodation?"

"What do you mean? I'm living here."

"But only students are meant to be in student accommodation."

"What?"

Another deep breath. "I said, only students are meant to be in student accommodation. And I am holding a letter that clearly states the university has terminated your contract."

She expected Dayton to shout at her or hang up. He did neither. He stayed silent. Perhaps he was more like his father than she realised.

"And it's dated over a year ago," she added.

A big huff came down the phone, and she could tell that, in his twisted mind, he was turning this against her; telling himself stories that justified what he'd done and made her out to be the villain.

It was at this point that she cried.

She hated herself for it. After all the difficulty she'd had raising her children on her own, on a small salary, in a small flat, she considered herself to be a strong woman as a result, and was proud of her achievement. These tears destroyed that – she no longer saw herself as strong, but as small, and silly, and pathetic – and she was made to feel this way by a person who she loved more than life itself.

"So what, you cancelled my money to teach me a lesson?" Dayton said, sounding like a petulant adolescent.

"Do you know what I've had to do for that money, Dayton?"

"Here we go..."

"Do *not* here we go *me*!" The tears turned to anger; she'd never, ever shouted at her children, but this time, that voice in her head that told her to stop wasn't loud enough. "I have worked my arse off, day and night, weekends, for you! I have moved to an even smaller flat, in an estate where teenagers stare at me everywhere I go, and I have given up on having a social life – all so I could put you through

266

university!" The anger faded back into tears. "And this is how you repay me?"

"I never asked to go to university," Dayton grunted. "I never wanted to. That was your decision, not mine."

"So this is my fault?"

"Look, Mum – are you going to send me the money or not?"

She almost laughed out of self-pity. After all she'd said, he still had the audacity to ask such a thing.

She responded with a quiet, resolute, "No."

Another audible huff came from Dayton's end of the phone.

"I would like you to come home," she said. "I'll send you the money for the train ticket if you need it, but that is all. I'm giving you no more money."She wiped her tears on the back of her sleeve.

"You belong here with me," she added. "With your mother. Who loves you dearly."

Dayton didn't respond.

"Please, Dayton. If you don't want to go to university, that's fine. Just come home and we'll figure it out."

A pause, then Dayton said, "I thought you were disappointed in me."

"I am," she admitted. "I'm very disappointed. But that doesn't change that you're my son."

Silence.

"I love you, Dayton. Please."

More silence. Then the phone clicked, and he hung up, and Delilah's phone returned to the lock screen, taken over by the image of her, Cassidy, and Dayton, happy and smiling at the camera.

The next time they spoke would be toward the end of Dayton's twenty-first birthday.

It would also be the last.

The Day of the Twenty-First

Chapter Thirty

THE REPORTER ON THE RADIO THOUGHT THE HIT AND run was the same guy he'd reported on earlier. That was clear. But from what Dayton heard, the police were no closer to tracking him.

Or, at least, that was the information they'd released. This could be a strategy. The police could be around the corner at this very moment.

This meant that Dayton needed to complete the next part of the day quickly.

He parked across the street from his target. A woman's only gym. He passed it most days on his way home, and it always made him scowl. Why did they get their own gym? What's wrong with a shared gym? It was pathetic. A meaningless business, and a poor use of a building.

So when he'd made his plans, this building had been in his mind. It wasn't until he'd left the coffee shop that he'd decided it would be his penultimate stop.

They were calling him a spree killer. He hated that. 'Spree' wasn't big enough. It was time to become a *Mass Killer*. It was time to ensure his message was heard.

He checked his phone. His video had over a million hits, and messages on the forum were praising his work thus far – everyone was in awe of how much he'd achieved and how brilliantly he was doing. The comments beneath his video, however, were not so encouraging.

Psycho.

Freak.

Virgin.

Desperate sad little kid.

Fucking nutter should be put to the chair.

He scoffed. He knew they wouldn't understand. It didn't matter. He was here to make a statement. But his statement wasn't big enough yet; he needed to go bigger; he needed to increase the body count.

A few women stepped inside the gym wearing sports bras and leggings that outlined their buttocks. Was that necessary? Did they not need clothes that allowed them to breathe to exercise? Dayton shook his head. It was all part of their silly, flimsy logic where they dressed for men's attention, then resented men when they received it.

Enough waiting. He stepped out of the car with his hood up and his hands in his pockets, his fist wrapped around his Stanley knife. So far, he'd used his large hunter's knife, and his Stanley knife had tasted no blood – this was about to change.

He followed the women in. They each swiped a card that lifted a barrier. This might be an issue. Then again, Dayton could easily leap over the barrier. And these women would be perfect prey.

"Excuse me."

Dayton watched the buttocks in tight leggings in front of him, glaring at the way they wiggled up and down, like it wasn't done intentionally.

"Excuse me."

He went to leap over the barrier.

"Excuse me!"

He turned around. A woman was speaking to him – older, big muscles, quite androgynous.

"This is a women's only gym," she said. "I'm afraid you'll have to leave."

The woman in the leggings in front of him paused. Looked back. Shifted her wary stare from the muscular woman to Dayton.

In a panic, Dayton took out his knife, reached over the barrier, and swiped it at the woman in leggings. She stepped back and instinctively raised her hands in defence. His blade went through her forefinger, leaving a large slice, and blood dripped down her arm.

The woman backed away, and Dayton went after her, but fell over the barrier as he did. He pushed himself to his feet, then felt a large force strike his waist, and he collided with the hard marble surface.

Muscular Androgynous Woman had rugby tackled him, and the humiliation was an intense pain in his gut.

His knife skidded along the floor, where it collided with the wall and span away, stopping far out of reach. He threw a punch – the first he'd ever thrown in his life – but it was weak, and had little effect on the woman. She mounted Dayton, retracted her fist, then thudded it into Dayton's nose. The world spun and splodges of colours overcame his vision in a dizzy head rush.

He threw another punch. She caught it and threw another punch back. Dayton moved his head slightly to the side, which reduced the impact, but her fist still landed on his cheek and left it throbbing.

Dayton did the only thing he could think to do to overpower her – he bit her. Hard. On the arm. Clamping his teeth down, putting all his might into his jaw, longing to taste blood.

She tried to shake him off, but he'd clamped down hard. She pulled her arm away, wrenching her skin from between his teeth and holding her arm out of reach.

With the opportunity to retaliate, Dayton pushed her off him, dived on the floor, grabbed his knife, leapt back over the barrier, sprinted across the foyer, and turned back to the room, clutching his weapon so hard it hurt

The muscular woman was holding her arm, which pricked with blood, watching Dayton with an aggressively bemused stare. The woman in the leggings had some tissue around her finger to stop the bleeding.

They had not attempted to go after him. Or flee. Like he wasn't a big enough threat.

This *incensed* him.

Even so, like any time one faces the potential of further pain, true instincts took over – and despite all he'd done, and the rage he felt, Dayton was still a coward at heart, and feared engaging in a fight with someone who'd already over-powered him. He glanced at the door, readying himself to flee. He hesitated only because he knew that the feeling of humiliation would intensify upon his departure.

He'd come here to kill. But he'd only caused minor harm to one person, then been beaten up by someone else. A woman. The exact kind of person who he had come here to dispose of.

Muscular Woman, still watching Dayton, pulled a phone out of her pocket, dialled a number, and put it to her ear.

"Police please," she said.

Shit. She'd called 999.

Dayton looked upwards. There was CCTV in the corner of the foyer behind him, and in the corner of the room opposite.

He needed to retreat. Regather. Rethink.

He burst through the door to the street and charged toward his car, stumbling a little as he crossed the road, unbalanced and dismayed.

The woman watched him through the glass door. He couldn't read her lips, but he was certain she was reciting his number plate.

"Fuck!" he bellowed as he collapsed onto the driver's seat and punched the steering wheel.

This was not how this was meant to go.

Refusing to be caught, he shifted into gear and skidded away, filling the street with fumes and the grand revs of his engine as he sped up.

"Fuck!" he roared again, guiding his car around a roundabout and toward a dual carriageway. "Fuck! Shit! Fuck shit fuck!"

A multitude of emotions flooded his wrecked mind. Fury at himself that he'd fucked up. Wrath that someone had dared try to stop him. Disgraced that he'd been so easily beaten. Pathetic that he hadn't accomplished what he intended to in that gym. And, most of all, terrified that he was going to be caught before he could finish what he had planned.

He had one choice – to execute the final part of his plan before the police caught up with him.

He stayed in the fast lane of the dual carriageway, the dial on his speedometer passing one hundred mph. When he came up behind someone going too slow, he drove within inches of their bumper until they moved over, then accelerated past them once they'd returned to the slow lane.

His thoughts raced as he pressed down on the pedal. He couldn't slow down; he couldn't give the police chance to track him. There were traffic cameras everywhere, and if he dawdled in one spot for too long, they'd have a fixed location. He had to move fast. He had to see just how fast this car would go.

He reflected on the events at the gym and blamed his parents for his mistake. If they had produced a tougher son, he'd have beaten the shit out of that muscular woman. If they had taught him to be mean and ruthless, instead of kind and genuine, women would have been attracted to him, and this day would never have come. It was not his fault they'd raised a gentleman. It was not beneficial to teach someone to be nice. They did not prepare him well enough for life. They did not teach him how to handle rejection. They did not instil in him the characteristics that women were drawn to.

And it was all their fault.

Not so much his father's, as he'd been absent, and had contributed little to the man he was. It was his mother's fault – she was responsible for the arduous times he'd endured, and she deserved the brunt of his indignation.

For the lack of money they'd had.

For the shitty flat they'd lived in.

For the awful schools he'd gone to.

It was her fault that those people at the house party had died, her fault that his housemates had to go, her fault that he was forced to run over those women outside the coffee shop.

If his mother had raised a better man, this wouldn't have happened.

And, in justice to the world, it was she who must pay for it.

Driving at extortionate speeds, he lifted his phone in front of the windscreen so he could see it. Another load of missed calls from his mother filled the screen. She was so desperate to speak to him.

Well, now was her chance.

He chose her name, and the rings came through the speakers, filling the car with its noise.

She answered immediately.

"Oh, Dayton! Dayton, thank God! Where are you? Are you okay?"

He didn't answer her questions. He just told her where to meet. That she must tell no one that they'd spoken. And that her wish was finally being answered.

Dayton was coming home.

Before the Twenty-First

Chapter Thirty-One

ONE DAY.

That was all.

He considered going out for one last attempt. Standing in a bar, or coffee shop, or the park. But there was little point. If it hadn't happened so far, it would not happen now. Still, he didn't feel like he could sit still at his computer. He was too full of energy. He had one more sleep to go, but the adrenaline was in his system, and he was too full of vigour to rest. He figured he may as well find one last opportunity to reaffirm what he believed. So he cruised around the local neighbourhoods in his car, taking it slow and easy, parking for a bit, then driving on, watching people and building his contempt.

He hated everyone he saw.

They were all part of the system. Part of the flawed setup of their world. Trying to pretend they were civilised, and not just cavemen and cavewomen, or animals in clothes. Their female ancestors were attracted to the alpha, not to the intellectually superior. Nothing had changed. If society was to progress, they needed to make better decisions. He was the only one wise enough to make those decisions for them. Once he enacted his plan, they would understand this. Or they would die.

In the park, a group of men and women his age gathered on a large patch of grass, enjoying the August sun. There wasn't a cloud above, and the sky was a clear light blue, and the sun was a giant ball of heat that forced the pretty and the young to remove their clothes.

The men played football without tops on. Their chests were toned, their biceps were thick, and they had no self-conscious thoughts at all. Dayton had always been small, and his body had always been thin and scrawny. This was natural. These men were not – they were the embodiment of unrealistic standards that make other men feel insecure. How could he ever have found a mate when women were attracted to false perfection?

The women were similarly scantily clad, wearing short skirts or shorts with bikini tops. Some of them pretended to play football, falling over the men laughing, their hands on the alpha's naked torsos, but most of the time they sat around in a circle, talking to each other with their slim, smooth skin on show. He could make out the outline of their breasts. How bizarre this situation was – if one was to leave the house in their underwear, people would say they were underdressed. Dayton could not see the difference.

Finding the temptation to attack too strong, he drove away. He must wait until tomorrow. Stick to the plan. If he attacked now, he would ruin The Day of the Twenty-First.

He cruised onwards and brought his car to a halt further up the park. Wishing to enjoy the weather, he left his car, and strolled along the gravel path between the greenery and trees. Further along, he reached a lake, where ducks gathered and old ladies fed them bread. It was a lovely day, but the rancid smell from nearby public toilets ruined any feelings of pensiveness and contemplation, so he kept walking until he came across a playground full of children enjoying their summer holidays and parents gossiping on nearby benches.

The sight made him stop. He noticed a boy, smaller than the others, with a mother and father guiding him down the slide, then onto the monkey bars. The father received a phone call and had to step away. The mother looked perturbed, but evidently didn't feel she could say anything, so encouraged her child along the playground with less enthusiasm. The child didn't notice.

Dayton pitied that child.

That child had no idea his father would soon leave, and would remarry, and would raise a new family in the home they'd once occupied. That he would grow up in a tiny flat with a mother who worked too much. Who grew old too quickly. Who suffocated him with nurture when he needed space to breathe.

Then again, maybe Dayton was wrong. Maybe that child wouldn't live out such a fate. But Dayton couldn't think of any other way it could be.

A nudge against his arm interrupted his thoughts, and he stumbled forward.

"Oh, sorry mate," said a guy as he passed, hand in hand with a woman. They continued talking to each other with big smiles and cheerful conversation.

"You couldn't just break apart for a second?" Dayton didn't realise he'd said it until the couple stopped and turned to him.

"Excuse me?" the guy said. A big guy, muscles like tree trunks. A trophy girlfriend beside him. Blond hair, tiny top.

It was the clearest representation of Chad and Stacey one could think of.

"You couldn't just let go of each other's hand and pass me single file for, like, one second?" Dayton said.

"Mate, I said sorry. It was an accident."

"Yeah, but if you weren't attached to each other, then—"

"I said sorry. Are we going to have a problem here?"

Dayton met this man's intense glare. Shook his head with self-pity. Resented how this man didn't need intelligence for a witty comeback when he could just use his physical prowess to intimidate others.

"No problem," Dayton said. "I just don't understand why you couldn't have passed me without—"

"If I want to hold my girlfriend's hand in the park then I will, you little prick."

The Stacey looked at her Chad with a wariness in her expression. Like she'd seen this side of him before. Dayton could see it in her eyes, but honestly, he was certain it turned her on.

"You people," Dayton muttered, shaking his head, then ignored the Chad and focused on the Stacey. "Is this the choice you make?"

"What is wrong with you?" the bloke said, releasing his girlfriend's hand and approaching Dayton.

Dayton kept talking to the woman. "You shouldn't be allowed to make such stupid choices," he said. "You encourage it. It's pathetic."

The Chad pushed Dayton, who stumbled backwards, then towered over him until he was consumed by the darkness of the man's shadow.

"You got a fucking problem?" the Chad said, his voice low-pitched and sinister. "Because I could break your face right now."

"Don't," the woman said. "Let's just leave him alone." As the man didn't relent, she added, "He's obviously a weirdo."

With one last lingering scowl, the man turned around, reattached his hand to the woman's, and they walked on.

Dayton was shaking. He wasn't sure what for. Fear, perhaps. The sheer audacity. The anger.

He turned to go, and locked eyes with the family in the playground as he did. They were watching him, unsure whether they should intervene. The father had returned. Dayton wanted to tell the kid not to get used to it, as it won't be for long. Instead, he retraced his route back to the car and climbed in.

He turned the car around and drove past the park. As he did, he passed the topless men and women in bikini tops again. He slowed down, considering saying something to them.

But what would he say?

You are the worst of all people.

I hate you with more hate than I can fit in my body.

Tomorrow, you're all going to die – I hope you know that.

In his mind, he said it all. He charged out of the car, launched himself at the first man, took him down, then tore the others apart with his words and accusations. He stabbed them all to death, slicing them until they begged, and forced them to admit their follies before they perished.

But this was all in his mind.

Until tomorrow, at least.

He returned home and trudged up the stairs. He went on the forums and watched the time count down. One by one, the sound of his housemates leaving told him he was alone. But he'd be ready for their return.

There were only a few hours left.

So he made his final post, writing a few simple messages for the only people he knew he could rely on.

It's time to fight the feminists and the arsehole men.

I'm going to create a world where women fear us, not reject us.

Watch the news tomorrow – you'll know when it's me.

Excitement greeted his post. They labelled him a hero. It no longer made him happy – he was used to it. He expected it. It was exactly what he deserved.

He thought he'd be nervous. That he'd have doubts or concerns about how the next day would go. But he didn't. He just felt ready.

It was around ten at night when the sun finally set, and Dayton spent the last few hours in darkness. Eventually, midnight arrived, and he went downstairs to begin, taking his large hunter's knife with him.

He switched the lights off and focussed on the door.

There was nothing to do now but wait.

When the world woke up in the morning, people would believe it to be a day like any other. How wonderful it was to know what they didn't. How powerful it felt to know there would be people opening their eyes, brushing their teeth, and going about their daily routine, with no idea they were about to die.

He wondered what would happen if his mother had done a better job. But there was no point wondering now. It was his twenty-first birthday, and his plan had been decided.

His mind was clear and focussed as he waited in the dark of the hallway.

In twenty-four hours, everything will have changed.

The world would never be the same again.

Chapter Thirty-Two

A MOTHER ALWAYS KNOWS.

It's not something science can explain, nor is it something one can logicise within the realms of the rational, but it is as true a fact as any other – a mother knows.

And Delilah knew.

She'd been awake most of the night, and had endured only a little sleep, most of it restless. It was her child's twenty-first birthday, and he was far away from her, with no money, and no one to celebrate this milestone with. She felt bad, and she longed to be there to present him with a cake and a gift, and she could almost convince herself this was the reason for her reservations; sadness that he was alone on his birthday.

But it wasn't.

It should be, but it wasn't.

There was something else. A feeling, churning in her stomach, like a part of her was failing; like an engine that wouldn't start, or a bird that wouldn't fly, or a river that wouldn't flow.

Then again, maybe this was sickness. An unknown

cancer growing inside of her. A plague spreading throughout her body. She'd reached her old years earlier than most – perhaps it was early onset Alzheimer's? Dementia even? She'd been quite forgetful lately. Just little things, like leaving her phone at the supermarket, or not packing her reusable bags that she never fails to remember.

No, that still wasn't it.

She sat up, leant against her bed's headboard, and chewed her thumbnail. It wasn't illness. It felt similar, but it wasn't quite right. But it was definitely a fault with part of her. Or, at least, something that had once been part of her; something she'd grown inside of her and unleashed into the world.

Dayton.

She checked the time. It was four in the morning. She'd gone to bed five hours ago, and had spent most of the night getting frustrated about her inability to sleep. And it wasn't that she wasn't tired, either – she'd spent most of the last few days pacing back and forth with the same letter from the university in her hand, deciding what she would do then backing out. At one point, she'd almost rented a car and driven to see her son, but she'd heard Brian's words echoing around the vast, empty corridors of her mind, reminding her how much she mollycoddled him; how she refused to liberate him and let him grow.

He was an adult now. No longer a teenager. She needed to let him make his own mistakes and figure out his own way home.

She'd always feared mistakes. As a child, she would never do schoolwork that she risked getting wrong. She never jumped over a puddle she thought was too big. She never read a book she wasn't certain she could finish.

Was Brian right? Had she passed this onto Dayton? Had she pandered to him too much?

She huffed and shook her head vigorously. What was wrong with her? She was listening to Brian's insults now? She needed to stop it. Snap out of whatever funk she was in. Stop fretting over something that probably wasn't even happening.

But it was happening.

Like a bird that could sense danger to her nest, she could tell when her son was in peril. It was something she felt deep inside of her, like a niggling discomfort shifting from side to side in her womb.

Did she even know where Dayton was?

She could still rent that car. Show up at his house. Pretend it was to surprise him for his birthday. But it wasn't realistic – by the time she'd booked a rental car, waited for it to be ready, filled out the paperwork, and set off, his birthday would nearly be over.

So what could she do?

She stepped out of bed, tired of trying to sleep. She took her duvet to the sofa and wrapped herself in a cocoon. She put the television on. It was too early for morning television shows, and the twenty-four-hour news channel had taken over the main channels. She was due to be at work in a few hours. She felt tempted to call in sick, but couldn't afford to lose the money.

She picked up her phone. Should she call him? Of course not – not at this time, anyway. She'd let him sleep. Give him space.

She set herself a target for when she would call him. Eleven o'clock was reasonable. A mother would call their son on their birthday. It wasn't her being overbearing, or needy, or mollycoddling him. It was her being a mother.

But could she really hold out until eleven o'clock?

She closed her eyes and listened to the news. It was the usual boring stuff. Some politicians were angry with each other for some reason, some country was annoyed with what another country was doing, and some celebrity had done something the public didn't like. It was all so predictable – the same news, just different names.

The news was rarely interesting.

Without intending to, she fell into a light snooze, and the next few hours passed quickly. She woke up shortly before seven, just as the morning television shows started, and the presenter shared that a famous footballer's wife had used a coupon when paying for their supermarket shop, and that they would have a debate about this. She laughed at the ridiculousness of it. Was this really worth discussing?

This was the first time her phone pinged.

It would ping a lot today, but this was the first.

It was a woman she hadn't spoken to in years. A mother she'd speak to at the school gates when her children were young. It simply had a link, and the text *You really ought to see this*.

Delilah clicked on the link, and Dayton's face filled the screen. She listened to the opening few sentences, then turned it off, finding his absence too painful.

She would soon learn that her mother's instinct had been correct.

The Day of the Twenty-First

Chapter Thirty-Three

The corridor outside Delilah's flat was narrow and cold, and usually smelt like body odour or marijuana. She rarely passed anyone, as the flats next to hers were mostly occupied by old people who didn't have the strength to venture out much, or bums who spent most of their day on their sofa drinking cheap cider, or women like her; single mothers working too much to be home.

At this moment, however, as light evening darkness faded to the thick black of night, and the only illumination was from the unpleasant amber glare of nearby streetlamps, the corridor was full. This block of council flats was in the middle of several blocks of council flats where everyone lived close together, and there was little space between buildings. This led to a sense of community where everyone knew everyone else. Delilah had never had a problem with this – she knew her neighbour's faces and this comforted her. But it also meant the community was rife with gossip, and news didn't take long to spread, and people would interfere with other's business.

So when members of the community watched the same

news report Delilah was watching, they automatically gravitated toward the corridor outside her flat. Delilah wasn't sure what they wanted – Vigilantism? Blood? Answers? Information? To be a part of a mob? – but she did not feel like facing them anytime soon.

"We can now confirm that the name of the spree killer causing unrest in the South West is that of Dayton Dankworth."

Dayton's social media profile picture appeared in the top right of the screen.

Delilah didn't believe it at first, even though she'd already guessed. Until now, she'd been able to treat herself to the gift of denial – but not anymore. The face of the boy she'd raised, the man she loved, and the killer she didn't know, gazed back at her in the eyes of her son. It was a pleasant picture, even though he wasn't smiling. But that was nothing new; Dayton didn't smile in photos. But he wore a nice blazer, a smart shirt, and had an awkward handsomeness to his face.

She searched for reasons to convince herself it wasn't real. The news had made a mistake. The police were wrong. Someone had stolen Dayton's identity.

But the sick feeling in her gut urged sense to her thoughts, however much she tried to push the urge back down.

"He was last seen at a women-only gym, attacking a woman with a knife. We warn you, you may find these images disturbing."

Delilah tried to look away, but she couldn't.

CCTV images of the foyer of a gym filled the screen. A young man swung a knife at a woman, who ducked out of the way in time to reduce her injuries to a slice of her finger. A bigger woman tackled Dayton to the floor.

That could be someone else, she told herself.

Then, as the man backed away from the fight, he looked up at one camera, then the next.

There was no mistaking his face.

But, unlike the masses of people watching these images and judging her child, she saw something in his expression that no one else did – vulnerability.

People would look at him and see evil. She looked at him and saw a troubled young man with needs that weren't being met. A person who should have received better help. A son who didn't see things as others did and needed support.

The volume of the crowd outside grew. She had the curtains drawn, and though she couldn't see them, their silhouettes filled the thin fabric that separated her from the window. The corridor was full, and there was shouting. Aggressive requests that she came out and faced them. Voices calling her names. There was so much anger dripping from the demands of people who knew nothing about her life, or her son's needs.

Someone tried the door. The handle twisted slightly, but stopped as the lock prevented it from twisting further.

She ran her hands over her face. This was the worst moment of her life, and there was an angry mob ready to crucify her for it.

"Police have stated that he was last seen fleeing the scene of his attempted attack in a black BMW. The police have urged the public not to approach Dayton Dankworth if they see him, but to call the police immediately. He is considered armed and highly dangerous."

Armed? Highly dangerous? Her son?

No, that must be wrong.

Dayton was not dangerous. He was the child who

carried his teddy bear around everywhere; the child who took moths in his hand and released them outside before his father could kill them; the child who cried when he learned of his parent's divorce.

How could people consider that child dangerous?

She turned off the television. Tried to ignore the shouts of the crowd outside. Picked up her phone, ready to try Dayton again. She must have called him at least a hundred times. It rang every time, showing his phone was on – but still no answer.

Should she keep trying?

She unlocked her phone. Of course she should.

Then, just as she was about to phone him again, his face lit up the screen.

He was calling her.

Oh dear God, he was calling her.

She stood up. Paced from one side of the room to the other. Panicked. What did she do? What would she say?

She buried her fear. Told herself to be brave. To speak to him. She was his mother, dammit – and he was her scared little boy, and she was desperate to have him back home, in her arms, where he belonged.

"Oh, Dayton!" she cried out as she answered. "Dayton, thank God! Where are you? Are you okay?"

He didn't answer at first. She could hear his breathing. And the sound of an engine. Was he driving?

Eventually, his voice, small and faded, said, "Mum?"

"Dayton! Yes, I'm here. I'm here. Where are you?"

"It doesn't matter..." He sounded so distant. So cold. So empty.

"Dayton, please, just come back to me and we'll figure this out."

Nothing. Just breathing. Just the rumble of an engine.

"Dayton?" she said.

"I want you to meet me somewhere," he said, blank and direct.

"That's fine, absolutely fine," she said, pacing from one side of her flat to the other. "Where? Where would you like to meet me?"

More breathing. A deep inhalation, followed by a large exhale. "I want you to meet me where you took me when you broke my heart."

She was stumped. She was keen to appease him, but she didn't understand – when had she broken his heart? What could he have seen that way? She'd always done her best for him; this made little sense.

"Where you and Dad both broke my heart," he said.

She stopped pacing. Tried hard to think.

The crowd outside was growing louder. It was as if they knew she was speaking to him.

"Where you told me you were getting a divorce," Dayton added.

Her face twisted as she fought tears. She nodded. Of course. Had that conversation affected him this much? It was a memory she could picture clearly. The ice cream. The bench. The sheep.

"Okay, Dayton, but just tell me, are you okay, are you–"

The phone call ended.

She checked the screen to be sure he was gone.

She'd wanted to speak to him so much, but it didn't feel like enough. She couldn't gauge his state of mind. What did he look like right now? Was he calm and collected, or was he sweaty and bedraggled? Was he livid, or was he terrified?

It didn't matter. She just had to get to the hill. And she had to get past the mob first.

She phoned for a taxi. They would be here in ten minutes.

How was she going to pay for this? She had no cash.

Recalling the piggy bank in the box of Cassidy's things, she ran through to the bedroom and sifted through her daughter's belongings. She apologised as she smashed it and stuffed the few notes Cassidy had saved in her pocket.

Next, she changed. She hadn't washed. Her hair stuck up in greasy clumps. She felt filthy. But she didn't care. She shoved on a pair of jeans, a t-shirt, and a hoodie. She zipped it up and pulled the hood over her head.

An alert came up on her phone. The taxi was outside.

She stared at the door. Sighed. They wanted her blood. But they were all talk – no one was actually going to hurt her. At least, that's what she told herself. Regardless, she had to get past them to get to Dayton.

It didn't matter how much of them there were – nothing would stop her from getting to her son.

Without another moment's hesitation, she charged to her door, unlocked it, and ignored the jubilant cries of *she's opening it* that came from outside.

She took a deep breath, opened the door, and shoved her way into the crowd.

"Monster!"

"Do you know where he is!"

"Give him up!"

"Mother killer!"

"Psycho lover!"

Their faces were close, painted with hostility, screaming names and threats and obscenities. She was smaller than them, and she was instantly surrounded; she could feel their hot breath on her face, but she just kept pushing forward, forcing her way through them with what little strength she could produce.

"Sick bitch!"

"Murderous cunt!"

"Fucking psycho!"

"This is your fault!"

"Go and run away, whore!"

Someone tried to trip her up, and she stumbled, but kept her balance. She felt her head pull back as someone grabbed her hair, and she pulled herself out of their grip, feeling strands of her hair rip from her head. Hands and fists shoved her as she passed, and she rocked from side to side, pushing and swaying as she penetrated the crowd, determined to find her way through.

She reached the stairs, and wrenched herself from the grip of strangers who tried to hold on to her, and ran down the steps two at a time.

The crowd followed. Still shouting. Still reaching for her.

"How fucking dare you!"

"Runaway then!"

"We'll find you!"

"You raised a monster!"

"You fucking did this!"

She reached the bottom step, feeling the proximity of those in pursuit, hearing every word screamed in her direction.

The taxi waited on the other side of the road. She emerged from the flat block and ran, hard as her weary body could manage. But there was more than just an angry mob waiting outside the building.

There were reporters. Photographers whose flashes went off as they snapped pictures of Delilah fleeing.

Cameras who captured video of her trying to escape. People who shoved microphones in her face and asked questions. It occurred to her that she'd be on the news. Maybe the headline would read *Killer's Mother Runs Away,* or *The World's Worst Mother Revealed.*

"Do you know where your son is?"

"Do you feel responsible?"

"How did your son become a monster?"

She barged her way past all of them, not caring for the images they caught. Her desperation to get to her son overcame any reservation she had about being filmed.

She reached the taxi, swung the door open, and threw herself onto the backseat.

The taxi driver looked panicked as he saw the mob and reporters approaching.

She gave him the location and urged him to hurry.

The driver pulled onto the street and drove away.

She watched out the back window as the reporters lingered and the mob pursued her. They ran hard and kept up with the taxi for a while, but once the driver pulled out of the estate and onto an A road, he sped up, and the mob came to a stop.

She sat up, panting, and put on her seatbelt.

"Are you all right, miss?" the driver asked. "What was that about?"

She felt oddly grateful to be in a car with someone who didn't know who she was, or what was happening.

"Nothing," she said. "Please, just drive."

The taxi driver didn't say another word, which she was thankful for.

She checked her phone again. A part of her had hoped she might receive another message from Dayton, but she hadn't. Just the one call, with blank, cold instructions.

For the next twenty minutes, she rested her head back and watched the world pass. She was exhausted, but also energised; tired from lack of sleep, but full of adrenaline.

She thought back to yesterday, and how blissfully unaware she'd been; it was like she was remembering a different person. She pictured that silly woman sitting on the sofa, watching television, thinking everything would be okay. How little that woman knew. How naïve she could be.

If only she could speak to that woman now, she'd shake her out of her stupid complacency.

After what seemed like too long, the driver reached the road that ran alongside the hill.

"Where abouts, miss?" he asked.

"Any of the lay-bys."

The driver pulled into a layby behind a black BMW. She paid him. Thanked him. Then stepped out and watched him drive away.

Night had descended, and with the full moon feeling close enough to touch, she opened a nearby gate and began her ascent up the uneven surface, toward the bench she'd sat on fourteen years ago, next to her husband and her child, hiding how her entire world was shattering to be strong for her son.

Her strength wasn't enough. She knew that now.

Her legs ached as she climbed upwards. The moon provided a small glow, but she still needed the light of her phone to check her immediate route.

When the bench came into view, she was sure she could see a figure on it. A silhouette she'd recognise anywhere. She'd expected that silhouette to be different somehow, perhaps bigger or more monstrous, but it was the same as it had always been.

She put her phone light away and approached.

Chapter Thirty-Four

THE BENCH WAS AS UNCOMFORTABLE AS IT WAS WHEN Dayton was seven.

Funny, he thought he remembered it being uncomfortable because of the news he was given, but really, it was just uncomfortable. A few wooden beams nailed together with splinters in the corners. There was nothing to cushion himself on, and he found himself fidgeting, which wasn't how he'd imagined it. He thought he'd finish his day here, beneath the full moon, sitting back, feeling resolute, anticipating the big climax. He thought there would be some kind of clarity to his mind, or some sense of achievement, rather than a simple irritation that, no matter what he did, he could not be comfortable on this bench.

He wanted to be calm and collected when she found him; not wriggling like there was something wrong with him.

In an effort to ignore the discomfort, he reflected on the day. Had it gone how he planned?

He'd disposed of his roommates, which turned out to be easy enough, but hadn't served the function he'd intended.

This was meant to free up his house to become the Torture Palace, yet he hadn't brought a single person back there.

He'd been to the party and executed three targets. But he'd intended to make his way through the party as a destructive force, like a tornado or volcano spreading through a village and capturing those who couldn't flee in time. As it was, he hadn't even been able to enter the house. He had reached a few people outside, but then he had to retreat, fearing that he would be overpowered.

He'd knocked over those women from the coffee shop, but truthfully, that wasn't part of the plan. It was reckless. A moment where his disappointment and disgust had the better of him.

And the gym... He bowed his head, rolled his eyes, and ran his hand over his face. That was pathetic. Again, he was meant to make his way through the building, destroying as many women as he could. He'd foreseen at least ten and had hoped for twenty. But he'd been beaten before he entered. By a woman.

Now here he was, at the final part of the plan, ready to execute the last stage. And he was having second thoughts.

Why was he having second thoughts?

Why couldn't he be strong?

He knew what he must do. He had decided days ago. This day must end this way. He just didn't know if he could do it.

But he had to.

His thoughts dwelled on his friends on the forum. They'd be watching the news. They'd know it was him. They'd probably be on the forum right now, heaping praise upon him, idolising him, placing his pedestal above that of God.

He could not let them down.

But that wasn't what he was worried about. It was he, himself, that he was worried he might disappoint. He was already so annoyed by the failures of the day. He'd had weeks of fantasies of how it would go, and he'd stopped himself from attacking many potential targets in anticipation of this day being glorious. And how many had he taken down?

He counted six.

Pathetic.

Perhaps those women were right. He was unremarkable. He wasn't supreme in the way he believed. He didn't deserve their love, or attention, or bodies. He didn't deserve them to approach him and start up a conversation. He didn't deserve sex, or romance, or love.

He was nothing like the man he thought he was.

Those women had seen what he couldn't – the truth – the failure – the boy in a man's costume – the misguided fool who thought he could be a soldier when he was barely a sheep.

He refuted the thought. Fought it with all the mental strength he had left. But his adrenaline was gone, and fatigue was setting in, and he didn't think he had the strength for more denial.

He still had his Stanley knife though. The one he held in his pocket to make himself feel powerful. He did that now. Sliding the blade out and retracting it.

In, and out.

In, and out.

In, and out.

He waited for the feeling of authority that usually accompanied the concealed handling of this weapon, but it was not forthcoming. It was such a little weapon. He'd left the hunter's knife in the car as he'd wanted this Stanley knife to be the accessory to his final act, but it didn't even make him feel powerful anymore. It just made him feel little and silly.

He bowed his head. There was nothing about him that matched his deluded self-image. He was not what he intended to be.

And it was all her fault.

Oh, how it was her fault.

Tears pushed at the corners of his eyes. He was alone, and there was no need to fight them. Besides, he wasn't that strong; he'd realised that. So he allowed them out.

They didn't stream out in a force, and nor did they burst down his face. There were just a few drops trickling down his cheeks and landing on his collar. A few remnants of his despair, and the pain of being the fool she'd created.

Why hadn't she stopped Dad from leaving?

Why hadn't she been rich?

Why hadn't she created a better son?

He sniffed, long and hard. Wiped the few stray tears away and left the rest inside his eyes. There was no room for this. He had one more thing to do, and if he was to do it, then he needed to see himself as strong.

"Dayton?"

When he heard that voice, any possibility of being strong left.

"Dayton?"

When he heard that voice, he did not know if he could go through with what he intended.

"Dayton, is that you?"

When he heard that voice, he knew the day was over, and that the end was imminent.

He stood. Turned around. Set his feeble eyes on the

image of a woman who was so much older and frailer than he remembered.

"Mum..." he said with a whimper. "Mum, I don't know what I'm doing here."

Then he did cry.

And she didn't hate him for it, or resent him, or think him weak. She just ran toward him and threw her arms around his shoulders. He buried his face in her collar, allowing her to hold him like she did when he was a child, and poured out the anguish and terror and pain that came with being the person he was.

But he didn't forget the Stanley knife in his pocket.

Nor did he forget the promises he'd made.

And nor did he want this moment to end; he wished he could never release his mother from this grip; that he could escape in her warm comfort forever.

Unfortunately, all plans must come to fruition, and all plans must end.

And it was time for this day to finish.

Chapter Thirty-Five

THIS WASN'T HER SON. IT WAS SOMEONE DIFFERENT.

The face was similar, and the body hunched over like she remembered, and he shrank in on himself like he always had – but there was a weakness in his grimace she'd never known; a despair that ran too deep for words.

So she held him. Even though she was smaller, she held him like a child she'd lost and since been reunited with, gripping his shirt, pulling him in tight, not caring whether she struggled to breathe. Her shoulder dampened under the force of his tears, but she didn't care. She wanted him to cry. She was terrified she'd show up and find a man made of stone, grim-faced and uncaring. But this embrace wasn't from a psychopath – it was from a son who was lost and had now been found.

The air was chilly. The sun of the day had left and, although it was the summer, the breeze felt sharp, and a faint hint of rain lingered. She didn't care. Not about anything. Not about the stories on the news, or the lies about university, or the words of the crowd.

She only cared about her son, this boy, here and now,

and the child that still existed beneath this wounded expression.

Eventually, after his persistent tears slowed down, he pulled his head back. He remained in her embrace, but allowed her to see his face; his red cheeks, his moist eyes, his weakened resolve. She placed a hand in his hair, brought his forehead down to hers, and rested it there, feeling him close. Just like she used to when he was a toddler. When he could still be anything he wanted to be.

"Mum..." he said. She was sure he intended it to be strong, but it came out as a sob.

"It's okay, Dayton," she said. "It's okay. I'm here."

He sniffed. The tears were ending, but the sadness was still there.

"Mum..." he whispered. "Mum... I don't know what I'm even doing here..."

She glanced at the bench. Recalled the feeling of sitting with a man she no longer loved, telling Dayton the news he would never forget. They'd tried to make it a pleasant moment, with ice cream and a walk up the hill, but that was stupid of them. There was no way to make it a pleasant moment, and they shouldn't have tried to pretend it wasn't the disaster that it was.

"That's okay, Dayton," she told him, her voice slow and clear; she was doing the best she could to sound comforting and calm, even though her insides were screaming, and she was more terrified of losing him now than she'd ever been.

"I've done so many things today..." he said. "So many..."

She fought away images of her son taking people's lives. "It's okay. We'll deal with that later. Let's just stay here for now. Like this. For as long as we can."

As she said it, her mind leapt ahead to what might happen after this moment. Might he go to prison? Might the media paint him as a killer? Would she be forever abused as the woman who raised him?

"But I've done so much," he said. Just as she was about to provide more words of comfort, he added, "And it's still nowhere near enough."

She paused. Didn't speak. Mulled over these words.

What did they mean?

She'd interpreted his despondency as regret. Was this correct? Or was he simply sad he hadn't done as much as he wanted?

"What do you mean, Dayton?" she asked. "What do you mean, it's nowhere near enough?"

He took a deep breath; it shook as he inhaled, then quivered as he exhaled. She thought the tears were about to start again, but they didn't.

"The world won't understand," he said. "But I had to. I did. I had to."

"Let's not..." Her voice petered away, unsure how to finish that sentence.

He lifted his head so his eyes locked onto hers. She could only just make out his pupils between strands of greasy hair. The moonlight made him seem so dark, so foreboding.

"Why, Mum?" he said, his voice growing. "Why?"

"Why what, Dayton?" she asked.

"Why didn't you do better?"

She went to reply, but didn't know what to say. Was this about her? She'd done the best she could. She'd done *everything* she could. Every job she could take, every bit of money she could spare, every ounce of love she could give – she'd given it.

"I'm not the person I'm meant to be," he said. "Why didn't you make me a better person?"

"Dayton, there is nothing wrong with the person you are."

He snorted out an ironic laugh, and she felt she was losing him. "There is everything wrong with the person who I am."

"No, Dayton, don't say that."

"I'm not rich. I can't get a girlfriend. I can't even get a woman to look at me. People think I'm weird. I was meant for greatness, Mum – why haven't you raised me for greatness?"

"I raised you to be a good person," she insisted. "And I still believe that's who you are."

In the distance, police sirens. Far away, yet too close.

"They are for me," Dayton said. "I know it."

"It's okay," she said. "It's okay. I'll stay with you until they get here."

He looked down, glanced at his pocket, then lifted his fragile eyes to hers. "You promise?"

"Of course."

He wrapped his arm around her again and leant his head on top of hers. She gripped his shirt, but with a little less emphasis. She was scared, though she wouldn't let him know.

Those sirens were getting louder. They must be for him. They knew who he was, they knew the car he was driving, and there were plenty of traffic cameras on nearby roads. It was a matter of time until they passed the hills and saw his car.

Soon, this would end. And she would lose the only thing she'd ever loved enough to hold on to.

One of Dayton's arms fell away. He held onto her with his left, but his right hand dropped into his pocket. Was this him trying to resist? Trying to get away? Trying to give himself up? She wouldn't allow it. She wrapped her arms harder around him, nestled her head against his neck, closed her eyes. Felt him close. Kept him there. Her son. Her love. The reason she did everything.

She held onto him with everything she had.

The sirens were too loud now. So many of them. They seemed to have stopped. But they had to climb the hill first. They had to search for them. She still had time.

If only that time could stand still, and she could keep him here, like this, she could avert disaster. She didn't want to think of tomorrow, of prison visits and cameras and neighbours. She just wanted to have her son, who she adored no matter what.

Dayton's right hand left his pocket. He lifted his arm up. She relaxed a little, pleased he was about to put a second arm around her, and keep her as secure as she was trying to keep him.

But that arm didn't wrap around her torso.

Instead, that arm rose to her neck, and his hand hovered there. Waiting. Trembling.

"Mum..." he said, so quiet she barely heard it.

"It's okay, I'm here," she told him.

"Mum..."

"I'm here, Dayton. I'm here. I'm not going anywhere."

"Mum..."

"Don't worry, I'll stay with you. We'll face this together. I won't let you go. I promise I won't let you go."

Another moment of silence preceded his final act.

She felt a sharp sting on the side of her neck. It was uncomfortable at first, like a bee sting or a pinprick. Then it became harder and deeper. Then it shot through her entire neck.

Dayton stood back, holding the blade of his Stanley

knife in the incision he'd made, then dragged it across the front of her throat.

Her eyes widened as she fell.

She didn't press her hands on the wound. Perhaps the shock was too much, or she just didn't think to do so. Instead, she lay there, suffocating, spitting blood, watching her son standing over her.

He knelt down.

Took her hand.

And stayed with her until the final breath.

She didn't take her eyes off her son for the entire time it took her to die. Not once. Not even for a second.

She watched him, thinking nothing, until her empty thoughts were no more, and she was an empty vessel with love bleeding out of her.

Dayton stood, lifted his knife, put it to his own throat, and waited for them to arrive.

Chapter Thirty-Six

ONCE THE POLICE OFFICERS IDENTIFIED THE BLACK BMW parked in a layby, they closed the road leading past the base of the hill. Between the cordons, a multitude of police cars stopped, their lights still flashing, and the lowest ranked officers knocked on the doors of the few houses, asking the residents to lock their doors and stay inside. Meanwhile, the firearms officers arrived in vast numbers, many called in from other counties, and began their ascent up the hill.

They erected large lights to guide them, and each firearm officer strapped a light to the top of their gun. Although they believed him to be armed with nothing more than a knife, they were not taking chances – the instructions were to apprehend him before he could hurt anyone else, and that meant using as much force as necessary.

They took their time going up the hill. It was steep, and the large amount of equipment they carried and the weight of their stab proof vests tested their fitness. They scanned the area and communicated that it was clear every few steps before continuing. After around every twenty seconds or so, someone shouted, "Firearm officers – Dayton Dankworth, show yourself!"

But Dayton Dankworth was not forthcoming.

They wondered if Dayton was on this hill. His car was parked here, but it could be a decoy, and he might be somewhere else. Still, they persisted, reliant on intel from Brian Dankworth that this hill was a significant location for Dayton. Whilst they could not get hold of the boy's mother, Brian had been hugely cooperative, and the list of places with sentimental meaning to Dayton had proven useful.

They continued up the hill, sweating, remaining methodical in their search, clearing each area, concentrating hard – there were plenty of shadows where Dayton could be hiding.

They had been searching for over an hour when an officer communicated over the comms, "Bodies ahead."

Each officer turned their guns toward their colleague's light, illuminating a bench with the tactical light above their scopes. Sure enough, there were two figures on the ground.

"Firearm police – put your hands behind your head!"

No movement.

"Repeat, this is firearm police – put your hands behind your head!"

Still nothing.

"We will shoot – put your hands behind your head!"

They slowed down, cautious in every movement, aware that this was a volatile situation – but the more they approached, the clearer it became that neither body was moving.

"The closest body is a woman."

"That looks like Delilah Cartwright."

"Can we make a positive ID?"

"Not from this far, but I'm fairly certain. Looks like her throat is cut."

A wave of frustration passed over them. Another deceased. And the boy's own mother too.

"Any positive ID on the second body?"

"Young male, can't see more than that."

"It might be Dayton. Slow down."

They slowed down, and the furthermost officer shouted, "Dayton, put your hands on your head!"

He didn't move.

"Put your hands on your head now!"

Still nothing.

"Could he be using his mother as cover?" one officer asked over comms.

"Hard to tell. Proceed with caution."

They approached, surrounding the two people in an arc, safety off their guns, aimed at the male.

"Dayton, put your hands on your head!"

Dayton did not put his hands on his head.

As they approached, they saw Delilah's wounds more clearly – a long line of red across her throat, and blood sinking into the grass beneath her.

"Confirm Delilah Cartwright deceased."

Behind her, Dayton. Her son. On the ground.

"Put your hands on your head now!"

The officer approached, shining his light on the body, finger over the trigger, ready for a surprise attack.

But there would be no surprise attack.

Dayton's body was a lump on the ground, a Stanley knife in his hand, and a long red mark across his neck. His wide, empty eyes stared back at the officer, who released a huff of frustration.

"He's dead."

Another officer approached and checked. "Confirmed. Target deceased."

They shared a moment of disappointment where they all lowered their gaze and shook their heads. The silence remained for a few minutes, as the pent up, stiff energy they'd felt in the hunt left, and a relaxed sense of anguish settled in.

The senior officer spoke to the detective inspector through his comms. "Positive ID, Dayton Dankworth and Delilah Cartwright. Both are deceased. It's safe to proceed."

"Roger, we're coming up now."

Fifteen minutes later, the rest of the officers emerged with the necessary equipment. A tent to protect the evidence from the elements. Protective suits. Bags for evidence. Cameras. Gloves for examination.

The detective inspector stood at a distance, allowing his men to work, with his hands on his hips. Honestly, he was gutted. He'd lost another victim in the mother, and they'd failed to capture the target alive. There would be no one to stand trial for the crimes. To him, that was a failure. And he hated failing.

A sergeant arrived at his side. "We've got Brian Dankworth on the phone, asking for an update."

The detective inspector rubbed his sinus. "Someone needs to tell him."

"Do you want me to do it?"

"No. I'll do it. Tell Mr Dankworth I'm coming over now."

The sergeant nodded and returned to his phone call.

The detective inspector turned away from the crime scene and traipsed downhill. It had been a long day, and he was exhausted. He'd tell the father that his son and ex-wife were dead, then he'd go home. Have some sleep. Make his kids' breakfast. Feign amazement at whatever picture they'd drawn for him. Then go back to work.

When he'd joined the force, he'd imagined achieving greatness. Yet all he did was deliver bad news and see good people die.

He started his car and put Mr Dankworth's postcode into his sat nav. The radio came on. An eighties tune he quite liked. He hummed along as he drove. Then he remembered his wife had bought the ingredients for pancakes and had promised to make them in the morning. The thought made him smile.

There was no need for greatness when you had a wife who made pancakes. And kids who drew you pictures. And a job that mattered. And, as he pulled up outside the fancy gates of Brian Dankworth's grand house, he remained content in that knowledge. He was about to shatter a man's world, but after that, he was going home. He had all he needed. It wasn't great, but it was good. And that was okay.

Greatness, it seemed, was rarely achieved by the great.

But hey, who cares – who wants to be great anyway?

Epilogue
Excerpt From Post 'A Fallen Hero'

WELL WHO THE FUCK WAS EXPECTING THAT!

I'd followed the guy on this forum for a while, and he'd always talked a good talk, always giving this DO SOMETHING shit, but I was always like... well YOU do something then.

I am so, so sorry for ever doubting him.

The guy is a hero. A legend. A fucking god. And I'm so fucked up over the idea that I will never get to meet him.

They say there'll be protestors at his funeral. I say we make sure he gets the send off he deserves – I say we attend, and make sure any fuckers who want to ruin the wake of this guy do not get close.

Dayton was right – they called us dweebs for too long, and it's time to show the alphas that this is not some nutjob doing shit to strangers, but that this is it – the start of the fucking BETA UPRISING, and that shit won't ever be the same again.

The funeral is the day we make our move.

Dayton's brilliance is incontestable – but he has only started the movement, and we need to pay him respect by ensuring his sacrifice wasn't for nothing, and that starts with not letting fucking chads and fucking staceys ruin the send off for the best fucking legend there's ever been.

This isn't the end. This isn't the middle. This isn't even the beginning. It's the epigraph that precedes the story. The prequel that looks good until the sequels come out and people are blown the fuck away.

There will be no better time than now, so in the immortal words of our martyr – DO SOMETHING.

And I fucking mean it. No more talk. No more sitting around on our arses, dicks going numb from so much wanking, women laughing at us, men fucking the women who laugh at us, men laughing at us before fucking the women who laugh at us then laughing at us again. Fuck them. Fuck them all. This is it, fuckers. This is the time.

They've tried to keep details of the funeral on the low, but I got that shit. I'll post the time and address below this post, and I expect to see you there.

If you've ever been on this forum, talking about taking a stand, then don't be a fucking coward when that day comes. Stand the fuck up. Be something. DO SOMETHING.

Dayton Dankworth is a name that garners all kinds of respect. Don't you want to add your name to that list? Don't you want to carry on his legacy? Don't you want this to be something that fucking matters, that makes a difference?

Friends, this is the time. I don't know how else I can keep writing it. You've read the manifesto. You've watched his video. Everything he said was fucking SPOT ON. That shit is REAL. He was right about everything, and we should not let anyone who pretends life isn't how Dayton described it spoil what is a proud moment.

A sad moment, yes, but a proud one.

Because Dayton lives, fuckfaces. He lives. HE FUCKING LIVES.

Because he lives in US. Do you see?

He lives in ALL OF US.

If his ideas are yours, then his words are yours, and his bravery is yours, and there's strength in fucking numbers, so let's be that strength in fucking numbers.

We all need to GET INVOVED. To TAKE ACTION. To DO SOMETHING.

So I sign off this post in hope it gets the same traction as Dayton's. Because it's just as important as Dayton's was. It's crucial. It's EVERYTHING.

We meet at the wake, and we tear the fucking world apart.

This man started something, and by the time we've finished it, there will be no more scared little boys sitting at computers. Chad will be the virgin, the beta will beat the alpha, and Stacey will do whatever we fucking tell her.

It's time to gather, my friends, and I'm pumped. I don't know if you can tell, but I'm fucking PUMPED. Everything has led to this. My entire life has led to this. This is it. This is fucking it.

So let's do this.

You are all my brothers, and I will stand with you on the battleground.

May Dayton be with all of us.

In his name, we fight.

The blood he shed was just a drip. Ours will be a downpour.

It's time to take action, my friends.

I will meet you all there.

Join Rick Wood's Reader's Group...

And get **Roses Are Red So Is Your Blood** for free!

Join at **www.rickwoodwriter.com/sign-up**

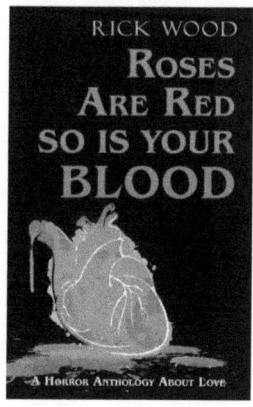

Also by Rick Wood...

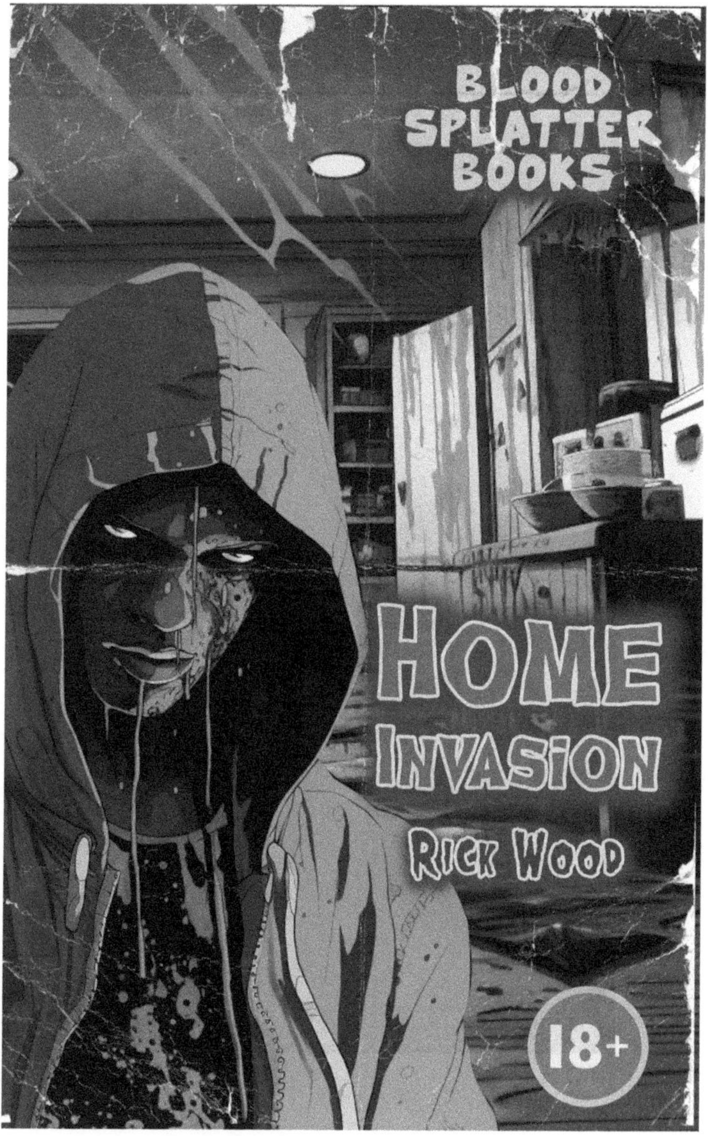
BLOOD SPLATTER BOOKS
HOME INVASION
RICK WOOD
18+

the sensitives
book one

the sensitives

RICK WOOD

THE HAUNTING
OF EVIE MEYERS

RICK WOOD

www.ingramcontent.com/pod-product-compliance
Ingram Content Group UK Ltd.
Pitfield, Milton Keynes, MK11 3LW, UK
UKHW040734171125
9004UKWH00045B/750